BOOKS BY

Brenda Adcock
====================

Pipeline

Reiko's Garden

Redress of Grievances

The Sea Hawk

Tunnel Vision

Soiled Dove

The Other Mrs. Champion

The Chameleon

Picking Up the Pieces

Brenda Adcock

Yellow Rose Books
by Regal Crest

Texas

ISBN 978-1-61929-120-1

First Printing 2013

9 8 7 6 5 4 3 2 1

Cover design by Donna Pawlowski

Published by:

Regal Crest Enterprises, LLC
229 Sheridan Loop
Belton, TX 76513

Find us on the World Wide Web at
http://www.regalcrest.biz

Printed in the United States of America

Acknowledgments

Once upon a time, Post-Traumatic Stress Disorder was better known as "shell shock" and was not considered by the military as a legitimate problem until fairly recently. The number of men and women who have suffered, and are suffering, with the affliction, for many years after a traumatic event, may never be known. However, those who live with those individuals also suffer in their own way. My own partner, who has always been the rock that keeps our relationship stable, was diagnosed a few years ago, after the shooting at Fort Hood, Texas, with a relatively mild case of PTSD. My own son, a victim of a roadside bomb in Iraq, denies he was affected and has, therefore, never sought treatment. I have the deepest respect for those who serve us all and come home unscathed, but have a special place inside for those who return a different person.

In helping me prepare and complete this story, there are those who must be thanked. As always I have to thank my publisher, Cathy Bryerose. We've taken a long journey together and I will forever be grateful for your support and friendship over the last years. I wish to thank my editor, Patty Schramm, and my copy editor, Heather Flournoy. Every change or correction you suggested, especially for my persistent POV problem, is greatly appreciated and makes me sound really good. As always Donna Pawlowski has produced another memorable cover. Finally, I thank Cheryl for everything she's given me over the many years we've been together. Patience has indeed been a virtue. Love you, baby.

To Cheryl, for everything and more in the future.

Chapter One

Ramstein Air Force Base, Germany
January 2010

LAUREN SHELTON RESTED her elbows on her knees and rubbed her forehead with the pads of her French-tipped fingers. Despite her heavy winter coat and the heat being blasted into the large waiting area, she could feel the weight of the winter weather outside settling into her bones. She blinked and took a deep breath.

"Why is it taking so damn long?" she asked, staring at the industrial carpeting that covered the seating area.

A warm hand slid up her back and across her shoulder, gently squeezing it in an attempt to reassure her that everything would be all right. Lauren turned her head slightly to look into her friend's face. "Tell me she's going to be okay, Mandy. Make me believe it."

Amanda Hardy wrapped her arms around Lauren and drew her closer. "Frank said she would be," she whispered. "I bet she'll jump right up and hug you."

"Not unless she's eager to get court-martialed," Lauren laughed humorlessly. "If I can just look into her eyes I'll be all right," Lauren managed. "We knew something like this could happen, but it's so damn hard."

"Frank's with her. It shouldn't be much longer, honey."

No matter how closely Mandy held her, Lauren couldn't get warm. She watched large, wet flakes of white drift in front of the huge terminal windows at Ramstein Air Force Base. It was less than half an hour from their home in Kaiserslautern, Germany. School was out for the long holiday season and she had spent hours getting their small cottage on the outskirts of the town prepared for her lover's return from her unit's most recent rotation. This wasn't what she had been expecting. There wasn't any way to acknowledge the impossible could happen. But it had.

"Look," Mandy said. "A plane's coming in."

Lauren stood quickly and rushed toward the windows, urging the plane to descend faster and be safely on the ground. She pressed her hands against the cold glass and watched as the huge converted cargo plane glided seamlessly to the runway. As soon as the plane slowed and turned back toward the terminal Mandy's cell phone chirped. She answered it immediately, but Lauren took it from her.

"Frank, Frank. Is she okay? Please, let her be okay," she

babbled helplessly.

"They sedated her for the flight, but they told me she'd be fine," he said, then paused and lowered his voice. "She's a little banged up."

"What's wrong? What aren't you telling me, Frank?"

"Tell Amanda to drive to Landstuhl. We'll meet you there."

"Why can't I see her here?"

"She's not looking her best right now, Lauren. You know how vain she is?" he said in an attempt to lighten the mood.

Tears ran down Lauren's cheeks as she handed the cell to Amanda. Amanda listened for a few moments before closing the cell.

"What did he tell you and don't you dare lie to me, Mandy."

"It's a head injury, Lauren. She was treated before they left Kandahar and sedated for the flight. An ambulance is waiting to transport her to Landstuhl for more tests. That's all he could say right now."

"How is he?"

"Claims it's nothing."

Lauren hugged Amanda tightly. "It's everything. He brought her back to me."

"That's what a good wingman does, Lauren. Let's go."

Amanda left the airport at Ramstein and turned onto L363 until she reached Kaiserstrausse and turned left into Landstuhl Regional Medical Center. It was the Army's finest overseas medical facility and served as the closest facility for treatment of soldiers injured in Iraq or Afghanistan. As soon as Amanda parked her car Lauren jumped out and began running toward the emergency entrance. Even if all she got was a glimpse, Lauren had to see her. She rushed to the triage desk.

"Have the ambulances from Ramstein arrived yet?" she asked nervously.

"Who are you expecting?" the nurse asked.

"Major Athon Dailey."

Amanda was suddenly at Lauren's side holding out her military identification card for the nurse. The nurse glanced at it and said, "You're both here for Major Dailey?"

"No," Lauren said at the same time Amanda said yes.

"We're together," Amanda explained.

"Who are you here for?" the nurse asked as she stared pointedly at Amanda.

"Captain Frank Hardesty. He flew in with Major Dailey."

"And who are you?" the nurse asked Lauren.

Lauren pulled her Department of Defense card which identified her as a teacher at the American high school in

Kaiserslautern. She thrust it toward the triage nurse. "Major Dailey's roommate. She has no family here or back home." Lauren hated identifying herself as Athon's roommate, just a friend with no more than a passing interest.

"I see," the nurse said. "Her roommate."

"Absolutely," Lauren muttered to herself.

The nurse gave Lauren a look and then said, "The ambulances are arriving now. If you'll take a seat, I'll let the doctors know you're both here."

It seemed like an eternity as they waited and paced. Nearly two hours passed before Amanda's name was called. She and Lauren had been holding hands and they both stood, reluctant to let go of one another.

"I'm fine, Mandy. Go to Frank," Lauren said.

"I'll see what I can find out," Amanda said as she hugged her friend. "We'll get you back there."

Amanda disappeared through the doors of the emergency room and Lauren sat down heavily. The next half hour passed slowly and Lauren closed her eyes, smiling at the pictures of Athon flipping through her mind. The playful, goofy look when she was teasing. The hazy look in her eyes filled with love and desire. The frown when she concentrated. She sensed someone sitting down next to her, but ignored them.

"Lauren Shelton?" a soft, female voice asked.

Lauren flashed her eyes open and saw a middle-aged woman wearing green scrubs seated next to her. "Yes, I'm Lauren Shelton," she answered hopefully.

"I'm Doctor Stephens. I examined Major Dailey when she arrived. The nurse tells me you're the Major's roommate."

Lauren raised her chin slightly. "I am."

"You're not legally a family member, but Major Dailey listed you as her beneficiary and next-of-kin on the paperwork that accompanied her. Her condition is serious, but she has been stabilized. She'll be flown to Walter Reed tomorrow morning."

"Please, can I see her?"

Stephens glanced at the triage nurse as she took another patient into the vitals area. "The bay doors only open for a few seconds. I can't officially allow you into room seventeen, but it is fairly busy back there and I have other patients to check on."

Lauren rifled through her purse and took out a business card. She handed it to the doctor. "I know you can't tell me much, but if anything...should happen between now and tomorrow morning, please call this number."

Stephens stuffed the card in her lab coat. Lauren rose and walked behind the doctor, waiting as she punched in the code to open the doors. She stopped at a water fountain near the entrance to the emergency department. As soon as the doctor walked through, Lauren stopped the door from closing completely with the toe of her shoe and counted to ten before pulling the door open far enough to slip inside. She walked down the hallway as if she belonged there, glancing at the room numbers. When she found room seventeen she looked around before stepping inside.

She moved quickly to the side of the bed and took her first glimpse at Athon in months. Her head was wrapped in bandages, covering her short blonde hair. Lauren reached out and hesitantly brushed Athon's cheek with her fingertips. Her face was swollen and bruised, obscuring her angular, but delicate features. Dozens of small cuts, along with two or three larger, stitched areas had torn her skin. IVs ran into her arms and her bandaged head was secured in place by a thick U-shaped yellow cushion. Various machines beeped monotonously.

Lauren bent down, lightly kissed Athon's forehead, and squeezed her hand. "I've seen you look worse, baby," she whispered. "I love you so much." She almost burst into tears when she felt a weak squeeze to her hand in reply. She stayed at Athon's side, telling her everything that had been happening since she'd deployed until Amanda stuck her head into the small room. Lauren leaned down and brushed her lips over a bruised cheek as gently as she could before leaving.

"How's Frank?" she asked as she hugged Amanda fiercely.

"Broken leg from a gunshot, but otherwise he'll be fine. And Athon?"

Lauren shrugged. "They don't know much yet. They're flying her to Walter Reed in the morning. I have to arrange for a flight to D.C. as soon as possible."

"Is she awake?" Amanda asked as they made their way down the corridor.

"No, but she knew I was there," Lauren answered. "Can I see Frank?"

Mandy grabbed her hand and led her to a triage room not far from Athon's. Frank pushed his body up slightly when he saw her. She went to him and hugged him. "Thank you for bringing her back to me, Frank," she said.

He nodded and swallowed hard. "How is she?"

"Still unconscious, but she squeezed my hand when I talked to her," Lauren said. "When I spoke to her a few days ago she said your team had a few days off."

"We did, but then all hell broke loose near a forward operating base in Helmand Province. A convoy hit an IED. Should have been a simple rescue."

Chapter Two

"MAJOR! MAJOR DAILEY! Dust off!" a voice called out through the darkness of her tent. She sat up quickly and looked around. It wasn't where she'd been moments before in her dream.

"What?" she rasped.

"Lift off in twenty," the voice said before leaving to awaken the rest of the flight crew. She looked at the clock next to her cot and shook her head hard to wake up. Three hours wasn't enough sleep for her crew. They had been in the air continuously for the past week. This was supposed to be their down time. Guided only by a stream of light from a nearby light pole she found her flight suit and stepped into it. She slid her feet into her boots before sitting back down to lace them. She yawned as she stood and yanked the heavy-duty zipper of the suit up to her neck and snapped the neck closure. Halfway to her chopper on the flight line, she saw members of the ground crew releasing the tether lines holding the rotor blades of her UH-60Q Medevac helicopter in place in case a sudden dust storm blew in during the night. She glanced to her left and saw Frank hauling ass toward his Blackhawk. Hers and a second chopper in her medevac group were preparing to lift off in the middle of the night. Her co-pilot, Chief Richie Ortega, tossed her a pair of night vision goggles as she pulled her flak vest on and climbed into the pilot's seat to begin her pre-flight routine. Ortega had joined her crew in Germany not long before their current rotation and seemed competent enough. Athon liked to keep a relaxed atmosphere for her crew and she wished Ortega would loosen up a little. The crew trusted her to bring them home after each mission, but hadn't yet developed the same rapport with their new co-pilot. Two medics assigned to her crew were running through a last minute supply count before storing everything in safety bins. She pulled on her helmet and adjusted the night vision goggles, allowing her eyes to adjust to the ghostly green glow.

"Everything set?" she asked through her helmet microphone. She waited until she received an affirmative from every crewman, then depressed her communications button to speak to the tower. "Dust off five-niner prepared for lift-off," she said calmly, reciting her chopper's call sign within the medevac group.

"You are cleared for lift-off, dust off five-niner," a disembodied voice crackled over the radio.

Ortega flipped switches on the panel above them and on his signal she pulled back slightly on the stick of the chopper. "Where we going, Starvin' Marvin?" she asked her navigator, a young man who never seemed to stop eating. Green lights illuminated the cockpit surrounding the flight crew as she waited for the coordinates to their destination to be set while she veered to the west. To her right she saw the comforting outline of the heavily armed Blackhawk escort helicopter. "You behind me, Junior?" Athon asked the pilot of the second helicopter over her headset.

"Seems to be my much envied lot in life to follow your hot ass around, Major," the pilot following her replied with a laugh.

She flipped the mic switch to speak to her crew. "What's the skinny?" she asked no one in particular.

One of the medics came over the headset. "A supply convoy just inside Helmand Province located a couple of IEDs. Estimate is six wounded. Bastards must have set them yesterday."

"Contact?"

"Off and on."

Thirty minutes later, Frank's voice broke the silence. "Medevacs hang back while we sweep the area." Athon banked the chopper into a holding pattern less than half a mile from the area of the attack. She watched the running lights of the Blackhawk as it criss-crossed the coordinates and saw no ground fire. "Proceed to LZ," Frank said.

Athon brought her chopper closer, following a low zig-zag pattern to avoid potential ground fire.

"Ready, Junior?" she asked.

"On your six, Boss," came the calm response.

Athon guided her chopper into the landing zone and set it down. Two medics jumped out before she settled and ran to help carry the wounded. She watched Junior land fifty yards to her right before she punched her safety harness release and left her seat. "Take the controls," she told Ortega. She went to the side loading door and pulled the first stretcher into the chopper. "How many?" she yelled over the noise of her rotors.

"Two more," a crewman yelled back. "Junior can carry the other three."

"Prepare to lift off, Ortega," she said. The words had barely left her mouth when she heard a loud whistling sound. "Incoming!" she shouted. She pressed her communications button. "Bug out, Junior. Now!" she ordered as she covered an injured man with her body.

The concussion of a nearby explosion knocked her against the bulkhead and she heard the whistling sound of a second incoming projectile. "Godammit! Get 'em off us, Frank!" she shouted into her helmet communications link. She saw sparks from ground fire strike Junior's chopper as it banked away sharply.

Stuttering shots from the Blackhawk's fifty-caliber machine guns strafed the area from which the projectiles had been launched, but smaller machine gun fire continued to strike the length of Athon's chopper. "Shit! Load that man!" Athon ordered as she jumped onto the pilot's seat and refastened her harness. "Go, go, go!"

As small arms fire pinged along the sides of the helicopter, she gasped when she felt a sudden sharp, stinging pain in her left side. She heard the side door slam closed and lifted off.

Chapter Three

"THINK SHE'LL MAKE it, Doctor?" a young nurse asked as she checked Athon's vitals and prepared her for the long flight back to the United States.

"She should, but with a head trauma, you never know," Dr. Stephens said softly.

The damaged body lying on the gurney in front of her was only one of hundreds that had passed through the hospital at Landstuhl. Dr. Stephens checked the tubing running into Athon Dailey's body to assure there were no kinks in the lines. She noticed the rapid eye movement beneath the closed eyelids. "Looks like she's dreaming about something," she said. She placed her stethoscope to Athon's chest and frowned. "Her breathing's becoming rapid and shallow."

"Increase the sedation?" the nurse asked.

Stephens nodded and stroked her patient's forehead in an attempt to calm her.

THE CHOPPER SUFFERED shrapnel damage from the rocket explosions as well as numerous strikes by small arms fire. A hole in the windshield let the cold night air rush into the cockpit, searing Athon's throat and lungs as she banked away from the LZ. Her controls were sluggish and she struggled to keep the chopper from slamming into the ground. It took all the strength she could muster to level off, dangerously close to the desert floor. She tried to rub away moisture that had gathered inside her goggles. "Ortega, take the controls," she told her co-pilot. "Ortega!"

When she didn't receive an answer she calmly ordered, "Get a medic up here."

"Pull up, Dailey!" Frank said.

Hearing his voice, she responded. "I'm hit. I think Ortega bought it. Got a little control problem. I'll keep us in the air as long as I can."

Athon was quiet for a few minutes. "Hey, Frank," she grunted as she fought to remain airborne.

"Yeah."

"Take care of Lauren. Tell her I'm sorry."

"Ain't nothing gonna happen to you, Dailey. Now shut up and fly, woman."

"Roger that. Dailey out."

She cursed as the engine sputtered and glanced at the fuel gauge. Her arms felt leaden as she used both hands to keep the chopper level. She was closer to the ground than she thought as the left skid struck it. The chopper bounced once and sparks from the metal striking rock flew into the air. She freed her harness. She had to evacuate her crew members before there was an explosion. She limped to the back and wanted to throw up when she saw the carnage. Blood was everywhere. She fell to her knees and searched for a pulse on each man now lying on the floor of the medical bay. Holes from ground fire had torn through the tail section. She tore off her night vision goggles and threw them as she screamed out her anger.

The sound of machine gun fire in the distance thrust her into flight mode. She wiped her arm across her face. She estimated her chopper only made it a couple of miles from the LZ and she had to put more distance between herself and the downed bird. The emergency lighting in the bay was dim and flickering. She managed to locate a towel and stuffed it inside her flight suit to staunch the bleeding before she lowered herself to the ground.

She ran as fast as she could, hoping the blackness of the night in a place where they never heard of streetlights, would hide her retreat. She glanced over her shoulder and saw electrical sparks inside her helicopter. It wouldn't be long before the area would be crawling with insurgents. If she had any hope of survival she had to increase the distance between herself and the crash site. The explosions at the LZ had been so loud her ears were still ringing. She stopped for a moment to wipe away sweat that, despite the winter weather, was running down her face. Her side throbbed and pain shot through it with every step. Push it away, she told herself. She heard a rustling sound behind her and reached for her revolver. A shot rang out and she fell to the ground as the bullet grazed her head.

"GAS IT UP!" Frank yelled as soon as he landed at his base. "Tell Evans we have a chopper down! Did Junior make it back?"

"Yeah!" a mechanic yelled back. "His bird was pretty shot up! What the hell happened?"

"They were waiting for us and didn't give a shit about the big red cross on the choppers. Dailey was hit and had to put down about a mile or two from the LZ. So put a rush on it."

"Fifteen minutes. Were you hit?"

"I don't think so."

"We'll check it out. Grab a cup of coffee."

Frank nodded and ran toward the unit command office. He flung the door open and strode inside. He rapped on the commander's door and tapped his foot waiting for the door to open. Colonel Stanley was rubbing his eyes when he opened the door. "Hardesty, come in," the older man said as he turned toward his desk.

"Dailey's down. They're prepping my chopper for take-off now."

"What happened?"

"It was an ambush. As soon as all hell broke loose, Dailey ordered Junior out of there. We laid down fire, but there must have been more than one group lying in wait. Dailey loaded as many as she could before she lifted off." He cleared his throat. "Her chopper was shot up pretty bad. The last communication I had with her she said she'd been hit and Ortega was dead. She was having problems with her rotors and was flying close to the deck. She put it down a couple of miles from the LZ. I didn't see an explosion so I'm assuming she'll find a place to lay low until we get back."

"Not tonight, Captain. The area's too hot and we can't afford to lose any more choppers. Wait until first light," the colonel said. "I'll send some armed men with you. It's too dangerous now."

"She's been shot! She might not make it until dawn, sir," Frank protested.

"Major Dailey knew the risks, like we all do. Send a message to the nearest unit. See how fast they can get there."

"They were under attack which is why we were there, to pick up their wounded. They're in no shape to send anyone," Frank argued, raising his voice. "We're the only chance Dailey and her crew have."

Colonel Stanley stood and leaned forward, using his fingers to balance his body. "Stand down, Captain," he ordered. "It'll be light enough in three or four hours."

Frank saluted and spat, "Yes, sir." He slammed the door as he left the colonel's office.

ICE COLD WATER splashed on Athon's face. She coughed and pain stabbed through her side. Her body twisted as she struggled to get her feet under her and remove the burning pain from her wrists. Her hands were tied with a rough homemade fiber rope that was looped over a nearby tree branch. The rough fiber had rubbed her wrists raw. After an instant of relief her legs were kicked from under her. The rope dug deeper into her flesh as her body weight jerked her down. She bit back a wave of nausea as she remembered bits and pieces of the frantic attempt by her crew to evacuate the wounded and escape the area. She remembered staring into the lifeless eyes of her chief medic. She felt warm tears mix with the cold water running down her cheeks. She was responsible for the safety of her crew and she had failed to protect them. She remembered the assault chopper that accompanied the rescue mission, piloted by Frank Hardesty, laying down cover fire. How long ago had that happened?

Her breathing became labored as she tried to ignore the pain in her side and the headache that pounded at her temple. Survival training had never seemed this real. She knew she wouldn't die from the training, but reality wasn't quite as certain. She saw movement off to her right and her breath stopped when she saw at least a dozen bearded men sitting in the snow around a small fire. She shook her head hoping it was a mirage or hallucination. She shivered slightly from the cold and closed her eyes. A voice in her head laughed. *You ain't got what it takes, kid.*

Chapter Four

Duvalle, Texas
September 1987

SIXTEEN-YEAR-OLD Lauren Shelton waited patiently while her mother filled out the registration papers to enroll her in a new high school. She hadn't been particularly happy when her father accepted the position as the new pastor of the Eastside Presbyterian Church in the small Texas town of Duvalle, just outside San Antonio, but she knew the move was her fault. They had spent most of the morning registering Lauren's younger brother, Devin, at the local middle school. The move from suburban Philadelphia, Pennsylvania to Podunk, Texas had not been well accepted by Devin. But, according to the Reverend Kenneth Shelton, God moved in mysterious ways which should never be questioned. Lauren's mother, Toni, seemed resigned to the move. For as long as Lauren could remember, her mother had stoically accepted her husband's decisions without question.

The sound of loud voices in the front office caught Lauren's attention as she watched a surly-looking girl with short, spiky blonde hair being escorted into the room and shoved into a chair. The teen was bleeding from a cut over her right eye. Blood ran down the side of her face and dripped onto a well-worn olive green t-shirt that advertised a product that had been popular several years earlier. Her eyes were heavily outlined by black eyeliner and drew attention to her pale skin. When she tried to stand and reach for a tissue box on the counter, an equally surly-looking man placed his hand on her shoulder and pushed her roughly back into the chair. She slapped the man's hand away and glared at him. She saw Lauren sitting in the nearby registration area looking at her.

"Whatcha starin' at, sweet cheeks? Never seen a real live juvenile delinquent before?" the girl snarled at Lauren, who quickly averted her eyes.

When her mother signed the last piece of paperwork, she smiled at Lauren and they both prepared to leave. On her way by the front counter Lauren grabbed a couple of tissues and handed them to the girl on her way out of the office.

"Thanks," the girl said as she looked up at Lauren and snatched the tissues. She pressed them against the cut over her eye.

Although she had never seen anyone who looked like the girl, Lauren was struck by her looks. She had delicate, but angular features with a straight thin nose. Her face was framed by unruly short blonde hair. But it was her pale blue eyes that made her face interesting. Minus the blood, Lauren found her quite attractive, in a dangerous, untamed sort of way. She felt her stomach clench and then release as she followed her mother into the hallway.

ATHON DAILEY HAD been trying to eat an undisturbed lunch when the fight broke out. Couldn't even enjoy a stupid Brand Z store brand baloney sandwich without being provoked by some jerk jock who thought he was being cool. She hated this school and she hated this town. She hated the way she was forced to live. She couldn't remember the last time she had actually spoken to her mother. Michelle Dailey spent her days sleeping off the night before and her nights stripping and getting drunk, strung out, or both, usually in the company of a drunken cowboy. She would never be a candidate for Mother of the Year.

That morning Athon got out of bed before daylight, managed to find reasonably clean clothing, relieved her bladder, and put together a breakfast of cold coffee and burnt toast with the burnt parts mostly scraped off. It was a long way to Carver High School from the semi-abandoned trailer park they called home. An elephant could have stomped through the trailer and Michelle Dailey wouldn't have noticed.

Athon hated everything about her life. Duvalle, Texas had originally been envisioned as a bedroom community for San Antonio, but someone forgot to tell anyone its purpose before the city expanded in the opposite direction. When San Antonio expanded to accommodate its burgeoning population, legal and illegal, it had moved west instead of east. Duvalle now had a reputation for absolutely nothing of importance and the only people who lived there were migrants who hoped no one would notice one more illegal Mexican in an area where there were thousands of others and hopeless people like her mother who were hanging on to the fringes of life by their fingernails. The smell of hopelessness permeated everything, even the air. Eventually it became a haven for trailer park trash like Athon and Michelle Dailey.

Athon lived on the edge of prosperity, but wasn't allowed to touch it. The only successful part of town was the original affluent subdivision surrounding the East San Antonio Country Club. New additions to the subdivision bulged into the Duvalle City Limits. Carver High School was constructed near the zone separating Duvalle and San Antonio and had an excellent academic reputation. Although Athon didn't live in Carver's attendance zone, she had discovered an ill-thought out Texas law that allowed homeless students or unaccompanied minors to attend the school of their choice, regardless of where they physically resided. Another section of the same law let a student declare themself homeless. She declared herself an unaccompanied minor and enrolled at the affluent school. She doubted her mother knew if she went to school, let alone where.

It was economically a long way from Buena Ventana Trailer Court to Carver High School. Now seventeen and entering her last year of high school, all Athon wanted was an uneventful year. She usually walked the three miles to school or hitched a ride if the weather was bad. She did everything she could not to draw unnecessary attention to herself, but it was becoming more difficult. Most of the students at Carver High School came from upper class families and there was no denying that Athon stood out in the preppie group. Her obvious Goodwill wardrobe clashed with the Neiman-Marcus clothing most of the other students wore. But only one year remained before she could leave everything she hated behind and make her own life without everyone and their damn dog telling her how worthless she was. She didn't need to be reminded about that. She knew it every morning when she rolled off that piece of shit her mother called a mattress. It was an old, ripped up twin mattress they had found on the curb and stank like pee. She'd tried everything to remove the odor, but nothing worked. It had probably belonged to a much younger kid who wasn't potty trained and it was too short for her thin five-ten frame. She looked down at her old t-shirt. It was one of her favorites, but it was ruined now.

"What did you do now, Athon?" the secretary asked.

"Nothin'," she said. "He attacked me." She smiled at Mrs. Fortenberry and added, "But I kicked his lily-white ass."

The man standing next to her smacked her on her shoulder. "Watch your mouth," he ordered.

"You know you'll be suspended for fighting," the older woman said, shaking her head. "Not a good way to start the new school year."

"I got things I need to do anyways," Athon said with a shrug.

"Your mama get a phone yet?"

"Nope. Things have been a little slow lately."

"You need to learn to control that temper of yours, Athon."

"Yeah, I been told that once or twice."

The teacher who escorted Athon to the office stepped out of the principal's door and motioned her inside. She dusted off her pants and sauntered into the office, keeping her defiant, don't-give-a-shit attitude in place.

"I hear you were involved in a fight at lunch, Athon," Mr. Tucker, the principal, said as he leaned back in his chair.

"Takes two to have a fight and I don't see the other participant in here," Athon said. "Why is that?"

"Coach Larsen says you provoked it."

"He's a liar," Athon stated.

Mr. Tucker sat up. "Why would Coach lie about it?"

Athon looked over her shoulder at the middle-aged man with the crew-cut and the prominent beer belly. "Probably because one of his pretty boy jocks let a *girl* give him a bloody nose."

"Who was the other student involved, Coach Larsen?" Tucker asked.

"Craig Hickson. He's a good kid," Larsen answered with his emphasis on the word good.

"As opposed to a *baaad* kid like me, I suppose," Athon smirked.

Larsen stepped closer. "That's right, Dailey. You've been nothing but trouble since the day you enrolled at Carver."

Athon turned to face Larsen. "But I still manage to make the honor roll every freakin' semester and can even count to twenty-one without using my fingers, toes, and dick."

Larsen's hands started to come up, but he stopped himself. "Can I return to my lunch duty, Mr. Tucker?" Larsen asked, never taking his eyes from Athon's.

When Athon and Mr. Tucker were alone, he leaned back in his chair again. "You know I'm going to have to suspend you, don't you Athon?"

"I know you probably will seein' as how I'm such a dangerous individual," she answered with a shrug.

"I know you're smart. All of your teachers say so, but you act like a common hooligan."

Tucker's words stung, but Athon would never let him know that. "I can't help who my parents are or the way I dress, Mr. Tucker. All I want is to finish high school and get the hell outta Duvalle. But right now I'm sorta stuck here. What am I supposed to do when some jerk starts shoving me around?"

"Walk away. It takes a bigger person to walk away from a fight. You're suspended until Monday," Tucker said. "Go to the nurse and get your cut bandaged. Then go home and think about trying to stay out of trouble. Let the office know if your mother gets a phone."

Not likely, she thought. She doesn't even know where I go to school. Athon left the office and walked to her locker to get her backpack. The bell rang and students dressed in fashionable back-to-school clothing began filling the hallways as she shoved her way through them and strode toward the front doors of the building.

Lauren listened to music on her Discman as she waited in the car while her mother ran back into the school to set up a lunchroom account. She closed her eyes and took a deep breath as the music flowed over her. When she opened her eyes again to adjust the volume, movement at the school entrance drew her attention. She watched as the girl who had been in the office slammed out the front door, shoving it open so hard that it banged against the bricks behind it. The girl cut across the street and jumped up on the curb, walking away from the school. Lauren couldn't pull her gaze from the almost seductive way the girl's hips swayed as she walked, her pants riding low on her hips as she sauntered away. She was having trouble tearing her eyes away from the way the girl's firm-looking ass pressed against the seat of her pants.

A gentle early fall breeze blew the girl's short blonde hair around, but Lauren could see her face clearly. She had noticed the striking clear blue of the girl's eyes in the office. Even though they had been filled with anger, there had been a hint of sadness the defiance couldn't hide. Lauren wondered what made the intriguing-looking girl sad.

Chapter Five

ATHON SLUNG HER backpack onto the work bench and grabbed a set of overalls from the hook on the wall. She stepped into the left leg first and worked the overall leg over her jeans.

"What the hell you doin' here, girl?" Tiny Hamilton, the owner of Tiny's Garage asked. He leaned his head back and snorted. "You got kicked out again, didn't ya?"

"Wasn't the plan, but that's how it worked out," Athon said as she slid her right leg into the overalls.

"How long this time?"

"I'm all yours until Monday, big man," she answered with a grin.

"You need to stay out of trouble. I can't afford to pay all these extra days you're gettin'." Tiny turned around and pulled a well-used rag from the back pocket of his work overalls. He wiped his large meaty hands and shook his head. "I got in a transmission that needs some work. Reckon you can start on that. Don't fuck it up though. Keys and ticket are in the office."

Athon had been working at Tiny's Garage for the last year and a half. Ever since he caught her trying to steal a hammer and a screwdriver to repair a leak in the roof of the old trailer she and her mother lived in. Tiny was the biggest man she had ever seen and ran faster than she had figured. When he grabbed her from behind, she was stopped instantly. The sight of the six-three man, breathing hard with sweat glistening on his ebony skin had knocked the bravado out of her. Rather than turn her in to the cops Tiny put her to work cleaning his garage, for free, until he thought she'd paid her debt. After she turned sixteen, he hired her and began teaching her to perform simple jobs, like changing oil, filters, and spark plugs. Later he taught her to tune an engine and work on transmissions. She didn't mind getting her hands dirty or scraping her knuckles. She was polite to Tiny's customers and even did some bookkeeping for him. She felt safer with Tiny than she did at home. Now because of her latest suspension, she had a chance to pick up a few extra bucks. Although Tiny worked on cars and pick-ups, the real money was in working on the big diesel rigs that frequented the truck stop down the road. She had been begging Tiny to teach her about working on the semis, but he thought she wasn't ready for the big jobs yet.

The days of late summer in Texas hadn't begun to shorten yet and there was at least an hour of sunlight left when Athon lowered the double garage door at Tiny's. He invited her to his house for a home-cooked meal, but, even though the half sandwich she'd managed for lunch before all hell broke loose had worn off hours earlier, she declined the offer. Her pride left no room for charity.

Tiny dropped her off near the entrance to Buena Ventana Trailer Court and she waited until he was out of sight before walking down the cracked asphalt road. She wasn't surprised when she found the derelict mobile home empty as usual. She threw her backpack onto the old mattress on the floor of her room and rummaged through the refrigerator and cabinets for something that hadn't expired the previous year. She picked dirty clothes off the floor and went through the pockets. She crammed her fingers under furniture and between cushions searching for loose change. She eventually came up with a buck thirty-eight. Combined with the five she had been saving for an emergency, she left the trailer and cut across an overgrown field behind it, headed for a burger joint run by a friend's father.

Gabriela LeBron had the same dream as Athon. To leave Duvalle, Texas far, far behind. Her parents worked hard, but still barely made ends meet. The burger stand was in another old trailer that the LeBrons towed behind their pick-up. Athon smiled when she saw it was in its usual spot in front of a deserted gas station. She stepped up to the window and looked over the hand-printed menu, checking out the prices. A teenaged girl leaned on her elbows and smiled at Athon. Her clothes were old and faded. A few places along the seams seemed to be unraveling, but everything was neatly pressed. A mass of dark hair surrounded Gabby Le Bron's head. Gabby was also a student at Carver High School due to a zoning mishap. Her family lived in an old house that was literally cut in two by the current school zone line. Given a choice between two school zones, Gabby's parents selected the more affluent Carver zone. When the line was finally corrected, Gabby was a senior and grandfathered for her final year. The whole thing had been an example of bureaucracy at its best.

"Hey, Athon. What can I get you?" Gabby asked while wiping down the already clean counter space.

"I got six thirty-eight. What can I get with that?" Athon asked.

"One burger or one cheeseburger or a couple of chili dogs, fries and a drink," Gabby rattled off. She leaned down closer and whispered, "No tax for you."

"Then I'll take the cheeseburger, fries and a drink," Athon said as she dropped the five and a fistful of change on the window counter.

Athon looked at the dusty area around the old travel trailer and waited. Finally, the side door opened and Gabby stepped outside. "Mind if I join you?" she asked.

"I'm not much company."

"Better than nothing," Gabby said with a grin.

Athon swung her leg over the warped and sun-bleached seat of a nearby picnic table and peeled the wrapper from around her cheeseburger. She knew it was fifty percent grease, but maybe it would be filling.

"I heard you got suspended again," Gabby said, dipping a fry into a splotch of ketchup.

"Yeah. Gives me a chance to work a couple of extra days."

"You'll never get out of here on what Tiny pays you," Gabby said as she nibbled at her own burger.

"I got a plan," Athon said, chewing her food thoughtfully.

"Ever'body's got a fucking plan." Gabby laughed. "What you gonna do? Get knocked up and draw a check?"

"I'll get out," Athon insisted. She picked up her trash and carried it to a trash can next to the trailer. "Did I miss anything in class?"

"Nope. Read the next chapter and..."

"Answer the questions at the end," Athon finished for her. She wiped her hands on the sides of her jeans and stuffed her hands in her pockets. "See ya Monday," she said as she started back across the weed-choked field.

As soon as she was back in the mobile home, she stripped and took a shower. Water and electricity were the only things that worked semi-reliably in the old trailer and for some reason had never been disconnected. She didn't want to be caught there when her mother came home. She collapsed on the mattress and flipped on the light over her bed after she slipped into a t-shirt and boxers and blocked her bedroom door with an old metal chair to prevent anyone from entering. She didn't remember dozing and didn't know how long she'd been asleep when she heard laughter in the front room. She recognized the shrill laughter and buried her head under a pillow. Just as she began to relax enough to fall back to sleep, banging on the door to her room brought her to her feet.

"What?" she yelled.

"Open the fuckin' door, baby," Michelle Dailey answered.

Baby? Athon couldn't remember the last time Michelle had called her that. In fact, she wasn't sure her mother ever had. Athon got up and pushed the chair away far enough to let the door crack open. Michelle's appearance was almost scary. She looked a lot older than her thirty-eight years. Her hair looked dull with split ends sticking out and plastered to her forehead by perspiration. Athon couldn't see any sign of life in her once-lively blue eyes.

"Got any money on ya, kid?" Michelle slurred as she incessantly licked her lips.

"No. I don't get paid until Saturday." Seeing her mother as the empty shell she'd become disgusted Athon and she started to push the bedroom door shut.

In a movement of strength Athon hadn't expected, Michelle lowered her shoulder and rammed it against the flimsy door. Michelle squeezed through the opening and pushed Athon aside. "I know you been squirrelin' money away somewhere, so don't be bullshittin' me, kid," Michelle growled.

Michelle Dailey was a shitty parent, but had never injured Athon. Now she turned to her daughter and attempted a crooked smile. Athon backed up to escape the foul odor of Michelle's breath. Trapped against the thin wall of the room, she cringed as Michelle reached out and grabbed her t-shirt with a fisted hand and pulled her closer. "I need it," Michelle begged while tears turned her mascara into sludge-like black rivers along her puffy cheeks. "I need it bad."

"I don't have any money," Athon insisted.

With a scream that came from somewhere deep inside her body, Michelle released Athon and took a step back before unleashing her desperate fury. She slapped Athon's face with all the strength she could muster and began pummeling her with her fists. Athon covered her head and tried to disappear into the foul mattress under her until Michelle's blows weakened and she collapsed on top of her daughter.

"Where the hell are you, woman? I'm waitin'," a man's voice echoed down the hall. "Let's get it on!"

Athon pushed Michelle away and stood up. She eased out the door of her bedroom and walked to the bedroom next door, holding her hand behind her back.

"She's sick. Go on home," Athon said in a flat voice.

The man lying naked on her mother's bed grinned as he scanned Athon from head to toe. "You look healthy enough," he said, licking his lips. His hand flopped to his crotch and he stroked himself. "How about it?"

"Get out," Athon said, her voice stronger.

"Oh, come on now. I'll show you a good time."

Athon brought her arm from behind her back and flipped open a switchblade. "Go now while you still got something to grab ahold of," she said.

The man jumped from the bed and grabbed his clothes,

keeping Athon and the knife in sight as he backed down the narrow hall toward the front room. As soon as he went through the front door, Athon slammed and locked it. She leaned her head against the metal frame and took a deep breath. "Y'all come back now, ya hear," she muttered.

She spent the remainder of the night taking care of Michelle as she shook and cried, begging for a drink or a fix. The next day she asked Tiny for an advance on her pay and took it home to Michelle, leaving it on the table next to her bed. When she returned home that evening her mother and the money were both gone, taking away a piece of Athon's dream of leaving Duvalle.

Chapter Six

THE FOLLOWING TUESDAY Lauren walked down the still unfamiliar hallways of Carver High School, her books and notebook clasped against her chest. She stopped at her locker and carefully turned the combination lock built into the locker. She hated combination locks because they never seemed to open for her on the first try. This one was no exception. In frustration she knelt down to place the load in her arms on the floor. She closed her eyes to concentrate and rubbed her hands on the sides of her jeans. Her locker was next to a short hallway that led outside and between the sections of the high school. The door opened every few seconds and students flooded in, jostling her slightly. After the immediate onslaught of students, she heard giggling. When no one walked past her, she glanced around the corner, her eyes growing wide. A couple was pressed against the wall and apparently enjoying a moment of semi-privacy as they kissed and ran their hands over one another's bodies. Lauren was stunned at such a public display of affection. She knew she was staring and pretty sure she was blushing. A student slammed a nearby locker, reminding her what she was supposed to be doing. She glanced at her wristwatch. When she looked up again hooded pale blue eyes outlined with heavy black eyeliner seemed to smile at her, daring her to say something. The second girl was engrossed in placing a hickey on the blonde's neck.

"Hey! Not so hard, baby," the blonde said, never taking her eyes from Lauren's. She smiled crookedly at Lauren and whispered, "Got a problem?"

Lauren shook her head and returned to fighting with the lock. The two girls parted with a quick kiss at the entrance to the hall. The blonde leaned against the corner of the wall and watched Lauren attempt to get into her locker.

"Need some help? These old locks can be a bitch to open," the girl said.

"And I suppose you have the magic touch," Lauren snapped.

The blonde pushed away from the wall and held her hands up. "Sorry I asked," she said.

A boy walking down the hallway veered toward the blonde and ran her into the wall. He laughed. "Sorry, Dailey. Didn't see ya."

"I heard there's a sale on glasses over at Wal-Mart," she responded as she rubbed her shoulder.

The boy reached out and touched her neck. "See you're still going out with one of the Hoover sisters," he said with a laugh.

"Fuck off, Hickson," Dailey said. "Unless you want me to kick your ass again this week." She looked around and grinned. "Larson's not around to save you right now. Bummer."

The boy looked at the girl with him and at Lauren. "You should wash that mouth out."

"Why?" Dailey sneered with a glance at the girl hanging on his arm. "Your dick ain't never gonna be in it."

It became obvious to Lauren that the situation might escalate as the boy made a fist and stepped closer. She grabbed Dailey's arm. "Do you really think you can open this thing?" she asked. "I don't want to be late for class."

"Sure. No problem," Dailey answered, glaring at the boy she'd called Hickson as the girl with him pulled him away. She finally turned her attention to Lauren. "What's the combination?"

Lauren told her and watched in amazement as the lock opened on her first try.

"Thank you."

"Like I said, no problem. And I promise not to come back later and steal your valuables."

"Unless you want more books you won't find anything worth having," Lauren said. She held her hand out. "I'm Lauren Shelton."

"I saw you registering last week. Athon Dailey," Athon said as she took Lauren's hand. "I think we share a class. English or something."

"That's an unusual name," Lauren commented as she took a book from the locker and put another one inside.

"I wasn't asked for my opinion about it. Gotta run," Athon said as she turned away and jogged down the hall.

The bell rang to begin the next class and Lauren hoped her teacher would take the fact that she was new into account.

ATHON OVERSLEPT THE next morning and didn't make it to school until the beginning of the second class.

"Hey, freak!" a boy's voice called out as he shoved her from behind. Athon caught herself and turned to glare at the boy. He tried to step around her, but she grabbed the belt loop of his baggy jeans and jerked them hard into his crotch.

"Leave. Me. Alone, you fuckin' re-tard," she hissed into his face. With a final shove against his chest, she stomped away. School hadn't been in session a month and already the gnats were swarming around her. She turned into the room designated as the location for her next class and found a desk in the back row. She slouched down in the seat as far as it would allow her five-ten frame to settle and ruffled a hand through her spiky blonde hair. She wasn't vain, but hoped the home-done haircut wasn't as obvious as she thought it probably was.

She stretched her long legs out and watched other students make their way into the classroom and eventually fill almost every seat. Two athletic-looking young men came in together and looked around. One nudged the other as they sauntered toward Athon, stopping practically on top of her.

"Move, freak," a tall, muscular young man with sandy hair ordered. As if to make his point, he reached down and shoved her on the shoulder. She glared up at them, but picked up her ratty backpack and moved forward one seat to allow them to sit together.

Just as she settled down again, she saw a familiar female student enter the room. It was the girl with the locker problem. She was shorter than Athon, maybe five seven or eight, and slender. Her skin was a toffee mocha color and looked like a perfect cup of coffee with creamer. Her dark brown hair fell smoothly to her jaw bone and framed fine, delicate features. Lauren smiled when she saw someone she knew and her light cinnamon-colored eyes seemed to sparkle when they met Athon's. Athon felt her heart flutter and dropped her eyes quickly to the top of her desk to avoid looking at her. She was suddenly fascinated with a groove someone had made in the surface and picked at it with her fingernail.

"You gonna try to tap that, Rafe?" the boy behind Athon whispered loud enough for her to hear.

"Oh, yeah. Sweet cocoa," the second jock said with a laugh. Rafe Stoneman was the quarterback of the Carver football team and all-around big man on campus. That meant he believed every girl on campus should fall at his feet and spread 'em.

"Her daddy's the new minister at my church."

"You'll have to invite me to your church next Sunday, dude."

"You'll never get past him."

"I got ten bucks that says otherwise. Preacher's kids are always the wildest."

"Think she'd be wild in the sack?"

"Is her daddy black?" Rafe asked, his voice husky.

"Nope, but her mama sure is."

"You know how they are," Rafe said with a laugh. "So, yeah, I bet she's plenty wild in the sack."

It bothered Athon to hear the two boys talking about Lauren like that, but she ignored it as the teacher brought the students' attention to what was written on the blackboard.

All morning Athon's mind refused to concentrate on her studies. She could be working, trying to save her money so she could leave Duvalle as soon as she graduated.

"Excuse me," a soft voice said as Athon was eating a can of Vienna sausages for lunch.

"What?"

"Is this seat taken?" Lauren asked.

"No, I'm done," Athon said, stuffing the last sausage in her mouth and standing up.

"You don't have to run away. I don't bite."

"I gotta go. Besides, maybe I'd enjoy gettin' bit by you."

Lauren Shelton's face flushed, turning her tan skin a golden brown. "This is my first year at Carver," Lauren said, steering the conversation to something less provocative.

Athon stared at Lauren for a moment. "This is my last year in hell."

Lauren ate quietly and then saw the girl Athon had been clinching in the hallway. "Looks like your girlfriend is looking for you," she said before she took a healthy bite of her sandwich.

"I don't have a girlfriend," Athon responded, her eyes turning steely.

"You always kiss girls you don't care about like that?" Lauren asked as she rummaged in her soft-side lunch container. She pulled out an apple. "You want this? I hate apples."

"They're good for you. I don't do charity," Athon said as she pushed up from the bench.

"It's not charity. I bit a worm in half in an apple when I was little and have hated them ever since," Lauren said with a shrug.

Athon laughed out loud and accepted the apple. "Thanks."

They ate silently for a while before Lauren asked, "So are you going to answer my question or not?"

"What question?"

"About kissing girls you don't like. You seemed to be enjoying yourself immensely."

"Jealous?"

"Curious," Lauren answered around the food in her mouth.

"Liz just wanted to try out something before her big date this weekend."

"So what are you, the kissing dummy?"

Athon shrugged. "More like a practice dummy. We started in middle school. Like kissing lessons, I guess."

Lauren laughed so hard she almost spit her food out. "Shut up! You're lying!"

Athon took another bite of the apple and shook her head. "You aren't born knowing how to be a good kisser, ya know. You have to know when to part your lips, when to slip 'em the tongue..."

"That's enough," Lauren said, holding up a hand. "Definitely more than I needed to know." She hesitated and looked at Athon out of the corner of her eye. "So who taught you?"

"I gotta go," Athon answered brusquely, tossing the apple core into a nearby trash can. "Thanks for the apple."

"Maybe tomorrow I'll bring a banana," Lauren said with a smile.

Athon looked at Lauren and let her eyes drift over her body. The corner of her mouth lifted in a grin. "Never cared much for bananas," she said.

Chapter Seven

Duvalle, Texas
September 1987

ATHON JUMPED OUT of the bed of an old pick-up that had given her a lift to the entrance of the Buena Ventana Trailer Court. She had shared the back of the truck with a couple of defeated-looking migrant pickers. Probably headed south to the Valley, she thought as she tossed a wave at the departing vehicle.

The abandoned trailer she shared with her mother was located near the rear of the park in the midst of several other derelict mobile homes that had seen better days. It had been a hot, but tolerable September day. She wiped her face with her hand as she kicked a rock she found near the entrance and turned the last corner that would lead to their trailer. She stopped in her tracks when she saw a black, official-looking vehicle and two patrol cars with their lights on parked across the cracked cement pad that once served as a parking space. She ducked behind a tree when she heard loud voices from inside the trailer and then the crash of something. The window into what served as a small living room shattered and Athon saw an old baseball bounce twice on the road and roll part way down the asphalt before it left the weed-choked road and stopped in an overgrown grassy area.

After more shouting, a state trooper stepped out of the trailer, straightened his uniform, and readjusted his Smoky the Bear hat before walking to his patrol car and jerking the back door open. Athon looked back at the trailer door in time to see Michelle Dailey, her brassy bottle blonde hair a tangled mess, being escorted from the trailer. She was barefoot, but still struggled against the hands leading her into the sunlight. She was wearing her familiar, barely legal Daisy Dukes that showed off a shapely ass. When she tried to jerk away from the officers her breasts quivered like Jell-O and threatened to escape her tight, low cut tank top. With her hands restrained behind her body she had little chance of getting away as a female trooper held her by the upper arm to prevent her from falling or attempting to run. A hand on Michelle's head protected it from striking the door frame of the waiting patrol car. Athon had no idea what Michelle had been arrested for this time. Could have been for any number of offenses. She was certain there were drugs hidden somewhere in the trailer. Or perhaps they were being evicted for trespassing again.

Athon turned away from the scene and hid behind another trailer about a block away. She sat down in a shady spot, pulled a half packet of stale Ritz crackers from her backpack, and waited for the vehicles to leave. When she saw the last patrol car go, she stood and made her way back to her home. The police had padlocked the front door to prevent anyone from entering. She almost laughed, certain there was nothing worth stealing inside. Athon walked to the back side and dropped her backpack. She pulled away a flimsy piece of plastic skirting, crawled under the trailer on her belly, and rolled onto her back. She pushed up a sagging piece of plywood that covered a jagged hole in the floor until it lifted and slid it to the side, making a space she could stand up in. She looked around in the hallway near her room and lifted her body inside. She rooted around in her room and found an old Army duffle bag she had scavenged from a pile of discarded items in front of someone's house. She liked the bag. It had a peculiar, oily odor, but was waterproof and sturdy. The olive green material was rough. The name Simpson, C. was stenciled on one side. When she first found it, she made up stories about who the unknown C. Simpson was. She stuffed several shirts and pants, along with underwear and socks into the duffle before gathering a well-used tube of toothpaste, a toothbrush, shampoo, and a few other personal hygiene things, at least enough to last a few days.

The room where Athon slept was next to her mother's and she hadn't gotten much sleep the night before. Michelle and her 'guest' arrived home after one in the morning and the rhythmic squeaking of the springs on Michelle's bed, as well as the grunting sounds from the guest, seemed to go on forever. Athon hated the sounds that kept her awake. It sounded like a hog rutting. It didn't help when the man Michelle claimed was Athon's father apparently couldn't find any place else to sleep.

Athon and Michelle rarely saw or heard from Hank Dailey. While Hank acknowledged he had fucked Michelle when he was high, he swore on a stack he wasn't the father of her 'bastard brat'. Athon didn't know how late it was when Hank barged into the trashy trailer and threw the grunting cowboy out. Athon heard cursing from the dispossessed 'guest', followed by a loud beer belch, and not long afterward more squeaking and grunting through the thin wall.

In the kitchen, she opened the refrigerator, not really expecting to find much and wasn't disappointed. She took the remaining generic peanut butter and a couple of cans of Vienna sausages and another of tuna. Once she was satisfied she had everything she needed to survive for a few days, she dropped her bags through the opening in the floor. She was making one last sweep of the trailer when she heard the deep, throaty rumble of a motorcycle engine. It slowed and idled in front of the trailer before the engine stopped. She quickly squatted down when someone banged on the warped aluminum screen.

"Open the goddamn door, Shelly," a man's raspy voice yelled. Athon recognized Hank Dailey's voice immediately. She pulled the wooden cover back over the opening in the floor. From past experience, Hank was probably drunk and would never go away. By the time she opened the trailer door Hank had jerked the already damaged screen from its hinges and it was hanging from the padlock.

"She's not here. The police took her away a while ago."

Athon started to close the door, but Hank bulldozed his way inside. "Any food in this dump? Anything to drink?"

Athon could smell his breath and backed away to escape the disgusting smell. "Nothin' here," she said.

Hank's hand dropped to his crotch and he scratched the area slowly. Athon closed her eyes and resisted the urge to throw up.

"What about you, girl? Got any money?" he growled.

"Do I look like I have any money?" Athon snapped.

Hank's hand flew out and slapped her. She tripped over something in the floor behind her and landed hard on her butt. "Don't get smart with me, kid. Where's your mama?"

"I told you the cops took her away. There ain't nothin' here for you," she repeated.

He leered down at her. "Shelly always done her best work on her back," he said. "How about you?"

Athon ground her teeth together. "Touch me and I'll kill you," she threatened.

He reached down and grabbed her by her t-shirt and jerked her to her feet, shoving her roughly into the trailer wall. As soon as she got her feet under her, Hank swung his arm and backhanded her hard enough to knock her down again. Instinctively she rebounded and lowered her shoulder. She charged at him, filled with uncontrollable fury, and buried her shoulder into his soft belly, knocking the air from his lungs. He grabbed the corner of the kitchen counter and managed to land a blow to her side with his steel-toed biker boots. Her hands went to her torso, leaving her open to his attack. His fist landed solidly on the side of her face and she dropped to her knees.

"You ain't got what it takes, kid," he said.

She winced as Hank grabbed her arm and yanked her onto wobbly feet. He twisted her arm behind her and shoved it hard up her back. She cried out when she felt her shoulder pop as he slammed her against the wall with enough force to crack the cheap, fake wood paneling. He spun her around and smacked her in the face again, opening the cut over her eye from the fight at school the previous week. He finally released her and delivered a crushing upper cut that lifted her off her feet. She didn't remember landing on the trashy floor or hearing Hank as he tore up the trailer searching for anything of value before leaving her bleeding and unconscious on the trailer floor.

DARKNESS GREETED ATHON as she groaned and half rolled onto her side. She brought her hand to her face and carefully felt the swelling over her eye that refused to allow her left eye to open completely. She tasted blood in her mouth and felt stabbing pain shoot across her ribcage. She took as deep a breath as her ribs allowed and panted as she struggled onto her knees. When she tried to use her arms to stand, pain ripped through her left shoulder and she gasped. Using the counter, she rose to her feet and staggered against the countertop. She felt her way along the wall into the small bathroom and brought handfuls of cold water to her face, patting it dry with a towel that hung from the shower rod. She straightened her clothing and slowly made her way to the now gaping entry door. She looked around to make sure Hank was gone before taking the duffle and duct-taped backpack in her right hand. She stepped carefully down the flimsy steps to begin her search for a place to spend the night.

Chapter Eight

Duvalle, Texas
October 1987

THE RUMBLING SOUND of thunder and distant flashes of lightning brought Athon's attention back to the present. She stopped to look around and could smell the heavy scent of ozone in the air. She was within about a mile and a half of Carver High School and needed to find shelter before the rain came. She increased her pace as much as she could, dragging the duffle and backpack behind her until she rounded a curve on the Fairfield Highway and saw a promising place off to her right. A six-foot chain link fence enclosed what looked like a junk yard. She followed the perimeter of the property until she located an opening. Her luck ran out as she entered the property the same time large, heavy drops of rain struck her head. She didn't see anyone around and ducked into the shadows. There were dozens of rusted out cars littering the property, but none of them provided much protection from the rain that had begun falling in sheets, causing her feet to slip in the mud. She tripped over something sticking out of the ground and went down hard, landing on her injured shoulder. White dots of varying sizes bounced around like pin balls behind her tightly closed eyelids as she tried to swallow back a scream of pain. She crawled to her knees and leaned her head back trying to take in a deeper breath, but the attempt only caused the pain across her ribs to increase. She pulled her arm up and worked it into the waist of her pants so it wouldn't move and cause more pain.

She was ready to give up and drown in a rain-soaked mud hole when she saw an old cab-over camper near the back property line. The top part rested on another old vehicle. She used what little strength she had left to stand and stumbled toward it. She ran her hand over her face as rivulets of water streamed over her eyes and pressed in the mechanism on the rusting screened door. She winced at the loud screeching sound of metal grinding against metal when she pulled the door open. She lifted her bags inside one at a time before crawling in behind them. She shivered uncontrollably from the cold wet clothes now glued to her body. Her shoulder throbbed with each shiver.

Flashes of lightning lit up the inside of the camper. It seemed to be in decent shape for something left out in the elements for God knew how long. She didn't know if the roof leaked from years of neglect, but saw an old mattress in the over-the-cab sleeping area. She forced her body up and pulled it to the floor. Layers of dust, nearly thick enough to choke her, flew up when she fell onto it. She tried unsuccessfully to suppress a coughing spasm. Despite the dust, the mattress wasn't any worse than what she'd been sleeping on, she thought. At least it didn't smell like piss. She was exhausted and within minutes the eyelid over her uninjured eye began drooping. She heard the heavy rain pelting the top of the aluminum camper and felt the gusts of wind that rocked it gently, lulling her to sleep.

BRIGHT LIGHT STABBED through her eyelids and pain shot through the area around her eye. The memory of the beating she'd taken from Hank Dailey came back to her and she tried to curl her aching body into as small a ball as possible. She flinched and yelped when a large hand touched her injured shoulder. Drops of water struck her face and dribbled down her neck. She panted in shallow breaths when the hand shook her and tried to roll her onto her back.

"It's all right. I won't hurt you. Just let me see how bad you're hurt," a deep, rumbling voice said. "Grit your teeth and you'll be safe soon. Bridget! Call an ambulance!" the voice called out.

"No," Athon managed. She heard heavy breathing as another person joined them.

"I told you I saw someone out here," a woman's voice said.

A hand stroked her head and Athon looked around wildly with her good eye. Although her vision was blurry she made out two faces. An older man with gray hair and at least a three day growth of stubble on his face leaned over her. What Athon saw in his eyes was concern and kindness. The second face was that of a woman in her early thirties holding a large umbrella and dressed in a nightgown that fell to her knees.

"Get me a blanket or somethin'," the old man said. "She's freezin'."

"That eye's not lookin' real good," the woman commented as she opened a compartment and dragged out a ragged old quilt.

"This shoulder is at least partially dislocated," the old man muttered as he carefully ran his big hand over it.

The woman stepped around Athon's body and knelt down behind her. She gently lifted Athon's head into her lap and covered her with the quilt. They heard the sound of a siren in the distance.

"You'll be in good hands soon, girlie," the man said.

Athon shook her head and gritted her teeth. "N-n-o d-d-doctor. N-n-no m-m-money," she said as she continued to shiver uncontrollably.

"Don't you worry about that, honey," the woman said, brushing Athon's hair away from where it was plastered to her forehead. "What's your name, baby?" the woman asked.

Chapter Nine

Helmand Province, Afghanistan
January 2010

ATHON WAS STARTLED by hands grabbing her roughly, holding her arms as they dropped. She was released and fell heavily to the ground. She struggled to get up, but only managed to crawl a short distance while trying to protect her side as she was jabbed with the barrels of several rifles. Her head throbbed. This was the end and she couldn't do a damn thing to stop it. A heavy foot rested against her hip and pushed her over. She grunted as a knee landed heavily in the middle of her back driving the air from her lungs, leaving her gasping to take a breath as her wrists were bound behind her. She was still trying to suck in a breath when she was jerked to her feet and dragged across the shaded clearing. She was lifted and body-slammed against a large, flat boulder. Pain stabbed through her wounded side. Black dots floated across her eyes as hands ran over her body and into her crotch, searching for God knew what. She saw meaty fingers grab at the heavy zipper of her flight suit. She yelled and glared at the foul-breathed man standing in front of her. The jarring blow of a rifle butt into her abdomen dropped her to her knees. Just as quickly someone grabbed a fistful of her hair and pulled her back to her feet, shoving her forcefully against the bark of a nearby tree. She felt the barrel of a weapon press under her chin hard enough to force her head back. The zipper of her flight suit was lowered and she closed her eyes as the clothing beneath the suit was thoroughly searched amidst the laughter of the group of smelly men surrounding her. To show their approval of her treatment, several fired off rounds into the air. Her feet were kicked out from under her and she hit the ground hard.

She tried to draw her knees up to protect her torso, but hands grabbed at her and forced her to stand. Suddenly she was filled with fury and resignation. This could go on until one of her captors finally got carried away and delivered a fatal blow. Well, why put it off any fucking longer, she thought as she jerked away from the hands and lashed out with her feet. She wanted to howl with laughter when her foot connected solidly after a lucky hit and she heard what sounded like cursing as a man hit the ground near her, clutching his crotch. Her resolution to end it all right there, right then, evaporated when her head was jerked back and metal pressed against her throat. Maybe she wasn't quite as ready to die as she thought.

Rapid voices, yelling in a language she didn't know, flew around her. She swallowed hard when her head was released and the knife, or whatever it was, left her throat. She shuffled her feet to steady her legs beneath her. Her efforts were stopped by another sharp blow to her abdomen followed by a staggering uppercut that sent her sprawling on the ground again, struggling to maintain consciousness. Her head was spinning as she was dragged roughly from one place to another until she was dropped into a snow-filled depression in the ground. She tried to roll onto her side in order to pull her face out of the snow that filled the depression, but a knee in the middle of her back held her in place. Hands held her legs down as her boots and socks were removed and her ankles bound together. Her head was lifted by her hair and something was pulled over her head, tied around her throat before being dropped back to the ground. Her heart stopped when a voice close to her ear spoke to her in broken English.

"You think you are so...what is the word...tough, yes, tough. Tell me what I want to know or I promise you will suffer. I have been to America. I know what you fear."

"What's that, frostbite?" Athon quipped. "Take this damn bag off my head and look me in the eye!" she demanded.

"We all look alike to you, don't we?"

"You all smell like a septic tank," she said. "That's for damn sure."

His low voice said, "We will play with you a while longer, I think."

The man moved away. "Continue," he said. "The whore will tell us what we want to know."

By turning her head slightly, Athon was able to find a way to breath. The snow around her was cold, but she was able to suck enough moisture through the fabric of the bag over her head to moisten her mouth. She felt her bound legs being raised, but didn't know why when they were dropped a moment later. She listened, hoping she would pick up something, anything she could use to help her escape. She was certain it was an impossibility, but hope kept her going. She had something, a new life, to return to. After hours of lying in the snow, she began to grow drowsy from the cold and couldn't feel her feet and hands any longer. She vaguely heard a slapping sound and was jerked across the ground by her ankles. Her head struck rocks beneath her and she lifted it. She heard someone make a clicking sound with their mouth. With each click her body was jerked forward again. She sucked in as much air as she could, but the fabric over her head was wet and clung to her nose and mouth when she breathed.

Her neck muscles screamed for relief as she continued to be periodically pulled over the ground. She could barely keep her eyes open between brief catnaps. She thought she heard a familiar sound in the distance and strained to hear. It was a helicopter. She was sure of it. Were they looking for her? As the sound came closer, she began to thrash around in the snow. Feet around her scrambled and her body was jerked once again, faster than before. She felt her body being rolled into the depression, her momentum stopped by something very hard. Her breathing rate increased. She couldn't see and didn't know what was happening. She turned her head to the side when she felt something landing on her body. Suddenly there was no more light coming through the fabric and the cold around her grew heavier. Oh my God! Her mind screamed. I'm being buried in the snow. The desire to survive was great and drove her body to continue thrashing. The weight of the snow over her head lessened and she gasped in a breath and lifted her head. A sharp blow to her forehead turned everything black.

WARMTH AND THE sound of pounding greeted Athon as she tried to open her eyes. She was no longer buried in snow. She tried to move her feet and hands, but they felt stiff and slow to respond to her mental commands. She was lying with her back bent over a log. Her ankles were tied to wooden pegs hammered into the ground and her wrists and upper arms were lashed to the log. Her head was tilted back, slightly lower than her shoulders.

She squinted into the blazing winter sun overhead and breathed in cold air that burned her nasal membranes. Her breathing rate had increased and her breath formed white puffs in the air as she exhaled. She twisted her head from side to side and observed a circle of men. No doubt about it, her situation was not going to improve any time soon. She closed her eyes and let the sunshine continue to warm her. A sharp, sudden blow to her abdomen forced breath from her lungs once again and her head jerked up. The cloth bag was jammed over her it again and loosely tied around her neck. Hands pushed her head back and she felt the edges of the bag being pounded into the ground. The muscles along her neck strained as she jerked her head and continued to fight against whatever was happening. A second blow to her abdomen served as a warning.

"What the hell?" she started as water began inundating the cloth bag, forcing the material into her nose and mouth when she tried to breathe, causing her to choke and sputter. Although her body needed water, drowning was not the way she'd hoped to receive it. She tried to move her head even slightly, but the material held her tightly. Her hands formed into fists as she gagged and fought for air. The flow of water stopped momentarily. She felt her chest expand when she was finally able to take a breath.

"I read about this in an American magazine," the voice returned next to her ear. "What do you think of our interpretation? Where is your base?"

"Go fuck yourself," Athon said between painful coughing spasms.

The flow of water began again before she could attempt to hold her breath. She had to struggle not to let panic set in. She wasn't sure how long she could endure this desert version of waterboarding before she either drowned or her heart gave out. She could feel it pounding against her chest wall, screaming for air. Then the water stopped again.

"Um, one of my friends has an interesting idea," the voice said.

"I can hardly wait," Athon choked out. Her neck muscles strained as she tried to move her head. From somewhere deep in her memory she recalled reading how Indians in the Old West tied wet leather strips around a captive's forehead and then left them tied out in the sun. As the leather dried, it tightened until the skull cracked. She didn't know if that had been true or not.

Her thoughts stopped as she felt something being dropped onto the wet cloth bag over her head. She could still breathe from the corners of her mouth with some effort, but at least she wasn't drowning. Suddenly small amounts of water began trickling onto the substance, creating an ooze of mud which seeped through the coarse material and ran into her nose. She tried exhaling in bursts to force the thick substance from her air passages, but nothing worked. Unable to find any air, her body began to thrash against the object beneath her. She was going to die in a sea of homemade desert quicksand. Bright lights danced in front of her eyes and she finally opened her mouth to let out the cry of someone dying. Her limbs went limp and the force of blood beating in her ears began to slow. Occasional muscle twitches moved her arms and legs as they began surrendering to death.

Chapter Ten

ATHON GASPED FOR air as she lay on her abdomen in the snow, her hands bound tightly behind her back. She could feel the gritty coarseness of sand and mud lining her mouth. Her stomach muscles clenched and she vomited water and brown, muddy slime. She could feel dried mud covering her face and hair. She could barely move her tongue, but she could breathe. A hand grabbed her hair and tilted her head back. Water flowed into her mouth and she gagged as more mud slithered down her throat. She couldn't remember ever being so tired. When the hand released her head, she didn't have the strength to stop it from hitting the ground. She heard the soft nickering of horses dancing near her. Too weak to prevent what was being done, her ankles were once again bound and attached to the rope around her wrists before being pulled together so tightly that her wrists touched her ankles. Her head fell forward, dangling helplessly from her shoulders. The hated bag was pulled over her head again before her body was lifted and moved. She was aware of feet moving around her, occasionally kicking her head. She groaned like the wounded animal she had become as she was pulled off the ground. Amidst raucous laughter, hands grabbed her head and delivered a blow hard enough to cause her body to spin helplessly, tightening the rope binding her hands and feet. A foot striking her head stopped the spinning, sending her in the opposite direction. Her body finally, mercifully went limp, continuing to slowly unwind.

The third, or perhaps the fourth, morning she was awakened by sharp kicks to her abdomen and ribs. Cold gusts of wind whipped at her hanging body. She was hungry and thirsty. She stiffened when she heard footsteps walking slowly toward her. Her body moved slightly before it fell to the ground. With no way to stop her fall, she slammed into the frozen ground and fell onto her side. She barely felt it when the rope holding her wrists to her ankles was cut and her legs dropped heavily to the ground. Moments later the bag was jerked from her head and the rope binding her wrists was cut away, allowing them to slide down her sides. The man stared into her eyes for a moment before pulling her numb arms over her head and re-tying her wrists. He ran a second rope between her bound wrists and looped the rope through a ring on the saddle of a nearby horse. He pulled Athon off her feet as he brought her arms to the ring and tied it off. Her feet were so cold she couldn't feel them other than periodic sensations that felt like a thousand needles stabbing into the soles of her feet. As she tried to keep her feet beneath her, he pressed his body against hers and whispered, "Do you fear what all women fear?" Athon jerked at the ring holding her against the horse. "Ah, I see that even a tough woman fears the invasion of her body," he said as he pressed his fingers down her sides and into her crotch. "You have raped my whole country," he spat. "Who will care about one weak American whore? My men have not pleasured themselves for a long time. Perhaps their wait will end this evening."

Athon closed her eyes, Hank's face flashing through her mind. "I'll kill myself first," she croaked.

He ground himself against her and she could feel his arousal. "I will decide when you die, whore. I think I will take you last so you will beg me to end your suffering. You see, some of my men are not as nice as I am. You remind me of a wild stallion," he said as he ran a hand through her hair. "I think I will enjoy breaking you."

Rage coursed through Athon's body as she fought with the only weapon she had left. She threw her head back sharply and smiled as it struck the man's face with a satisfying crack. He yelped and shoved her forehead against the saddle before he walked away wiping blood from his face. He paused to slap the rear of the horse, watching it drag Athon as it trotted to join others in the small herd.

Once the camp was packed up, Athon was released from the ring and dropped heavily to her knees. Periodically, the rider holding the rope which bound her wrists tugged it, forcing her to walk faster or dragging her if she fell before stopping to allow her to stand. The sun beat down on Athon's head as she stumbled along barefooted, leaving bloody tracks in the snow. She tried to produce enough saliva in her dry mouth to moisten her split lips. She heard a familiar sound in the distance and searched the sky, but was unable to tell which direction it came from. The horses stopped and danced around amid a flurry of voices. She fell to her knees in the snow and brought a handful to her mouth. Just give it up, she told herself. Don't get up again and this will end.

Gunfire erupted around her and chaotic yells seemed to come from everywhere. She fell into the snow and covered her head the best she could with her bound hands. A Blackhawk was laying down rows of machine gun fire through the group that held her, spraying puffs of snow into the air. Not far from where she lay she saw the lifeless eyes of the heavily bearded man who had taunted her. When she blinked Hank's face momentarily replaced that of the terrorist. She forced the vision away to low-crawl toward him and pull his pistol from his hand. She ran her hands beneath his clothing, smiling as she withdrew a dagger from his waist. She clawed her way toward a dead horse and slithered behind it.

Holding the dagger between her knees, she sawed at the rope around her wrists. She was weak from lack of food or water and the dagger slipped a couple of times, causing her to cut herself, but she ignored the blood and continued sawing at the rope. Once it fell away, she looked over the body of the large dead animal in front of her. Four of her captors remained alive. Two were firing at the Blackhawk while the last two were putting a missile launcher together. She pushed her body up and willed her legs to move. Bent at the waist, she ran up behind the closest man and drew the dagger across his throat. As he grasped his throat in a futile attempt to staunch the bleeding, she grabbed his automatic weapon and swung it toward the remaining men. She yelled as loud as she could and felt her anger release as the rounds left the barrel of the weapon and slammed into two of the men. A return round burned into her shoulder, but she barely felt it and dropped to a prone position to return fire. The helicopter disappeared over a rise, but she could still hear the whirling sound of its rotors as it prepared for another pass. She thought, as she took aim and fired, just don't fire your missiles.

She fired at the remaining enemy until the click from the trigger told her she was out of ammunition. The Blackhawk still hadn't returned and she saw the man rise to his feet, his weapon aimed at her. She ducked her head and covered it with her arms, a prayer speeding through her mind. She was so close, so close. She heard the report of a weapon, but felt nothing. Could it really be that painless? Then strong arms were pulling her onto her back as she continued to cover her head with her own arms.

"Dailey! I gotcha! Let's get the hell outta here."

She lowered her arms and looked into the eyes of Frank Hardesty. She threw her arms up and hugged him fiercely as tears ran down her face creating a muddy, blood-tinged rivulet.

"My crew. They're all dead, Frank," she whimpered.

"I know. But you survived. Let's get you home," he said.

He patted her on the back and stood to pick her up. The look on his face changed from jubilation to disbelief as a shot rang out, followed by more gunfire from the men who had accompanied him. They both fell to the ground and Athon crawled closer to him.

"Son of a bitch shot me," Frank groaned.

"Medic!" Athon screamed.

"SHE'S SEIZING, DOCTOR!" the nurse said as she rolled

Athon's body to the side to make sure her airway remained clear. Stephens quickly forced Athon's jaws open far enough to slide a padded instrument into her mouth to prevent her from biting or choking on her tongue. "Ativan," she said calmly. Gradually, not long after the injection was given, Athon's body seemed to relax. "Get her ready for transport and make a note to the doctors on-board about the seizure."

Dr. Stephens left the emergency room and walked to the nurse's station, pulling a chart down and flipping to the page containing doctor's notes. She sat down and read through what little information there was regarding Major Athon Dailey's treatment in the field and during her evacuation to Landstuhl. She turned back to the personal information page and glanced down at her emergency notification sheet. There was no family listed. Stephens reached into her coat pocket and withdrew a business card. She tapped it against her chin before picking up the desk phone and dialing. The phone rang four times and Stephens was preparing to hang up when she heard an out-of-breath voice on the other end.

"Miss Shelton? This is Dr. Stephens at Landstuhl Medical Facility."

"Is Athon all right? Is something wrong?"

Stephens cleared her throat. "She suffered a seizure while we were preparing her for transport."

"Oh, God," Lauren moaned. "I have to see her again, please."

Stephens looked up to see Athon's gurney being rolled toward the ambulance bay. "We've stabilized her and she's being taken to the ambulance for transport now. Are you flying to the States?"

"I was going out the door to catch my flight when you called. It leaves in two hours."

"I'll call a colleague at Walter Reed. When you get there ask for Colonel Beverly Thompson. She'll be expecting you."

"Dr. Stephens, thank you. I...I don't know what to say."

"It's what I'd want. Having a loved one nearby is important for a patient's recovery. Have a safe trip."

Chapter Eleven

Duvalle, Texas
October 1987

GENTLE ROCKING LULLED Athon into a deep sleep. The pain was gone except for a dull lingering throb around her eye and through her shoulder, along with a persistent headache. Her mind drifted back to the beating she'd suffered at the hands of the man who was supposed to be her father. The man who was supposed to take care of her. He'd taken care of her all right. Although she thought she'd die at the time, she vowed it would never happen again.

The sun was already climbing its way toward noon on Friday when the woman, who introduced herself as Bridget Fitzgerald, pushed Athon's wheelchair out of the emergency room doors. Her father, whom Athon learned was Pudge Fitzgerald, had left to bring his car around to pick them up after Athon refused to stay in the hospital. She tried to find a comfortable way to sit in the wheelchair, but there was no place on her body that didn't ache. Only medication had lessened the dull throb in her shoulder, which the doctor discovered had indeed been dislocated. A sling held her left arm close to her body to prevent further damage to the fragile joint.

The car stopped in front of Athon and Bridget and Athon tried unsuccessfully to lift her sore body using only her right arm. Pudge swung the back door open and he and Bridget were able to help Athon stand and rotate in order to sit in the back seat. When everyone was reasonably situated, Pudge started the car and looked at his passenger in the back seat.

"Where to, girlie?" he asked. Athon was growing accustomed to the deep, gravelly voice. Pudge Fitzgerald had stayed as close as possible to Athon during the long hours she had spent in the emergency room and held her hand as the doctor stitched up a couple of deep cuts on her face.

"Buena Ventana Trailer Court," Athon answered through gritted teeth.

"Why you wanna go there?" he asked. "Ain't nothin' there but a bunch of abandoned old trailers."

"Home, sweet home," Athon mumbled.

"Where's your mama?"

Athon took as deep a breath as her body allowed. "Jail," she muttered.

"And your daddy?" Bridget asked.

"Don't know or care. Drunk or high somewhere."

Pudge squinted into the rearview mirror. "Well, I can either take you to my place where we can look after you, or to that shitty old camper we found you in," Pudge said.

"Just take me to Buena Ventana," Athon said. "I can get in."

"Maybe I should call Child Protective Services," he said, turning his head to look at the battered teenager in his back seat.

"I ain't no child!" Athon said, pulling her body up by grabbing the front seat with her good arm. "Stop the fuckin' car!"

Pudge pulled the car to the side of the highway and stopped.

"Daddy?" Bridget started, but Pudge waved her off.

Athon jerked the car door open and forced her body to swivel into the opening. She slid out and tried to stand up. Her knees buckled and she fell face first into the grass and weeds next to the car before rolling down the embankment. When the pain in her shoulder and ribs subsided, she struggled in an attempt to get up as Pudge watched her, a grin on his lips.

"How long you gonna let her lay there like that, Daddy?" Bridget huffed.

"Until she figures out she needs help," Pudge answered.

After several failed attempts, Athon dropped onto her back, panting.

"Well, this is about the stupidest thing I've ever seen," Bridget grumbled as she opened the passenger side door and stepped out of the car. She squatted down and lightly touched Athon's abdomen.

"Girl, you ain't never met any human as stubborn as my daddy," Bridget said as she looked into Athon's pain-filled, bloodshot blue eyes. "He'll sit out here all damn day in this heat watching you squirm around like a worm on a hook. We been up most of the night and I'm plumb tuckered. The beds at Daddy's house are a lot more comfortable than these weeds and rocks. So how about I help you back into the car and we all get some rest?"

"I...I can't pay him and don't want no ch...charity," Athon managed. "I gotta go to work."

"He'll find a way to make you pay so don't you worry none about that," Bridget said with a laugh. She looked into the car. "Daddy! Daddy! Wake the hell up! I can't lift this girl by myself."

Pudge sat up and shook his head, rubbing a meaty hand up and down his face. "Finally come to her senses, did she?" he grunted.

"Let's get her home," Bridget said.

Athon was surprised at the old man's strength when he lifted her into his arms. He backed into the back seat and sat down, still cradling her body. "You drive, Bridge," he said. He scooted to the far side of the vehicle and let Athon slide out of his arms with her head resting on his lap. As Bridget started the car and pulled back onto the highway, Athon felt his rough, callused hand stroke her hair and she felt safe for the first time she could remember.

THREE DAYS LATER Athon sat at the small table in Pudge Fitzgerald's kitchen shoveling a mound of scrambled eggs into her mouth and washing it down with a cup of the best hot fresh coffee she'd ever tasted. Her shoulder still ached, but the sling was thankfully gone.

"You gonna be okay to return to school today?" Pudge asked.

"I don't have a choice. I'm behind enough already."

"Don't let anyone run into you today. You're still pretty bruised up. What did you do to deserve such a beatin'?"

"I don't wanna talk about it. I probably deserved it."

"Nobody deserves a beatin' like that. I'll drive you to school and give them your note from the hospital."

"I can do it. You ain't my daddy, you know," Athon bristled.

"I 'spect I'm a damn sight better than your daddy, girl," Pudge snapped.

Athon scratched her bruised cheek, hoping the old man didn't catch a glimpse of the hurt in her eyes.

He cleared his throat and softened his voice before saying, "Since neither of your folks is around, I'll watch out for you until you can take care of yourself."

"I appreciate what you did for me, Mr. Fitzgerald. I'll find another place to stay by next weekend. I can go back to work tonight."

"You can stay here. Or in that old camper. I figure in another week or so you can start workin' off what you owe me. If you leave I'll never get my money back. Where you workin'?" Pudge eyed Athon and took a deep breath.

"Tiny's."

"I'll go by and tell him why you ain't been there."

ATHON HATED THE thought of everyone staring at her and snickering as she followed Pudge into the main office of Carver High School later that morning. She brushed her shaggy hair over her forehead and tried to keep her head down as much as possible as she shoved a hand into the front pocket of her jeans. When Mrs. Fortenberry saw her she winced and sucked in a breath.

"Lordy mercy! What on earth happened to you, Athon Dailey?"

"Had an accident."

"Did you walk in front of a vehicle?"

"No, ma'am," Athon said, trying not to move her jaw any more than necessary.

Pudge slid the hospital release form, along with a doctor's order, across the counter. He leaned closer and whispered something Athon couldn't hear to the secretary. Mrs. Fortenberry nodded and smiled at Pudge. "How's Bridget doing?" she asked nonchalantly. "She get her beautician's license yet?"

"Takes the state test in a couple of weeks, Ellie. Then she can start gettin' paid to fix hair. I been settin' up a little shop for her in the old garage. Looks real nice."

"Tell her to give me a call when she's ready," Mrs. Fortenberry said. She wrote a pass out and handed it to Athon. She stuffed the pass in her shirt pocket and turned to leave.

"I'll pick you up when school lets out," Pudge said. "Out front."

They watched Athon sling her backpack over her good shoulder and walk slowly into the hallway.

"Know much about her?" Pudge leaned his elbows on the counter. Everyone knew Ellie Fortenberry was the biggest gossip in town and never minded spreading what she knew. Ellie looked around to make sure no one else was nearby.

"I knew her mama when she was a student here at Carver, but that was years ago. Come from a real good family. I think her daddy was a lawyer or something. Then she discovered drugs, booze, and boys, not necessarily in that order. She left home and was working over at the Rusty Spur before she even graduated, servin' drinks and strippin' for the men until she got pregnant. With Athon, I guess. I heard Hank Dailey is Athon's daddy. He went to school here too, off and on. Always in trouble, like Athon, and dropped out because he was so far behind. He claims he isn't Athon's daddy, but who knows."

"The girl says her mama's in jail," Pudge said.

"Probably is then, again. I suppose Athon's raised herself for the most part. It's a shame because her teachers all say she's smart as a whip." Ellie paused and lowered her voice even further. "I heard she's a...lesbian."

Pudge chuckled. Ellie shushed him and leaned closer. "She don't exactly make it a secret and that's what gets her in trouble, mostly for fighting. She's got a hair-trigger temper and the other students know it. All they have to do is say something she takes offense to and the fight is on." Ellie drew herself up and looked at Pudge. "Otherwise she seems like a nice enough kid. She's always been polite to me and Lord knows she hasn't had many breaks or role models in her life. At least this is her last year at Carver."

ATHON OPENED THE door to her classroom and walked in, her jaw raised defiantly. Snickers rippled through the room when the other students saw her face. She handed the pass to the teacher and limped down the aisle to her desk. Out of the corner of her eye she saw Craig Hickson grin as she sat down and began pulling her notebook and pen from her backpack. She ignored them and leaned back to wait for the teacher to begin the day's lesson. Once everyone had begun working, Ms. Davenport made her way to Athon's desk and knelt down next to it.

"Before you leave you can pick up the folder of make-up work from my desk. Are you all right?"

"Yes, ma'am."

"Let me know if you have any questions."

Athon nodded and glanced up to see her classmates still staring at her. She'd avoided any mirrors in Pudge's house that morning, but guessed her face was pretty messed up. When Ms. Davenport stood and ordered the students to resume their work, Athon noticed Lauren Shelton continued looking at her. Athon lifted the side of her mouth in a semi-smile. It hurt too damn much for a real grin and when she did the stitches on her cheek and over her eye pulled. She lowered her head to work, but periodically glanced in the girl's direction. A tap on her sore arm startled her and she visibly winced.

"Guess you ran into someone tougher'n you," Craig muttered. "Sucks to be you, Dailey," he said with a giggle.

Athon turned her head toward him and forced a smile before responding, "Catch you later, dickhead."

"You threatening me, perv?"

She simply smiled at him and continued with her work. About five minutes before the bell rang Ms. Davenport called Athon to the front of the room.

"The note requested I let you leave a few minutes early to make it to your next class." When Athon started to return to her desk to get her backpack, Ms. Davenport said, "Lauren, can you assist Athon to her next class?"

Lauren nodded and packed her things quickly before retrieving Athon's old backpack and walking to the door.

As soon as they entered the hallway, Athon said, "I can handle it," and reached for the backpack.

"I got it," Lauren said. "What happened?"

"A disagreement. No big deal."

"When someone kicks the crap out of you, it is a big deal,"

Lauren said with a frown. "Will you be okay?"

"Yeah. I'm always okay."

Athon glanced around the hallway to avoid looking at the attractive mocha-skinned girl next to her. She had cinnamon eyes accented by the reddish tint of her hair. She was beautiful. It was all Athon could do not to stare at Lauren's moist, full lips. She wished she could think of something suave to say, but the truth was she didn't feel very suave at the moment.

Athon limped slowly down the hall. Periodically Lauren reached out to steady her. Athon felt the warmth of her hand on her back and tried to ignore it.

"So do you like the school?" Athon asked.

"Yeah, it's okay. Not as many students as my old school so that's kind of nice."

"Your parents moved here on purpose?"

"My father's the new pastor at Eastside Presbyterian Church."

"You're really pretty," Athon blurted.

Athon watched Lauren's skin turn that amazing, indescribable color when she blushed at the remark.

"Thanks." Lauren laughed at the compliment and Athon enjoyed the sound of it. "You can be my first friend here," Lauren said.

Athon shook her head. "Hangin' with me isn't a good idea if you care about your reputation. I'm okay alone. Always have been." She took her backpack from Lauren and rested against the wall outside her next class to wait for the bell. "Thanks though." Athon refused to look at Lauren as she walked away. She couldn't stand to let anyone see how defeated she felt despite her bravado. She wouldn't let anyone see that.

Chapter Twelve

ALTHOUGH ATHON WAS grateful to Pudge for helping her, once she was back on her feet she convinced him to let her convert the cab-over camper into her temporary home and offered to pay rent. He flatly turned down the rent, but agreed to let her use the camper. Tiny gave her the rest of the week off while Bridget helped her carry a load of cleaning supplies to the camper before hauling a pile of sheets and cleaning rags back to the house to be washed and dried.

Any light coming through the camper windows was muted by several years' worth of dirt and grime. Athon found two large plastic cat litter containers and filled them with water and poured a few capfuls of cleaning solution into an old bucket and wrung out the excess water to begin cleaning up the inside of the camper shell. By the time she finished there were no more dust motes floating around her and she could see out the window next to the elevated sleeping area. It was the cleanest place she'd ever lived. She made a list of things she would need to live independently.

Every day Bridget picked Athon up from school and drove her to the junk yard. When she entered the camper, she almost always found something Pudge no longer needed or used that made her life a little easier. She was particularly glad when she found a couple of old lanterns, a camping stove, and a rusty cooler stacked outside the camper door. She checked books on survival out of the school library and, in her spare time, learned to set up a cooking area and a solar shower. She dug a hole outside the camper in a shaded area and buried the cooler three-fourth of the way in the ground, leaving the drain open. She kept a few items in it and bought a bag of ice every two or three days. It wasn't ideal, but she felt comfortable and safe. Bridget always cooked too much food and dropped off a plate for her most nights or she made something simple on the camp stove. Occasionally, Pudge stopped by to chat and kill time while they sat on a couple of old car seats Athon found and was using as lawn chairs. No matter how much she fought it, Athon was becoming attached to the gruff old man and his daughter.

EXCEPT FOR THE one class they shared, Athon didn't see Lauren often. Once or twice Lauren attempted to chat her up, but Athon saw the way other students looked at them and brushed her off. It was a blustery October Saturday when Athon opened the bay doors at Tiny's Garage and prepared for another day at work. Early that morning she walked to a small diner downtown that was looking for a dishwasher for the evening shift during the week. She'd never have a social life, but the extra money would come in handy. Neither of her jobs required more than t-shirts and jeans. She wasn't required to talk to anyone or smile at people she had to pretend she liked. Each job allowed her to remain anonymous to everyone around her and she preferred that it remain that way. She only had seven months left before she could escape Duvalle.

Athon put away the tools Tiny had used during the week, wondering how he ever found the one he needed on the cluttered work bench. Her job that day was to take all the old oil gathered during the week and pour it into fifty-five gallon barrels. The recycling truck would be by at the beginning of the next week to haul it away. She would rather be working on a car, but in every job there was a chore no one really wanted to do. There was always sludge in the bottom of each oil pan and she had to scoop it out. It took a miracle to avoid coating her arms with the black substance. When a miracle didn't occur, Tiny accused Athon of trying to make herself as black and beautiful as he was.

Usually during the week Bridget picked Athon up at school and dropped her off at the diner and picked her up around eleven. On the weekends she walked to Tiny's and he drove her to the diner after he closed. Because the diner closed later on Saturday, Athon walked the three or four miles back to the junkyard and collapsed into her clean bed, usually still dressed. When she woke up on Sunday she spent the day doing homework and helping Pudge strip parts for customers. So far today was just another Saturday.

The loud honking of a horn drew Athon back to what she was doing. She glanced over her shoulder in time to see a tall, well-dressed white man in a gray suit climb out of a car driven by a young girl. When the girl stepped out from behind the wheel, Athon smiled. The man shook hands with Tiny and the two discussed something while Lauren looked around and checked out the displays of hoses, belts, and filters. Athon looked at her hands and arms and finished emptying the last oil collection into the barrel. She grabbed a rag from her back pocket and wiped away the thickest collection of sludge before dipping her hands in the mechanic's goop and rubbing it on her hands and arms. She loved the gritty feel of the gel and was glad that it removed most of the slick, black sludge except from around her fingernails. From the corner of her eye she saw Lauren waltzing toward her as she checked out the last display of key rings.

"I didn't know you worked here," Lauren said, her voice soft.

Athon shrugged and grinned. "Something wrong with your car," she said, leaning against the work bench and taking a look at Lauren's car. "Nice ride," she offered.

"Don't ever buy one," Lauren replied. "They might be eye candy, but are a maintenance hog. Always in the shop for something."

"What's the problem today?"

"It's missing."

"Might need new spark plugs or a timing adjustment."

"You any good?"

Athon grinned again and stepped a little closer. "Depends on what you're talkin' about."

Lauren blushed, her skin turning that amazing color Athon liked and pushed Athon playfully. "You're really bad, you know?"

"Haven't had any complaints so far." With a wink Athon turned on the water in the stainless steel sink with her elbow and filled her hands with soap to wash away the goop"

"Athon, c'mere a minute," Tiny called out.

She turned the water off and dried her hands with a shop towel as she walked toward Tiny.

"Athon, this is Reverend Shelton," Tiny introduced the man with him. "His daughter's car is missing and I can't get to it right now. Listen to it and see what you think."

"She's only a kid," Reverend Shelton said with a laugh.

"She's been workin' for me two years now and I've taught her pretty much all I know. I guarantee all her work." Tiny looked toward Lauren. "Can you start it up, please?"

Lauren slid behind the steering wheel and turned the key in the ignition. Athon leaned over the engine and turned her head to listen for any unusual sounds. "Rev the engine a little," she said loudly.

Lauren pressed down the accelerator slowly. Athon reached into the engine compartment and grabbed the accelerator rod. As the engine whined loudly, Athon leaned in farther and closed her eyes. "Timing sounds off a little. Minor adjustment." She stood up and looked at Reverend Shelton. "I need to ride in it or drive it to see when it's missing."

Reverend Shelton raised an eyebrow and looked at Athon's greasy clothes. She unzipped her overalls and stepped out of them. Lauren stepped out of the vehicle and met Athon's eyes as she stripped out of the overalls. Athon bent over to untie her work boots.

"Guess you'll have to drive," she said. "I'm not supposed to drive without shoes."

Lauren returned to the car while Athon placed a protective paper on the passenger seat and floor board before getting in. "We'll be back in a few minutes," she said confidently. "Just go down the highway a ways and turn into the nearest housing area," she instructed Lauren.

Athon turned the radio off and crouched down on the floorboard, pressing her ear against the carpeting. She finally sat back in the seat. "Let me drive," she said. "I'm insured."

"What about your shoes?" Lauren asked.

"I won't tell if you won't."

Lauren pulled to the curb, removed her seat belt and scooted across the seat closer to Athon. Athon laughed. "You could just open the door and get out," she said.

"It's more fun this way. Crawl over me," Lauren said with a grin that made Athon's heart miss a beat.

Athon cleared her throat and lifted her body, careful not to touch Lauren, and dropped onto the driver's seat. She shifted into gear and pulled back onto the road. After a series of stops and starts, she pulled over to let Lauren drive back to Tiny's. She scooted over and Lauren raised her hips to slide over Athon. When Lauren paused briefly, her butt hovering over Athon's lap for a moment, Athon inhaled a deep breath and held Lauren's earthy scent in her nose and lungs as long as she could. Lauren dropped into the seat and drove back to Tiny's. Athon saw the frown on Reverend Shelton's face as Lauren brought the vehicle to a stop and they both got out.

"Whatdaya think?" Tiny asked.

"New plugs and a little adjustment," Athon answered, shoving her hands into her pockets.

"Can you fix it today?" Shelton asked.

"It should be ready by the time we close," Tiny said. "Leave your phone number in case it's ready sooner. Otherwise we'll see you around five," he added as he shook Shelton's hand.

Shelton turned to his daughter. "Call your mother. She had to take Devin to practice and I need to get to the church."

The Reverend and Lauren waited inside as Athon pulled the vehicle into a bay and popped the hood. She began removing the old spark plugs and noticed a few of them seemed burned. She checked the gap on each plug and set them aside for Tiny to double check. She wiped her hands and headed to the bins where new plugs were kept. As she walked back toward Lauren's car she saw a tall, attractive woman with dark skin get out of her car. Shelton kissed her lightly on the lips and took the car keys from her while

Lauren greeted her and started talking. Athon could easily see where Lauren got her good looks. She carried three sets of plugs to Reverend Shelton and explained the advantages and disadvantages of each brand, letting him decide how much he was willing to pay. She personally recommended a medium-priced set of plugs because she had found them more reliable than the more expensive plugs. They looked fancy, but didn't perform any better than a cheaper plug. Once she had Shelton's approval she walked back into the bay, with a glance at Lauren as she got into the back seat of her mother's car.

Just before closing, Athon removed her overalls and scrubbed her hands and arms to wash away any lingering vestiges of oil and automotive grime. Reverend Shelton and Lauren parked in front of the garage and Lauren stared at her vehicle. It had been a relatively slow day and Athon spent a little time washing Lauren's car and cleaning out the inside. Tiny went inside and settled the bill for the repair as Lauren walked around her car, reaching out to touch the shiny surface occasionally. She waved at her father as he drove away before settling behind the wheel. Lauren saw Tiny leave the office and go to where Athon was standing, resting a large hand on her shoulder. Athon nodded and picked up her backpack. She cast a wave at Lauren as she jogged across the highway and began walking.

Lauren pulled onto the shoulder ahead of Athon. When Athon reached the vehicle, Lauren lowered the window and stuck her head out.

"Need a ride?" she asked.

"No thanks. I'm good," Athon answered.

"So you keep telling me," Lauren said with a suggestive grin as her eyes scanned down Athon's lean body and she moistened her lips. "Where you headed?"

"I got a job downtown."

"When do you have to be there?"

"Six."

"Well, get in and I'll drop you off. I promise not to bite."

Athon grinned. "There you go with that bitin' thing again." She shook her head and walked round the vehicle to the passenger side. "Thanks," she said as she slid in.

Lauren checked the traffic before merging onto the highway. They rode in awkward silence for a while before Athon asked, "How's it handlin'?"

"What?"

"The car. Seems to be runnin' okay now."

"Yeah, but knowing it the way I do, today won't be its last trip to the garage." Lauren sighed and ran her finger into her hairline near her temple.

"Maybe you should sell it."

Lauren shook her head. "My father's a nice enough man, but totally into status symbols, which includes this car. So where do you work downtown?"

"I wash dishes at Gus' Diner on Main," Athon said. "You can drop me off in the alley in back."

"How do you get home?"

"Someone usually picks me up or I walk."

"What time do you get off? I can pick you up," Lauren offered with a tinge of excitement in her voice.

"I get off late. I can walk. It's Saturday and you should be out having fun with your friends."

"I'd rather drive you home."

"I get off about one, maybe a little sooner. Your parents might not like you out that late just to give someone a ride."

"I'll handle that. Hey, maybe we can grab a burger or something before I take you home."

Athon laughed. "I work in a food joint. They feed me dinner."

"Well, at least bring me a drink."

Athon lowered her head. "Thanks. Be careful." When Lauren pulled into the alley and stopped Athon pushed out of the car and took the concrete steps to the back door of Gus' two at a time.

"WHERE YOU BEEN, *chica*?" the short order cook, Pedro Martinez, asked as Athon tied the strings of an apron around her waist.

"Had to get a ride," she said, glancing at the growing stack of glasses, dishes, and silverware around the sink.

"Tiny had a last minute rush come in," she added while she ran water in the deep, dented stainless steel sink and started washing.

An hour later she slid two racks of glasses into a large oven to dry them off. She wished for the umpteenth time that Gus would buy an industrial dishwasher. It would cut her time in half. She grabbed a pail and mop and cleaned the bathrooms. She refilled the soap dispenser and made sure there was plenty of toilet paper. She swept the main dining area and scrubbed down the tables. It was going to be a long night, but she would appreciate it on pay day. The dinner rush never started until around seven and everything was prepped and ready by six-thirty. She helped Pedro chop onions, lettuce, and tomatoes before they decided to take a break and relax a little. Athon jumped up on a short retaining wall that ran along the alleyway behind the diner. Pedro offered her a cigarette and she took it. He opened the back door and found the basketball he always brought to work. Gus had brought an old basketball goal left at home when his kids moved out for Pedro to use. Pedro tossed the ball to Athon and prepared to defend the old goal. Athon dropped her cigarette and jumped from the wall. At five-ten she was as tall as Pedro and a decent long-range shooter. They ran around the alley and laughed when either one did something stupid while pretending to be a professional basketball player. Pedro had just finished the last letter of their game of horse when Gus stuck his head out the back door.

The next couple of hours went by quickly as Athon bussed the tables when customers left and even managed to get ahead on the dishwashing. A little after eleven a group of teens who had just come from a movie loudly entered the diner. Athon had been hoping to make it back to the camper before two in the morning, but figured the group would hang around at least an hour. As soon as they left, Athon cleared the table while Gus locked the front door and lowered the blinds. Athon scraped off the plates and dumped the discarded paper and food into a large garbage bag. Pedro scrubbed down his grill while Gus refilled salt and pepper shakers and napkin holders. Tying the bag securely, Athon hoisted the garbage bag over her shoulder and carried it toward the dumpster in the alley. She swung the bag into a large arc and let it fall. She wiped her hands on her apron and turned back to the diner. Before she had taken two steps, a large, shaggy-looking man stepped out of the shadows and wiped his nose with the back of his hand.

"What do you want?" she spat.

"Got any cash on ya?" he asked.

"Not for you. I don't work every damn day to support your habits," she snapped as she tried to push past him

He grabbed her by the shoulder he'd dislocated a month earlier and squeezed, causing her to grimace. "Now that ain't no way to talk to your dear ol' daddy, girl."

Athon couldn't stop the harsh laughter that bubbled up inside her. "My daddy? The only time you claim that title is when you need money. Otherwise, I'm just Michelle's bastard brat!" She pushed him away roughly. "Leave me the hell alone, you pathetic son of a bitch."

Hank grabbed Athon's shoulder roughly and spun her toward him. He shifted his hand and grabbed the front of her shirt, holding her as his hand snapped across her face. She stumbled backward and hit the metal dumpster behind her. Dazed, she shook her head and stood to face the now angry drunk. A car horn distracted them both and Athon saw Lauren's car pull into the alley.

"Hey! What's going on?" Lauren demanded as she stepped

from the vehicle.

"Just a little family disagreement," Hank slurred. "Take a hike."

"Are you all right?" Lauren asked, turning her attention to Athon.

"Get out of here," Athon ordered through clenched teeth.

"This what you're into now, girl. She's a pretty little split-tail even if she is a little on the dark side." He hitched up his pants and stepped toward Lauren. "I ain't had me no sweet dark meat in a long time," he sneered.

"Back off, Hank!"

Hank spun back around to Athon again. Before he could move closer she pulled her switchblade from her back pocket and snapped it open. "Don't make me hurt you," she said.

Hank suddenly roared with laughter and advanced toward Athon. She moved away from the dumpster, but held her ground. As soon as he was within her reach she flicked the switchblade out and cut his arm. He hollered, his voice now filled with pain and rage. Athon's head snapped around and she covered her head when the sound of a shotgun blast broke through the darkness. Gus stood in the back door of the diner, his shotgun aimed at Hank.

"You go!" he said.

Blood had soaked through Hank's shirt and dripped from his fingertips. "She cut me, you stupid wetback," he argued. "Call the fuckin' cops!"

"You alive," Gus barked as he cocked the hammer on his shotgun. He came slowly down the steps and waited for Hank to move away. He followed him, but stopped next to Athon. "You leave now. We finish."

"I'm sorry, Gus," Athon murmured.

"No you fault." He smiled at her. "See you Monday." He released the shotgun long enough to pat Athon's shoulder while keeping an eye on Hank.

Athon removed her work apron and handed it to Pedro who had joined them. "Give me knife," Pedro whispered. "I keep for you."

She nodded and closed it before handing it to him. "Thanks, man."

Lauren grabbed Athon's hand and dragged her toward the car. Athon climbed in and slouched down in the seat as Lauren backed out of the alley. Athon directed her to the main highway and stared out the side window into the night.

"You always carry a knife?" Laura asked.

"Since I was ten," Athon said, exhaling a deep breath.

"Are you okay?" Lauren asked softly.

"Hunky damn dory," Athon muttered. "Let me off at Tiny's," she added. "I can walk from there."

"I can drive you home," Lauren said.

"I said drop me off at Tiny's!" Athon repeated angrily.

"Was that your father?"

Athon shrugged. "Hell if I know." She looked across the car seat and her eyes narrowed. "My mother is an addict and a whore. She fucked so many men she wasn't sure which one knocked her up and just picked one. Happy?"

"You didn't have to tell me all that, Athon."

"Everyone around here already knows anyway."

"Is that why they treat you like shit?"

"Doesn't matter. Pull over. I can walk from here. Go back where you belong, Lauren. Stay away from me."

Chapter Thirteen

Duvalle, Texas
October 1987

ONCE THE WEATHER began to cool slightly into what Texans laughingly called fall, Pudge put Athon to work helping him clean up the large lot of his junk yard. It took her several tries to start the gas-powered weed eater and her shoulder ached from pulling the rope. He woke her up early on Sunday and fed her a good breakfast before walking with her to the far side of the junk yard. She spent most of the morning cutting down tall grass that had grown up around the discarded vehicles. She had no clue what he planned to do with the rusting hulks and doubted he did either. By noon her t-shirt felt like it was glued to her body from a mixture of sweat and dust. Her hands tingled from the vibration of the weed eater and she sat down on the torn seat from an old car and leaned her head back. She was so tired she was sure she'd fall asleep. She closed her eyes and readjusted the old, faded green John Deere baseball cap Pudge had given her.

"I ain't payin' you to sleep, girlie," Pudge's voice said, forcing Athon to open her eyes. He was on the old golf cart he used to get around the property.

"You ain't payin' me period and I needed a break, old man" she said as she unscrewed the lid on a canteen of water and squinted at him. "I'm allowed."

"Fall asleep out here and you'll turn into a lobster in nothin' flat."

"I know," she snapped as she stood up.

"Don't get smart with me, kid. I come to tell you Bridget has lunch ready and you got company."

"Nobody knows where I live."

"Reckon someone does. Kinda cute little gal, too."

"What?"

"You losin' your hearin', girlie?"

"I got a name, old man."

"So do I. Mine's Pudge. Actually it's not, that's just a nickname. What's yours?"

"I don't have a nickname, but most people just call me perv."

"Be proud of your name, Athon Dailey. You ain't your folks. Now get in the damn cart and let's go. Leave the weed whacker. You'll be back."

Athon stepped onto the old golf cart next to Pudge and sat back. She swung off the torn seat a few minutes later before it came to a full stop. When they entered the mud room of the old house she heard laughter coming from the kitchen. She approached the room and stopped to peek around the corner. Her breath caught when she saw Lauren sitting at the small table. Athon looked down at her filthy clothes. Her sneakers were coated with green and pieces of grass and weeds hung from her jeans. She wiped her dirty hands on the butt of her jeans. Pudge strode past her and took a seat at the small kitchen table.

"Where's Athon?" Bridget asked.

"Standin' out in the mud room tryin' to figure out how to make herself look more presentable, I reckon," Pudge said with a chuckle as he picked up his sandwich.

"Athon Dailey! Get your skinny ass in here!" Bridget called out.

Athon stepped shyly into the doorway and rubbed her hands together. She nodded at Lauren who was smiling at her broadly. Athon finally took a breath and walked to the kitchen sink to scrub the dirt from her hands and arms. Lauren looked too cute for words in shorts that were a little baggy and fell to just above her knees, showing off well-toned calves. She was relieved that Lauren had topped her shorts off with a baggy long-sleeved t-shirt. Athon squeezed her eyes shut and swallowed hard. There was no way in hell she'd be able to stop herself from taking a peek at Lauren's touchable body otherwise. She dried her hands on a hand towel hanging from the oven door and pasted a smile on her face.

"So, what are you doing here, Lauren?" Athon asked, hoping she sounded casual, and felt the heat rise in her face as her voice cracked when she said Lauren's name. She cleared her throat as if something was blocking the vocal chords. "Sorry," she added. "Dust in my throat."

Lauren shrugged. "Just checking to see if you might be free for a movie or something."

"I can't." Athon took a large bite of her sandwich. The quicker she finished eating, the quicker she could leave again. "I'm busy today," Athon said, flashing a glance at Bridget. "I have to finish cleanin' up around the vehicles."

"I can help you and then maybe we'd have time to grab a burger or something before the movie," Lauren volunteered.

"No," Athon said hastily. "You can't do what I'm doin' in shorts."

"I have an old pair of jeans she can borrow," Bridget offered with a shrug. "Might have to tie the waist though since I ain't been that skinny since I was twelve."

Athon turned toward Bridget. "You're just a world of helpfulness today, aren't you?" she said sarcastically. "Thanks."

Two hours later, Athon stopped the weed eater and set it down. Lauren had been sitting in the shade watching her. Even though Athon was a little self-conscious about the way she looked, she still moved fluidly. She knew her face was flushed from the autumn heat and exertion. When she walked toward where Lauren was sitting, she wiped her hands along her long waist and tried to ignore Lauren's eyes as they watched her.

"Guess that's everything, at least for today," Athon said as she pulled a hand towel from her back pocket and wiped her face. "I'll clean up a little if you'll help me," she added. "I'm pretty ripe about now." Athon walked toward the camper as Lauren stood and followed her. "How did you know where I live?"

Lauren shrugged. "I followed you after I dropped you off the other night."

Athon reached inside the camper and lifted out two large kitty litter containers. She hoisted one onto the roof of a nearby vehicle. "If you'll tip this over a little at a time, I can at least wash off the first layer of dirt," Athon said as she removed the cap on the first container.

Lauren braced it with her hands as Athon bent over slightly. At first the water dribbled out of the container, but when Athon began rubbing her head briskly Lauren allowed the water to flow out more freely. The bottom of the container slipped in Lauren's hands and over half the water poured onto Athon's head and ran down her t-shirt and into the waist of her jeans. She jumped a little before running her hand under her shirt to rinse her sweaty body. Lauren laughed as water ran down Athon's face and dripped from her hair. When the water was gone Athon replaced the first container with another one, making sure the water ran down her back. Lauren ran a hand under the back of Athon's t-shirt and rubbed her hand over the smooth skin beneath her fingers.

Athon arched away and turned to look down at Lauren. Lauren reached up and ran her hand through Athon's hair and down her face, pausing at the reddish spot along Athon's cheek. Athon brought her hand up and covered Lauren's. "You shouldn't do that, Lauren," she said softly. "You shouldn't be here."

Athon shook her head and looked in the camper for a towel. She felt exposed standing there in wet clothes. The coolness of the wet jeans against her skin made her shiver. She blushed as she saw her hardened nipples pressing against the fabric of her t-shirt. She turned away from Lauren and ruffled her hair with the towel.

Lauren tilted her head to the side. "I like you, Athon."

"You don't know a damn thing about me."

"I know enough."

"Trust me, you don't."

Lauren picked up the second container and dumped the remaining water over Athon's head, sending a sheet of water over her body. Lauren laughed and tried to step away. Athon grabbed her by the wrist and pulled her into the camper. She drew Lauren close and let the palm of her hand sweep down Lauren's side. She held her at the waist as she leaned down and kissed her lightly. She felt Lauren flinch and was sure she would pull away, angry that Athon had taken such a liberty. Instead she ran her hands down the back of Athon's jeans and over the tight muscles of her butt to pull her closer as their lips met again, more demanding the second time.

Athon slid her hands under Lauren's shirt and moved them up until she felt the soft fabric covering her breasts. "You're so beautiful," she whispered. She pressed her face into Lauren's hair and held her tightly. She didn't know why she wasn't maneuvering Lauren toward the bed inside the camper. She had seen the hungry look in Lauren's eyes even before the kiss, but backed away from the temptation. "You deserve better than me. You should get home before it gets too late," she said.

"I think it's already too late. Can I come over again sometime?"

"Your parents wouldn't approve. I'll see you at school tomorrow."

"HERE'S THE DEAL, girlie," Pudge rasped over breakfast the following weekend. "I ain't got the time to be running you all over the place for school and work. And now that Bridget's got her beauty license, she won't have as much time either."

"I can walk to school and work or hitch a ride," Athon said with a shrug. "I used to walk farther."

Pudge held up his hand. "So I was thinkin'," he continued. "I got this old car somewhere on the lot. Ain't a thing of beauty, but she's got a good engine. You got a license?"

"Yeah."

"If we can get it runnin' and through an inspection, it's yours while you're here."

"I can't afford a vehicle," Athon frowned.

"Since I ain't gonna charge you nothin' for it, I reckon you can afford that, can't ya?"

"Why are you being so nice to me, Pudge?"

"Just givin' you a break. We all need that once in a while, that's all."

Athon picked up her plate and rinsed it off. She didn't want

Pudge, or anyone else, to see the tears in her eyes. She stopped next to the table and wrapped her arms around the old man who let her live on his property. "Thanks, Pudge. Someday I'll pay you back."

A month later Pudge watched as Athon slid into the driver's seat of the old blue and rust Toyota. She closed her eyes and said a small prayer before she turned the key in the ignition. She and Tiny had been working on it in their spare time. She had pulled seats from another old car in Pudge's junkyard and drilled new holes to fit the Toyota frame and body. The engine sputtered and tried to turn over. She bounced up and down on the seat as the engine finally kicked over. She left it running and jumped out, leaping into Pudge's arms and slapping him soundly on the back.

"Can I take it on the road?" she asked excitedly.

"When was the last time you drove a vehicle?"

"Not since I took driver's ed," she admitted.

"Maybe I better go with you."

"I'm good," she called out as she leaped back into the seat and tugged the door closed with a pop as she revved the engine.

"Don't push it and drive slow," Pudge yelled. "Been a while since this baby seen the highway."

Athon waved out the window as she eased the car out of the parking area in front of Tiny's and turned onto Fairfield Highway. Even though she was only going twenty-five miles per hour, the November wind coming through the window felt cool and refreshing. Gradually, she increased her speed and found it exhilarating as she cruised along the stretch of highway that eventually would lead her into San Antonio. Before she hit the city limits sign she pulled over and waited for an opening in the traffic to turn around. She ignored the speedometer as she drove and was surprised to see red and blue lights flashing behind her. A siren whooped and she slowed down as she pulled onto the shoulder of the road. She glanced into the rearview mirror and immediately recognized the stout figure exiting the police car. Sheriff Raynelle Cosper never seemed to smile.

"License, registration, and insurance," Sheriff Cosper said as she stepped next to the driver's window, her ticket book attached to a clipboard.

Athon looked at her own reflection in the sheriff's mirrored sunglasses. "I only have my license," she said.

"Get out of the vehicle," the sheriff ordered as she stepped to the side of the door and rested her palm on the butt of her weapon.

As soon as Athon got out and slammed the door to make it close, Sheriff Cosper shoved her toward the front of the vehicle. "Hands on the hood and spread 'em," Cosper said.

"What did I do?" Athon asked, starting to turn around.

Cosper shoved her roughly against the hood leaving her hand firmly planted on Athon's back. Athon jerked her elbow back and spun to face Cosper. The glint of sunlight striking the sheriff's firearm greeted her. "Hands on the hood," Cosper repeated through clenched teeth.

After a thorough search of Athon's loose clothing, Cosper asked, "Where'd you get this vehicle?"

"Can I stand up now?" Athon replied.

Cosper grabbed her by the shoulder and turned her around, allowing Athon to lean against the front of the car. "Where'd you get this vehicle? And I'm getting tired of repeating myself."

"It belongs to Pudge Fitzgerald. Pudge, Tiny, and me just finished giving it a tune-up and I was test driving it."

"Shove your hands in your pockets," Cosper said as she looked down both sides of the vehicle.

Athon stuck her hands in her front jean pockets and shifted from foot to foot. "Runs good," she muttered.

"Tell Pudge he needs plates and insurance on this heap," Cosper said. "Now get this POS off my highway."

"Yes, ma'am," Athon said. She carefully stepped around the sheriff and slid into the driver's seat. She smiled when the motor started immediately. I did that, she thought. Her work made it run. She felt her chest puff out with pride as she watched the sheriff open the door to her patrol car, remove her hat, and lower her body inside. Athon signaled to enter the highway and pulled slowly off the shoulder. Sheriff Cosper followed her all the way back to Tiny's and continued on her patrol when Athon signaled and turned off the road, breathing a sigh of relief.

Chapter Fourteen

Duvalle, Texas
December 1987

ATHON HAD BEEN living at Pudge's for only three months
yet it seemed like she'd been there forever. He and Bridget treated
her like a member of their family and she owed them more than she
would ever be able to repay. She cleared the table while Pudge
stretched out on his recliner for his nightly nap in front of
television shows he never watched. Bridget put leftovers in
containers and made a place for them in the refrigerator.

"Got a date tonight?" Bridget asked as she snapped a lid on a
plastic container.

"What makes you ask?"

"Just that you been actin' different since that cute little gal was
here a couple of months back."

"She's only a friend."

"Uh huh," Bridget said with a look. "Tell me another story,
sugar. A blind person could see you like her."

Athon turned from the sink and leaned against the counter as
she dried her hands on a small towel. "I do like her, but I don't
want her to get in trouble. She might if she hangs around me too
much. Her father's a minister."

"Her father's a man and will do what he thinks he has to to
protect his daughter." Bridget planted her fists on her hips and
shook her head. She stepped toward Athon and placed a hand on
her shoulder. "Just be careful and don't let yourself get hurt. And
don't you hurt her neither."

"I—" Athon started to protest.

"I haven't known you long, Athon Dailey, but I know you like
girls the same as a man does."

Athon glared at Bridget and threw the hand towel on the
counter. "I haven't done anything wrong!"

"Depends on who you talk to. I 'spect that minister wouldn't
be too happy that you might have been lovin' up on his daughter.
Just be careful, that's all I'm sayin'."

Athon left the house and ran to the camper. Her own words
echoed in her mind. *I haven't done anything wrong.* She stretched out
on the mattress with her hands behind her head. Bridget was right.
Athon did like girls—a lot, but she'd never been with one she
wanted to be with all the time. Until she met Lauren. She was

comfortable to be with and they could talk about anything. It was the first real friendship Athon could remember having with anyone.

It was a Saturday night and Gus had given her the night off. She needed to get ahead for her classes, but couldn't convince herself to leave the comfortable mattress. She glanced at her clock. It was still early and she wondered what Lauren was doing on a pleasant Saturday night. Thoughts about Rafe Stoneman crossed her mind. He'd been hounding Lauren to go out with him for weeks. Maybe she finally gave up and accepted a date. Athon closed her eyes tightly and didn't want to think about that. She knew Rafe's reputation. Mr. One and Done.

In an attempt to shake the image of Lauren and Rafe together, the fullness of her lips against his, the smoothness of her skin beneath his fingers, Athon stormed out of the camper. She dug a cigarette from the cabinet inside the camper door and lit it with shaking hands. What the hell was wrong with her? The thought of a girl she had kissed once in the arms of some guy never bothered her before. In fact, she expected it to happen, knew it would because she was only a practice dummy. As much as she longed to, she had never really touched another girl intimately. The thought of kissing Lauren again made her stomach muscles clench.

Athon plopped down on a discarded car seat and rocked back and forth as she held her head in her hands, biting back the groans as her mind relived the feel of Lauren's lips against hers. She wrapped her arms around her waist against the chill of the evening and laid down on the car seat.

A hand on her shoulder startled Athon awake and she blinked as she looked around. Her eyes slowly began to focus on the face kneeling in front of her. Dark hair plaited into cornrows and held in place by multi-colored beads surrounded the slender caramel face staring at her. Athon reached out and slid her hand over the back of the neck and pulled the image closer until their lips met. She deepened the kiss hungrily, wanting to devour the beautiful girl of her dreams. She felt warm arms slip around her as she broke the kiss slowly and traced her mouth and tongue to the slender neck. It was more wonderful than she remembered as she felt a strong rapid pulse beneath her lips. A hand caressing her face brought her fully awake.

"What are you doing here?" Athon asked as she blinked and stared at Lauren.

"Looking for you," Lauren breathed.

"I'm sorry. I guess I fell asleep," Athon said, nervously rubbing her face.

"I don't know what you were dreaming about, but I liked it."

She brought her mouth closer to Athon's ear and whispered, "Was I in your dream?"

Athon fingered a dread and smiled. "I like your hair this way. You're beautiful."

Lauren rubbed her hands up and down Athon's bare arms. "You're cold. Can we go into the camper?"

"You shouldn't stay," Athon said as she stood and pulled Lauren up.

"Why not? It's Saturday night."

"You should be out on a date or something. With Rafe."

Lauren snorted. "That gropasaurus! I don't think so. Definitely not my type. Besides I have more fun with you." She opened the door to the camper and stepped inside. "I never did get the grand tour of your humble abode."

"Not much to see. It's just an old camper. But it doesn't leak when it rains. You want something to drink?"

Athon turned on one of the lanterns as Lauren sat on the bench seat on one side of the camper's table. Athon stared at her guest, her hands shoved into her jean pockets, wondering what to do or say next.

"Tell me what you're thinking Athon," Lauren said quietly.

Athon shifted her gaze to the floor.

"Maybe you could give me a kissing lesson," Lauren suggested.

"You definitely don't need kissing lessons," Athon mumbled with a grin.

Lauren stood and moved closer to Athon. "You've been avoiding me at school. Have I done something to make you mad?" She took Athon's wrists and pulled her hands from her pockets. "Talk to me. Please."

Athon frowned and closed her eyes. "Do...do your parents know you're here? Do they know I kissed you?"

Lauren sat back down and traced a crack on the table with her finger. "I didn't tell them where I was going," she started. She took a deep breath and exhaled. "They know I like girls. It's the reason we moved here." She looked up at Athon. "And I wanted you to kiss me."

Athon slid into the bench seat across from Lauren and took her hand. Lauren laced her fingers with Athon's. "When we lived in Pennsylvania, I met a girl and we spent a lot of time together. Her parents were members of my father's congregation. She was in her first year of college and was two or three years older than I was." Lauren cleared her throat before she continued. "We had fun going shopping together or to a movie. I spent the night at their house one weekend and we started horsing around. The next thing I knew she was kissing me and touching me." Lauren's eyes met Athon's. "I liked it and one thing led to another." Lauren laughed humorlessly. "I didn't have a clue what I was doing. Based on what she was instructing me to do, it wasn't her first ride on the carousel."

"Did you like her?"

"I liked kissing her and the way I felt when she touched me," Lauren said with a shrug. "But next thing I knew she pushed me away, pulled her blouse back together, and slapped my face. Before I could ask her what I'd done wrong I heard her mother order me to pack my stuff and get out. Her parents took me home and claimed I'd made unwanted sexual advances toward their daughter and would have raped her if her mother hadn't come in the room. I admitted I kissed her, but only because she kissed me first. The suggestion was that I'd forced her to kiss me. After all, as everyone knows, people of my *ethnic persuasion* are all sexual predators because we simply can't live without having sex like alley cats. Her mother launched into a lecture about rampant sexual diseases and reproduction statistics because all 'black people' are promiscuous," Lauren went on using her fingers to make quote marks. "The bright side of it was, as enlightened Christian white folks, they were willing to sweep the whole sordid incident under the rug—if my father resigned and we left town."

"What did your parents say?"

Lauren released Athon's hand and leaned back, spreading her arms. "Here we are. My father prays for me every day and my mother, well, she just doesn't say much. They don't have an ideal marriage. It's always been stressful because he's a lily-white Southern boy who was seduced by a wanton black woman and led astray. His parents disowned him and my brother and I have never met them. To learn his daughter is gay was just the icing on the cake. So, I guess my family is just as screwed up as yours. At least we have something in common," Lauren said with a bitter laugh.

Athon pulled Lauren up and held her close. She ran a finger lightly over Lauren's lips and saw them part slightly. She lowered her head and touched the full, tempting lips with her tongue before her lips followed and she lost herself in the heat of Lauren's mouth. She heard a low moan escape from Lauren's throat as the kiss deepened. Lauren's hands ran into Athon's hair and held her tightly.

Athon pulled away from the kiss and searched Lauren's eyes. "I promise I won't ever hurt you," she rasped.

"Could you hold me for a little while?" Lauren breathed.

They climbed into the camper bunk and spooned against one another. Athon nuzzled into Lauren's neck as they molded together and whispered how she felt until they both fell asleep.

ATHON HAD NEVER looked forward to a Christmas before and she felt like the little kid she should have always been. For the first time in her life she had people she wanted to give presents to and looked forward to wrapping them. She had a reason to get up each day and knew when she went to school she would see Lauren. Everything would be all right. She felt connected to something more than herself when she held Lauren's hand or wrapped her arm around her shoulders. She was content. She could see a future worth living.

She smiled to herself as she wrapped Lauren's Christmas present using sparkly red paper and a huge bow that dwarfed the small box. She had used over half her savings to buy the present. She hoped it was true that the best presents came in small packages. Lauren agreed to meet her at the diner after it closed. She hadn't been able to spend much time with Lauren once school was out for the holidays. She had worked as many shifts at the diner as she could get and Tiny had paid her for working overtime. It seemed that everyone wanted a tune-up or oil change before the New Year. She was exhausted, but she hoped the look in Lauren's eyes would make it all worthwhile.

After Gus and Pedro left for the night, Athon rushed around the small diner setting up a special table for just her and Lauren. She hadn't told anyone it was her eighteenth birthday and there wasn't anyone she wanted to celebrate it with more than Lauren. She stood back and admired her handiwork, straightened the balloon and flower arrangement in the center of the table along with a small cake. In front of the arrangement she placed the box. She lit a candle and turned off the glaring overhead fluorescents. She pulled out a bottle of perfume she'd borrowed from Bridget and sprayed the air around the table. She looked at the clock and rubbed her hands together. She walked to the back door and scanned the alleyway. She couldn't remember the last time she'd been so nervous. She looked down at her clothing and ran her fingers through her hair. She shivered as the cool outside air mixed with the nervous perspiration on her body and stepped back inside the restaurant. What if Lauren didn't come? What if she had second thoughts about being with Athon? What if the things other students told her about Athon mattered more than she let on? Her excited nervousness and doubts began to shift her thoughts to anger as she paced back and forth between the table she had prepared to celebrate a special evening and the back door of the diner. Ten minutes late. Lauren was ten minutes late for the most important evening of Athon's life.

The knock on the back door was so light Athon almost didn't hear it. She felt frozen in place for a moment before rubbing her sweaty palms down her upper thighs and rushing to the door. Lauren was dancing from one foot to the other. Her coat collar was pulled up high on her neck and all Athon could see were those incredible cinnamon eyes. She reached out and took Lauren's arm, pulling her inside. She locked the back door and wrapped her arms around Lauren's shivering body.

"I thought you changed your mind about coming," Athon confessed.

"Sorry, honey," Lauren said. "Halfway here I looked at my gas gauge and discovered I was sucking fumes. The cold wind blowing under the canopy at the station was freezing."

"You're here now," Athon said, taking Lauren's coat. "That's all that matters." She swept her arm toward the front of the diner and escorted Lauren to the table she had prepared. Pulling a lighter from her pocket, she lit the candle on the table and watched as its glow was reflected in Lauren's eyes.

"It's beautiful, Athon," Lauren said. "The only thing missing is soft music."

Athon smiled and held up her index finger. "Gus showed me how to do this," she said as she walked to the jukebox, reached behind it and flipped a switch. She chose a selection and waited for the song to begin. She stepped behind the counter and pointed a remote device at the jukebox. The sound lowered a little at a time until it was much softer.

"Dance with me?" Lauren asked when Athon rejoined her.

Athon cleared a small area of tables and took Lauren in her arms. They moved slowly around the makeshift dance floor. Athon placed kisses along Lauren's cheeks, forehead, and ears, inhaling the fresh scent of her hair. Athon's lips met Lauren's and drank in her essence as they stood in place and swayed in one another's arms. When the music stopped, the two teenagers held hands and walked to the table. Athon pulled a chair out and waited for Lauren to sit. Her eyes lit up as she glanced at the cake and then at Athon. Her lips curled into a smile when Athon joined her.

"I bet you thought I didn't know today was your birthday," Lauren said. She withdrew a small package from the front pocket of her sweatshirt and placed it on the table.

"No way," Athon said, looking surprised yet pleased. No one had ever given her a birthday present. She blinked away the itchy sensation in her eyes.

"I asked Mrs. Fortenberry."

Athon teased the side of Lauren's face with a fingertip. "Why did you want to know?"

"Because you're the most special person in my life." She looked at Athon and fluttered her eyelashes. "Do you know my birthday?" she asked coyly.

"February eighteenth," Athon answered confidently.

"Can we have another party then?"

"Anything you want, baby," Athon said as she leaned toward Lauren to kiss her cheek.

She was thrilled when Lauren turned and met her lips as she whispered, "Happy Birthday."

An hour later Athon closed the back door of the diner and locked it. She took Lauren's hand and walked her to her car. Lauren opened the door of her car and turned to look at Athon, still fingering the shiny new necklace around her neck. "Someday I won't have to go home," Lauren said. "Unless it's with you."

Athon drew her closer and kissed her lightly. Before she could step away, Lauren took her hand and met her for another blistering kiss. "Someday soon," Athon said, resting her forehead against Lauren's.

Lauren got in her car and backed it out of the parking area. Athon watched it depart before walking slowly to her own vehicle. She glanced at the gold link bracelet that encircled her wrist and smiled.

Chapter Fifteen

Duvalle, Texas
January 1988

PUDGE SHUFFLED TOWARD his front door on New Year's Day, wiping bread crumbs from the stubble on his face. A tall, distinguished-looking man wearing a three-piece-suit under a black and gray tweed coat stood on his porch when he opened the front door.

The man turned. "Mr. Fitzgerald?"

"Yeah, but I ain't buyin' nothin'," Pudge rumbled.

The man extended his hand. "My name is Kenneth Shelton. I'm Lauren's father. Could I speak to you for a few minutes?" In his other hand he held a large manila envelope.

Without accepting the hand, Pudge walked back toward his kitchen, leaving the front door open. Reverend Shelton followed him.

"Coffee?" Pudge asked as he refilled his own mug.

"No, thank you," Shelton answered, clearing his throat.

"Take a load off," Pudge said. He picked up his breakfast dishes and set them in the sink. "What can I do for you?"

Shelton unbuttoned his coat, but still looked uncomfortable. "Are you the guardian of Athon Dailey, Mr. Fitzgerald?"

"No, but she lives here. She became her own guardian when she turned eighteen. Is she in trouble?"

"That depends on your definition of trouble, I suppose. Her soul is in terrible jeopardy and as a result, so is my daughter's."

Pudge choked as he swallowed a sip of coffee and set the mug down. He finally managed to say, "Athon's a good kid, Mr. Shelton."

"She's an affront to God, sir, and a sexual deviant."

Pudge stood up quickly. "I think you need to leave my home before I kick your ass out," he said through clenched teeth. "Who the hell do you think you are?"

Shelton stood. "Please, Mr. Fitzgerald." He placed the manila envelope on the table and ran a trembling hand over his face. He opened the metal clasp and withdrew several eight-by-ten photographs. His hand was still shaking slightly when he held them out to Pudge. "I'm a father," he said, his voice cracking. "I received these last night. From my son."

Pudge pulled his glasses from the top pocket of his overalls and adjusted them. The photographs clearly showed Athon and Lauren in a steamy clinch somewhere. There were four pictures, each one a closer shot of the same scene. He thrust them back at Shelton. "So what? Have you talked to Lauren?"

Shelton shook his head and slid the pictures back into the envelope. He lowered his body back into his chair and waited for Pudge to sit as well. "I...I will tell you that I'm not surprised by these pictures, Mr. Fitzgerald. We moved to Duvalle because of a similar situation," Shelton said.

"Looks like that didn't work out so well for you," Pudge noted.

"My family and I are moving back east. In fact, Lauren, my wife, and son are leaving very soon. I will follow them after my New Year's service. I plan to resign from the church and begin a new profession. I can't lead my flock to redemption when my own child is condemning her soul."

"You think separatin' them will solve everything?"

Shelton exhaled a long breath. "I don't know. I have no doubt Lauren will attempt to contact the Dailey girl. I'm asking you to not let that happen. No letters, no phone calls, no nothing. My daughter believes we are making the trip because my wife's mother is ill. I have already made arrangements for a new school."

Pudge tapped his fingers on the table top. "None of this will change who they are. You know that, right?" he asked.

"I need time to reason with Lauren. To seek help for her. You surely cannot condone this kind of immoral behavior."

Pudge chuckled. "Oh, I don't know. At least I'll never have to worry about Athon gettin' herself knocked up."

"I want my daughter to be normal and happy, Mr. Fitzgerald," Shelton insisted.

Pudge shook his head. "No, I think you want her to be your definition of normal and don't want to be embarrassed by what she does or who she does it with." He rubbed his forehead and thought for a moment. "Tell you what I'll do," he finally said. "I'll intercept the mail. There's no reason for Athon to ever answer my phone. If they find each other after that, there's nothing I can do about it." He looked at Shelton. "The only reason I am willing to do any of this is not because I think what they're doin' is wrong. I'm just not sure I want Athon mixed up with a family like yours. I know you're a preacher and all, Mr. Shelton, but I don't trust anyone who says one thing and does another." Pudge pushed his body out of the chair and looked down at Shelton. "You have a blessed day now, ya hear?"

ATHON HURRIED THROUGH the back door of Pudge's house and went directly to the telephone in the living room. It was dark inside, but she could still see the numbers. She had been trying to call Lauren all evening during her breaks from work, but there had been no answer. Now fear that something was wrong nagged at her. She waited, standing in the semi-darkness as the phone rang and rang. Still no answer. It was nearly two in the morning. Where the hell was Lauren? Had something happened to her?

"She won't answer," Pudge's voice said, startling Athon.

"What?"

"She won't answer. They're gone," Pudge said as he walked into the living room, tying the belt of his old robe.

"Gone where? When will they be back?"

Pudge plopped down on the couch and rubbed his face.

"Her daddy was here this afternoon. He's taking his family back east somewhere. You'd be better off to forget about her."

"They left because of me?"

"In a way, but it's not your fault, Athon."

"No!" Athon shouted. "She would have told me!"

"She doesn't know she's not coming back." Pudge stood and walked closer. He put his arm around her shoulder.

Athon shoved him away and ran out the back door.

ATHON SAT SHIVERING under a large tree in front of the Shelton's house. There were no lights on inside and she hadn't seen any movement through the windows. It was unseasonably cold and all she saw were the white puffs that rose in the early morning air as she exhaled. The sky had finally lightened when a large moving van pulled into the driveway and backed toward the front door. Athon's body was stiff from sitting in the cold as she forced herself from the ground. She waited until the front door of the home opened and a group of men and women entered the house. Athon made her way up the steps and stood in the entryway, stepping aside as men began carrying furniture out and loading them on the truck. Women were putting boxes together and beginning to fill them with smaller items.

"You need something?" a man asked.

"Yeah," Athon said. "Looks like they're moving, huh?"

"Yep. Reckon the house will go on the market soon."

"Where'd they go?"

The man shrugged. "Beats me."

"Where are you supposed to deliver the furniture?"

"We're just packing it up. It'll go into storage until they find a place and let the moving company know."

"How long will that be?"

"I'm not a mind reader, kid. You better split now, okay?"

Athon stuck her hands in her coat pockets and turned away. How could Lauren leave without telling her where she was going? Leave as if they meant nothing to one another? Tears filled her eyes as she trudged away. Gradually, anger filled her and replaced the sorrow she felt. She didn't need Lauren. She didn't need anyone to promise they cared. No one had ever cared. She had been stupid to believe Lauren had, that anyone would. She could only depend on herself. Her anger would sustain her. She only had to hang on five more months.

Chapter Sixteen

Kaiserslautern, Germany
January 2010

FRANK'S INJURY WAS only enough to get him back to the unit in Kaiserslautern and a few months of desk duty while he healed. The bullet had shattered a section of his right femur, but his orthopedist was hopeful the metal rod placed in his leg to connect the two sections of bone would knit together. If the procedure failed, it was unlikely he would ever fly again. Satisfied that Frank was resting before his surgery, Mandy drove Lauren to the airport for the long flight home.

"I don't know when I'll be back, Mandy," Lauren said as she exhaled a deep breath. "Or if I ever will."

"You just take care of Athon. We'll handle everything here. If you need me to pack your furniture and other things, let me know. My housekeeper is a whiz at packing for the military."

"I'm not military," Lauren said softly.

"Helga doesn't know that. She'll pack everything under Athon's name and the military will ship it."

"I've only been here a year," Lauren said as she looked at the fresh snow beginning to fall. "It's beautiful here and feels like home. We loved it here so much."

They remained silent the remainder of the trip. Lauren checked three or four times to make sure she had her ticket home to occupy her time. She looked up when she heard the sound of a large airplane passing overhead. If the medical transport from Ramstein left on time, the plane she saw could be Athon's.

"The transport has a layover in Greenland," Mandy said. When she saw the look on Lauren's face she added, "I asked the doctor when I saw Frank last night. You could make it to Andrews before it lands."

"What's the difference?" Lauren said with a shrug. "They probably won't let me see her anyway."

"It's just the way things are, Lauren. You know that."

"It doesn't make me feel any better about it."

"You got the name of that doctor Colonel Stephens gave you."

"Yeah," Lauren said as Mandy wheeled into the terminal entrance for the airport.

"I'm sorry you'll be alone, honey," Mandy said as she opened the back of her vehicle to remove Lauren's luggage.

Lauren rolled a large bag to the skycap desk and checked it in before turning and hugging Mandy. "You just go back and take care of Frank. Let me know how his surgery goes. He saved Athon for me. I can never thank him enough."

A whistle warned Mandy she had stayed too long in the loading area and she hurried back to her car while Lauren walked briskly into the terminal to find her gate. Before she could get comfortable her flight was called for boarding. At exactly their departure time, the big airplane was pushed away from the gate to begin its taxi to the take-off point. She hadn't slept well the night before. After the plane reached its flight altitude, she pulled a book from her shoulder bag, but thoughts of Athon that lingered in her mind forced their way to the front not long after she fell asleep.

Duvalle, Texas
October 2006

THE SOUND OF crashing furniture immediately brought Lauren Shelton's attention to what was happening in the outer office she shared with two other assistant principals. She handed the student sitting in front of her desk a half-sheet of pink paper assigning his punishment for breaking the rules established to control the students at Carver High School. She cast a quick, tight smile at the student as she escorted him out of her office.

Despite the disruption created by the two armed campus police officers intent on controlling a belligerent, uncooperative young man, the daily routines of the secretaries who ran the office seemed to proceed undisturbed. Lauren signaled with two fingers that the student be brought into her office. Hector Olivera was a dump student. He had been kicked out of every possible educational facility in the county before establishing his residence within the Carver attendance zone. At least it was his residence this week. Lauren felt certain his residence was almost like a floating crap game. Depending on his behavior, the young man had been shuttled from uncle to uncle, aunt to aunt, or various other suspicious "relatives" to avoid both local and school authorities. The fact was, no one wanted Hector Olivera. With the help of the school's interpreter, Lauren had managed to have one conversation with Hector's mother. Shortly thereafter mom had been mysteriously called back to Mexico to care for a sick relative. That had been nearly a year ago and Hector's behavior had plummeted from ditching classes and the occasional macho fist fight and cursing intended to make him appear tougher than the average tenth-grader. Lauren had heard rumors that Hector had become involved with a group of gang-bangers who might or might not be bringing drugs onto the campus.

For the most part, Lauren enjoyed her job, especially working with the students who actually gave a damn about getting the best education they could. There were a number of advanced and special programs specifically designed to better the lives and minds of Carver students. But no matter what the school did, there was a persistent ten percent who did nothing and constantly made Carver look like a home for wayward, delinquent youth. Because of its location in a low-growth area of the town, Carver, once an affluent school, had been dubbed "a ghetto school" and local real estate agents had been overly zealous in their efforts to make sure newcomers did not mistakenly buy a home within the Carver zone.

"What's up that's so important so early in the day, Hector?" Lauren sighed with a glance at the police officers. From the red eyes and uncoordinated speech, Lauren was sure the boy was high again. "Did you search him?" she asked the officers.

"Yes, ma'am. Didn't find anything, but definitely on something."

"I got a cold, man," Hector sniffed.

Lauren reached for the phone on her desk and looked at her computer screen as she dialed. "I'm suspending you for the remainder of the day for resisting arrest. You can return Monday morning."

"I want my lawyer," Hector mumbled.

"You don't need one for this," one of the officers said.

Lauren explained the circumstances of Hector's problem to his current guardian, who promised to retrieve him within the hour.

"Escort him to the detention hall until his guardian arrives," Lauren instructed.

Hector Olivera became the first in a procession of students involved in various teen drama scenarios Lauren had to deal with. The flow of students in and out of her office continued until she was forced to grab her walkie-talkie and make her way to her duty station in the cafeteria lobby. In spite of the raucous noise made by the myriad conversations taking place at each table, Lauren was relieved by the change of scenery. She wondered if they had been as predictable when she was a student as they were now. Regardless of changes in the laws around the nation, students insisted on self-segregating into ethnic groups.

"Miz Shelton!" a girl called out as she approached, shoulders slightly forward, reminding Lauren of a small, determined steamroller.

Lauren greeted the student by wrapping her arm around her shoulders and squeezing lightly. "What's up, Tiara? Having a good day?"

"Except for that fool Markees. The boy is following me around like a lost puppy. He's gettin' seriously on my last nerve."

"Maybe he's working up his courage to ask you to the prom," Lauren said with a smile.

"As if I'd go anywhere with his sorry self. I'd rather stay home."

"Try to imagine what he might look like say in ten years. He could be a righteous hunk when he's all grown up."

Tiara bent over at the waist, laughing hysterically. "Well, he looks like Erkel now."

"I dated a guy once who was skinny, wore glasses, and was shorter than I was. I finally caved and asked him to the prom. Then I found out he didn't even have a driver's license and I had to pick *him* up."

Tiara patted Lauren's back. "That had to be a hundred on the humiliation meter."

"I shouldv'e hung on to him since he's now a rich engineer who drives a fancy sports car. The last time I saw him, he had grown into a very handsome man."

"Well, I'm not that confident in Markees' ability to grow into much of anything."

"The line's gone down some so you better get some lunch while you still can." Lauren glanced at her wrist watch. She would have to leave soon and it wasn't something she was looking forward to.

LAUREN STEPPED OUT of her vehicle and straightened the skirt of her black suit. It was a moderately warm day, but she reached into the car and took out the suit jacket, slipping her arms into its sleeves and pulling it up on her shoulders. She adjusted her sunglasses and began her way up a small rise, following others paying their last respects to Marvin "Pudge" Fitzgerald. Lauren first met Pudge when she was a teenager and knew he was a man who should be respected. From the top of the rise she saw six uniformed men standing at the back of the hearse. She was surprised the coffin had not yet been removed. To her left she watched as an officer in full military dress stepped out of the family limousine and extended a white-gloved hand to assist Bridget Fitzgerald Hauser, Pudge's daughter, out of the long, black vehicle.

Everyone around the family stopped as Bridget took the officer's arm and was escorted to a seat beneath a canopy next to the grave site. The officer leaned down and spoke to Bridget for a moment, then pivoted and walked to the back of the hearse. The coffin slowly slid on a set of rails until it stopped in front of the officer. Lauren heard a low, crisp order being issued, followed by the six military pall bearers grasping the rails on the coffin. They carefully side-stepped away from the hearse before turning to face the gravesite. The officer gave a subdued "forward march" and followed as the pall bearers took one step and stopped, one step and stopped, until they were ordered to halt. They lowered the coffin onto the bier over the open grave and stood at attention as the minister recited a prayer to comfort the assembled mourners.

Sharp verbal commands led the pall bearers through the ceremonial folding of the flag that had been draped over Pudge's coffin. Lauren watched intently, absorbed by the significance of the ceremony and the honor being paid to a former warrior against whatever cause Pudge had once fought. When the final edge of the flag was tucked into the familiar triangular shape, the officer at the head of the coffin grasped the folded flag and pressed the edges together securely, then placed one gloved hand beneath it and another on top and accepted the flag. The officer drew the flag against his chest, took a step back, did a sharp right turn, took four steps forward and a left turn that ended immediately in front of Bridget.

The officer leaned over and presented the flag to Pudge's daughter, saying, "On behalf of a grateful nation." The officer came to attention and slowly brought his right arm up into a salute. The officer held the salute as Lauren heard the first strains of a bugle beginning the haunting and mournful strains of "Taps". A second bugler, farther in the distance, echoed the first and Lauren felt her throat begin to constrict slightly as a shiver ran down her spine.

As the final note of the bugle and its echo faded away, the officer slowly lowered his arm. A precise about face and the officer marched away, the pall bearers following. The military portion of the service was over and Lauren heard a collective sigh from those gathered for their final farewell. The service had been emotionally moving and Lauren was surprised at the number of people who had turned out to bid Pudge Fitzgerald goodbye. She didn't really know Bridget Fitzgerald, and hadn't seen her since she was a teenager, but moved along the line of well-wishers. The Army officer returned and stood next to Bridget, almost acting as a bodyguard. The temperature had become warmer as the graveside service went on. The officer lifted the low dress hat off and used a handkerchief to wipe his brow. Someone spoke to him and he turned, flashing a dazzling smile at the individual speaking. Lauren felt as if someone had sucker punched her in the abdomen and forced the breath from her lungs. She would know that smile anywhere, even though she last saw it nearly twenty years earlier.

She debated stepping out of the line and retreating to her vehicle before the military officer with short, blonde hair and piercing blue eyes looked at her. But something drew her forward and within minutes she was offering her condolences to Bridget. Lauren shifted her rusty brown eyes up slightly and fell into the blue she had once known so well.

"Thank you for coming, Lauren," the officer said softly. "Pudge would have liked that."

"How have you been, Athon?" Lauren asked as their hands touched. She wondered if Athon still felt the same, familiar electrical current that had always passed between them when they touched one another. The passage of time had not diminished the shock of it. Nor the sting. Not waiting for a reply, Lauren hurried away from the people beneath the canopy and made her way back to her vehicle. She would have sworn she felt Athon Dailey's eyes staring into her soul again, but refused to look back. The past was the past and deserved to remain a distant memory. Lauren didn't really believe that, but thinking it saved her from bursting into tears.

Chapter Seventeen

Duvalle, Texas
October 2006

AFTER BRIDGET SPOKE to the last well-wisher, Athon escorted her back to the family car. She slid in next to Bridget and her husband and removed her hat, setting it on her thigh.

"It was a very nice service," Bridget said after blowing her nose. "Daddy would have liked it." She gripped the folded flag and held it against her chest.

Athon took Bridget's hand. "I'm sorry I couldn't get here sooner, Bridge."

Bridget squeezed her hand. "You did a wonderful job today. Daddy was always so proud of how you turned out, honey. It was like you was his own daughter."

"He was the father I never had," Athon said as she stared out the window

"You stayin' at the house while you're home?"

"If it's all right," Athon said.

"That old camper is still parked at the back of the lot. Just like you left it," Bridget chuckled.

Athon laughed. "I can't believe Pudge didn't get rid of that thing."

"It reminded him of you, honey. It was your home."

When the conversation seemed to dry up, Bridget asked, "How long you plannin' to stay?"

"I told them my father passed away and got ten days leave," Athon said with a grin. "I have to report back to Benning in about a week."

"Lauren looked good today, don't you think?" Bridget asked, watching Athon's reaction.

"She's changed, but I guess we all have. I didn't know she was back in Duvalle."

"Been back two or three years now, I think. Listen, Athon, we'll never eat all that food people brought over. How about I bring half of it over to the house for you while you're here?"

"That's fine. You need to come over and get whatever you want anyway, so plan to eat dinner at Pudge's tonight."

ATHON PICKED UP her rental car at the funeral home and

drove to Pudge's. She took in the changes that had taken place along the way. She hadn't been back to Duvalle in nearly five years although she called Pudge every couple of weeks. A few years earlier she had a laptop delivered to him and asked Bridget to teach her father how to use e-mail. It was cheaper than calling when she was stationed overseas.

A whoop-whoop sound snapped her back to the present. She looked in the rearview mirror of her rental car and glanced at the speedometer as she signaled and pulled to the shoulder of the highway. She was sure she hadn't been speeding, but pulled her wallet from the inside pocket of her dress jacket, opened the console under her right elbow and fished out her rental agreement before lowering the driver's side window and letting the warm outside air flood in. She turned toward the window in time to see a gun belt about eye level.

"Step out of the vehicle, please," a gravelly voice ordered.

Athon opened the door and stood up. She placed her hat back on her head and waited.

"Still breakin' my speed limit, Dailey?" Sheriff Cosper asked, hooking her thumbs in her belt.

"I didn't think so, but this is a rental. Speedometer could be off," Athon said, handing over her license and a copy of the rental agreement for insurance.

"You here for Pudge's funeral?" Raynelle Cosper asked as she gave the paperwork a cursory glance and handed them back.

"That's right, Sheriff. Leaving again in a few days." Athon couldn't stop a grin as she looked at Sheriff Cosper. The woman had always worn aviator-style sunglasses with a silver coating that hid her eyes. Now Athon was wearing a similar pair.

"Where you stationed?"

"Georgia right now, but we're transferring to Germany in a few months."

Athon saw the sheriff's head move slightly as she looked her up and down. "You're lookin' mighty spiffy all dressed up in that uniform, Dailey."

"Thanks, Sheriff."

Sheriff Cosper leaned closer and lowered her voice. "Just so's you know, me and old Pudge have been mighty proud of everything you've accomplished." She clapped Athon on the shoulder. "Just wanted you to know that. You take care and come home safe."

Athon grinned and swallowed past a lump in her throat. She'd never had anything but trouble in Duvalle, Texas, but it felt good to know there were people there who had believed in her. She clasped the sheriff's hand firmly before settling into the car again.

Athon unlocked the front door to the old house and removed her hat when she stepped inside. She tucked it under her arm as she walked slowly around the house. The air inside smelled musty and she set her hat on the dining room table to open the windows in the front and back of the house. A nice breeze sent the curtains fluttering as she smelled the mustiness leave. She was shocked when Bridget told her Pudge left the house to her in his will. Athon protested that she traveled too much to take care of the place, but Bridget promised to look after the property until Athon could decide whether to keep it or sell it.

She removed her uniform jacket and hung it neatly on the back of a dining room chair. It had been a long, emotional day. She was surprised to see Lauren Shelton at the funeral, but years of military training had taught her to suppress her feelings. It had been twenty years, but Lauren was no longer the skinny girl Athon remembered. Today she was a beautiful, sexy woman, her mocha skin still flawless and temptingly touchable. Lauren's cinnamon-colored eyes had flickered slightly, but had been unable to break away from the magnetic hold of Athon's eyes. Now Athon didn't want to remember what had happened between them. In the end Lauren had left her and she'd never heard from her again.

"Smells better in here already," Bridget said from behind Athon.

Athon turned and smiled. "It doesn't take long for a good breeze to make everything fresh again."

Athon walked into the kitchen and opened the refrigerator. She was thankful when she found a bottle of water.

"Why don't you change out of that uniform and into something more comfortable?" Bridget asked.

Athon shrugged and went into the old guest bedroom she had slept in when Pudge first found her, bloody and beaten and soaking wet. She left the guest room a few minutes later dressed in slightly baggy, faded jeans, a white t-shirt, and a pair of comfortable-looking sneakers.

"Now that's the Athon Dailey I remember," Bridget said with a laugh. "Still don't have a lick of fashion sense."

"Probably never will," Athon said. "Don't need much when Uncle Sam tells you what to wear every day."

"Well, you're a fine-looking woman in uniform, Athon. A real pistol."

Athon sat on the edge of the couch and finished tying the laces on her sneakers.

"I thought, if you weren't too tired, that you might help me go through some of the crap Daddy couldn't seem to part with."

"Where do you want to start?" Athon asked as she stood.

"Upstairs," Bridget said. "In the attic."

"Jesus, Bridge, it's probably over a hundred degrees up there."

Bridget flipped a switch on the hall wall. "Daddy installed an exhaust fan up there a couple of years back. Might only be ninety."

"Sounds balmy," Athon quipped.

Bridget reached up and pulled on a rope hanging from a hidden stairway into the attic. Athon grabbed the rope and pulled the folding steps down, making sure they were locked into place. Since the attic had once been a home for stray cats and squirrels that sneaked in, Athon turned on the lights in the attic and looked around before Bridget followed her up.

"Don't be staring at my ass, Bridget," Athon teased.

"Like I'd be interested in your scrawny butt," Bridget huffed.

"You never know until you try it."

Athon stepped onto the loose planks that had been placed across the attic support beams and turned to offer a hand to Bridget.

"Lotta crap up here," Athon said as she looked around and brushed her hands on the seat of her jeans. "Where do you want to start?"

"How about I take the left and you take the right?" Bridget answered with a shrug. "If we can get it downstairs, I can go through it and get Marty to haul most of it to the dump. Daddy kept some stuff up here that belonged to my Mama. I might want to keep some of that."

Bridget and Athon pushed dusty boxes closer to the folding steps and stopped periodically to lower them to the floor. Under a heavy duckcloth tarp, Athon uncovered an old camelback trunk. She got on her knees and tugged it across the planking. It was about three feet long and two feet wide. The humped lid was made of embossed metal of some type. As she pulled on one of the old leather handles, it snapped in two sending her backwards onto her butt. Bridget rushed to her side to help her up.

"Sorry about that, Bridget. I'll get the handles replaced," Athon said.

"Don't worry none about that, Athon," Bridget said as they pushed it to the edge of the attic opening.

"You go on down," Bridget said, "and catch it when I slide it over the edge."

Athon scrambled down the folding steps far enough to grab the sides of the small trunk and ease it down to the hall floor. She paused as the dust from the attic finally got to her sinuses, causing her to sneeze several times. She shoved the trunk out of the way and helped Bridget down the ladder. After the last items were removed, they closed the opening and began hauling boxes into the front room to go through them. Athon picked up the trunk and ran her hand over the intricate design on the lid. Might as well start with the trunk, she thought, but noticed it was padlocked.

"You got a key for this?" she asked.

"Just get a hammer and bust it off," Bridget said as she rummaged through a large box that contained old quilt tops her mother had made.

"I don't want to ruin it," Athon said.

"Daddy had a thousand keys stashed in one of the kitchen drawers. If you want to mess with them, that's up to you." Bridget shrugged and turned to open another box.

Athon walked into the kitchen and went through the drawers, finally lifting out the biggest key ring she'd ever seen. There looked to be over a hundred keys of various shapes and sizes on the ring, some old and rusty, others looked brand new. It reminded Athon of one of those old jailor's key rings she'd seen in movies. She plopped on the couch and tried the first key without success.

Bridget laughed when she saw the number of keys on the ring. "We probably won't find a lock on this whole place those will fit," she said.

Athon grinned at Bridget. "That hammer is sounding pretty good right about now," she said as she tried another key. She was able to eliminate several keys because of their size or shape. She had worked her way through half the keys when she tilted the old lock up and inserted another. Her eyes widened when she turned the key and the mechanism snapped open. She removed the padlock and said loudly, "Hoo-rah!"

Bridget moved to sit on the couch next to Athon. "Maybe it's a pirate treasure," Bridget said in a hushed voice.

Athon took a deep breath and carefully opened the lid, revealing a half dozen small and medium-sized boxes still wrapped in brown postal paper. Mixed in with the boxes were envelopes tied in small bundles. Athon picked up a stack and examined it. All the packages and envelopes were addressed to her at Pudge's address. She looked at the return address and her eyes flew up to meet Bridget's.

"They're from Lauren," Athon said. "I don't understand. Did you know about these?" she asked, waving them in front of Bridget.

Bridget leaned back on the couch. "I didn't know, Athon. I swear. But when Daddy was dying he said something I didn't get until now."

"What?"

"He said he hoped you'd forgive an old man for doing what he thought was the right thing at the time."

Athon picked up the rest of the bundles and looked through them. "There's five years' worth of letters in here. He didn't have any right to keep them from me. He knew I was looking for her." Athon swallowed hard. "He let me believe she just up and left me without a word."

Bridget patted Athon's arm. "I'm sorry, honey."

"She gave up because she never heard anything back. She thought I didn't care."

They sat in silence for a while as Athon stacked the letters and packages by their postal date and stared at them. Five years was a long time to keep trying.

"Maybe Daddy thought, with you both still being kids, that eventually you'd forget each other and find someone special after you was grown up."

"That should have been our decision." Athon patted Bridget's hand. "Thanks, Bridge. I really want to be alone right now, okay? This is kind of a shock."

"I understand, darlin'. Call me after you've read them if you want to talk about it. The past is about to rise up and bite you in the ass, girl," Bridget said.

ATHON DIDN'T KNOW how long the sun had been up when she carefully folded the last letter and slipped it back into its envelope. Lying before her was a chronicle of Lauren's life. At least through her graduation from college The first few letters begged Athon to call her or write so Lauren would know she was all right. She loved Athon and her writing told of a deep depression. Lauren apologized for the actions of her parents and wanted Athon to know that she had no part in their separation. Lauren wrote about her loneliness and her fear she would never see Athon again or hold her in her arms. She would never feel the solidness of Athon's body or the softness of her lips. By the time Athon finished she was emotionally drained and had never felt so exhausted. She remembered the last Christmas she had been with Lauren and the simple heart-shaped necklace she had given her. Athon fingered the gold link bracelet on her wrist as she wondered what had become of the necklace after Lauren gave up on her.

Athon cut open the first package Lauren had sent. It would have been Athon's gift the Christmas after Lauren disappeared. Tears filled her eyes as she lifted the lid. Inside, resting on a thick bed of downy cotton was a gold ring, similar to a wedding band. It was inscribed on the inside with both their names. Ornate scrollwork covered the outside. A note inside the box said that Lauren had one identical to it. She promised to wear it...forever and always. Athon picked the ring up carefully and slid it onto the ring finger of her left hand. "Forever and always," she murmured as she clenched her fingers together. The remainder of the boxes contained small trinkets. Some were from events during Lauren's college years that she wished Athon could share with her. There were wallet-sized photographs, pictures of Lauren with friends or a dog. And finally there was a picture of Lauren at her college graduation. So much had happened.

Athon flopped back on the couch and stared at a photograph of Lauren. She looked exactly the way she had the last time Athon saw her. Athon twisted the ring on her finger and finally stood. She took a hot shower and collapsed onto her bed. Within seconds sleep overtook her.

Chapter Eighteen

Duvalle, Texas
October 2006

MAKING HER WAY to lunch duty two days later, Lauren took a deep breath and let her eyes travel slowly around the cafeteria lobby. They lingered for a moment on the courtyard outside the lobby area. Floor-to-ceiling windows allowed a relatively clear view of the students lounging on the benches surrounding the once beautiful fountain. The fountain had been a gift from a past graduating class, but had become the site of too many practical jokes involving bubbles and food coloring over the years until the school administration closed it down, filled it with soil, and tried vainly each year to grow flowering plants.

As she rocked back and forth on the balls of her feet she noticed a cluster of students gathered near the center of the courtyard. They weren't loud enough to indicate a fight in progress or a potential fight, but such a gathering was definitely not normal. Gradually the students, many of them girls, moved to create a corridor. Kneeling inside the cluster of students, Lauren saw an individual dressed in military camouflage and wearing a maroon beret that sat jauntily on the center-left of the head covering short blonde hair, holding what looked like a large remote-control device. The beret was slightly forward on the person's head and Lauren wasn't able to fully see their face. As the students widened the path, a medium-sized olive green helicopter began to lift off the sidewalk, gaining momentum until it lifted into the air. Lauren watched as the front of the remote-controlled helicopter dipped and the copter moved forward, barely missing the plate-glass windows into the cafeteria. Lauren had been holding her breath as she watched the object approach and suddenly let the air explode from her lungs. She would definitely have to speak to the ROTC people about safety issues. One at a time, students came forward and were allowed to maneuver the helicopter. Lauren could see the alertness and excitement in their eyes. The adult in charge only stepped in if it appeared a student was having a difficult time or losing control. Finally, a few minutes before the bell ending lunch, two ROTC instructors moved the students back and cleared a space large enough for the helicopter to land. The adult with blonde hair stepped forward and looked up as the copter was brought down to land softly in the semi-circle. There was no doubt that the remote control pilot was a female. She spoke to the students while she waited for the rotary blades to come to a stop. Then she approached and knelt down next to the helicopter. She picked it up and pointed to parts of the machine, apparently explaining the function of each.

Lauren carefully observed the expressions of the students as they listened to her. The speaker was tall for a woman and quite slender. The sleeves of her camouflage top were rolled up to just below her elbows and Lauren saw a gold bracelet dangling from her right wrist. A large, black wristwatch with a webbed band, its face covered by a strip of olive green material encircled her left wrist. Everything about the woman's uniform was...perfect. Lauren smiled when she remembered hearing other women talk about how hot someone they knew looked in their uniform, whether it was police, fire, or any other kind of uniform. She had to admit that the woman in the courtyard filled out her military uniform extremely well. The way in which she stood and moved was the picture of pride, confidence, and sex appeal. Lauren looked away and cleared her throat, hoping she wasn't blushing.

"She's turned out rather impressively, hasn't she?" a voice behind Lauren said.

She glanced over her shoulder and saw the officer in charge of the ROTC program at Carver High School, Colonel Wilson Fruge.

"I'm sorry?" Lauren responded.

Colonel Fruge took a step forward to stand beside Lauren. "When she was a student here everyone was positive she would wind up in prison," he said with a smile.

"You were here when she was a student?"

"It was my first year here. I remember her, but don't think she was ever in ROTC."

Lauren turned her head and stared at the striking figure. There was something very familiar about her. The bell rang and students began making their way to the next class, some shuffling and others walking rapidly into the hallways surrounding the cafeteria lobby. The door from the center patio opened and Lauren glanced toward it in time to see the woman shaking hands with a few students, a brilliant smile lighting up her face. Athon Dailey.

Athon handed the helicopter and remote to the two ROTC instructors with her and said something. The two men came to attention and saluted her before she turned and strode toward the cafeteria door. As she stepped inside, she removed her beret and sunglasses and turned slightly to catch the glass door before it slammed shut. She saluted Colonel Fruge and Lauren would have sworn Athon's face froze when she saw her standing next to the colonel.

"Excellent presentation today, Major," Fruge said as he

returned the salute.

"Thank you, sir," Athon said crisply. "It was my honor, sir."

"Ms. Shelton, let me introduce Major Athon Dailey. Major Dailey is in town on personal business and was gracious enough to speak to our cadets today. Major, this is Ms. Lauren Shelton, the Dean of Students at Carver."

"A pleasure, ma'am," Athon said, shaking Lauren's hand as if they'd never met. Lauren was surprised at the electric feeling she used to feel when she touched Athon. It was still there. She could see in Athon's eyes that she felt it as well. The twenty years that had passed changed nothing.

"Welcome home, Major," Lauren said with a smile.

LATER THAT AFTERNOON, when school ended for the day, Lauren looked out the window of her office and saw Athon standing on the sidewalk in front of the building talking to Colonel Fruge. A few minutes later the colonel walked away leaving Athon standing alone on the sidewalk, glancing at her wristwatch. Lauren left her office and exited the building. She needed to say something to Athon and this would probably be the last time she'd ever see her.

"Major Dailey," Lauren said. "Could I speak to you before you leave?"

"Of course, Ms. Shelton. What can I do for you?" Athon said as she adjusted her sun glasses.

"Are you staying at Pudge's house?" Lauren asked as she stopped in front of Athon.

"Yeah. In fact, Bridget is supposed to pick me up in a few minutes." Athon smiled. "The house seems strange after all these years. I don't know what I'm going to do with it."

"What do you mean?"

"Pudge left that little chunk of property to me in his will." Athlon laughed. "I don't know what he was thinking."

"What about Bridget?"

"She's got her own place with her husband now. She didn't really want the old place."

"How have you been, Athon?"

"I'm doing fine. As you can see I have a career that lets me see some pretty interesting places. I like what I do."

"What is it that you do?"

"I'm an army aviator, specifically a helicopter pilot. Mostly my crew and I do rescue work. In fact, I'll be preparing to deploy again not too long after I report back to my unit in Georgia."

"Where will you be going?"

"Germany. Probably Afghanistan from there. There's some talk that our permanent base will move to Germany and then go on a rotating schedule with other helicopter units doing medevac missions." Athon cleared her throat and looked up and down the street. "I...uh...think about you sometimes, Lauren."

"Would you consider having dinner with me this evening?" Lauren asked, looking down at her hands.

"I'd like that," Athon said with a smile. "Where are you living now?"

"I have a place here. My parents passed away a couple of years ago."

"I'm sorry to hear that. I'll pick you up around seven, if that's all right." Athon opened the cargo pocket of her BDUs and pulled out a small notebook and a pen. "I'll need your address," she said as she handed the items to Lauren.

"I'll look forward to it."

Chapter Nineteen

Duvalle, Texas
October 2006

A FEW MINUTES before seven, Athon pulled to the curb in front a small brick house on Crabtree Street. The sporty-looking rental car she had picked up at the airport the day she arrived seemed a little much, but she smiled as she stepped out and straightened her uniform. She pressed the doorbell and waited. She wasn't sure what she should tell Lauren about the letters she'd never received or if she should mention them at all. If she had found Lauren, would she be where she was now? Would Lauren? She had tried to overcome her anger about the letters, but had only been partially successful. Screaming and yelling would be counter-productive after twenty years. She smiled when she heard a noise indicating someone on the other side of the door. When it opened, Athon couldn't stop her smile from spreading across her face. Lauren was beautiful. Athon wished she could have been there to watch her morph from the pretty teenager she remembered into the stunning woman in front of her now.

"It's good to see you again," Athon said as she removed the cap of her dress uniform. "Are you ready?"

Lauren nodded and stepped outside to lock the door. Athon placed her hand on the small of Lauren's back and escorted her toward the vehicle at the curb while repositioning her hat.

"Fancy car," Lauren said as Athon leaned around her to open the passenger door.

"It was about all the rental company at the airport had, but I like it."

Athon walked around the car and slid into the driver's seat, removing her cap again. "Wait until you see the dash. Looks like a 747. Where to?" she asked as she started the engine.

"Unless you've become a vegetarian since the last time I saw you, there's a new steakhouse on the other side of town everyone's been raving about. It's on Belmont."

"Carnivore City, here we come," Athon said with a laugh.

They drew a few looks when they entered the restaurant and were seated. Athon tried to ignore the customers who looked at them and then whispered behind their hands. Some things would never change.

When they were settled at their table Lauren cleared her

throat. "How long will you be home?" she asked.

Athon took a drink of water before she answered. "I'll hop a ride from Randolph in a few days. They'll fly me to Robins Air Force Base near Atlanta. My crew chief will pick me up and drive me back to Benning. I spoke to him this afternoon. My unit's in the process of prepping before we deploy."

"Do you enjoy being a pilot," Lauren said as their waiter set a salad in front of her.

"I like being an Army aviator. We'll be starting a rotating assignment with two other units already on site."

"A rotating assignment?"

"We'll be assigned to Ramstein Air Force Base and will stay there most of the time. Every six months one of our units will deploy to Iraq or Afghanistan for medical evacuations."

"Do you know yet where you'll be going?"

"With things winding down in Iraq, probably Afghanistan. How long have you been back in Duvalle?"

Lauren looked up and seemed to be thinking.

"About three years. I was with a district just outside of Houston for a few years. An administrative position here came open, so I applied and was hired."

"Do you like it?"

"It's different than teaching."

"And pays more."

Lauren nodded and laughed. The sound of it brought a smile to Athon's face. "And pays more." Her face grew solemn. "The thing is I wanted to teach, not just teach long enough to become another administrator. I'm not sure how long I want to be out of the classroom."

"Only you know what you want, Lauren."

"I went to visit Pudge when I came back. He told me you received your college diploma."

"Couldn't become an officer without one."

"He was very proud of you. What's your degree in?"

"History. Can't do much with that, but now I'm really stoked about going to Europe. I can finally see everything I studied."

"Maybe you could teach?"

"If I have to stop flying I might be able to teach at one of the military schools. I can retire just about any time now, but I'm too young to think about that yet. I like what I do."

"Remember Liz Gordon?"

"Yeah."

"She's back in Duvalle. I ran into her at the grocery store a few weeks ago. She married Rafe, but they're divorced now."

"Ever see anyone else from the distant past?" Athon asked stiffly.

"Surprisingly, a lot of them still live in Duvalle," Lauren said without looking at Athon. "Have you heard anything about your parents?"

"Bridget said Michelle died after a long weekend of partying and tweaking. I got a letter from Pudge a few years back telling me Hank was found stabbed to death in an alley in Dallas." Athon flashed a smile at the waitress as she stopped to check if their food was all right.

Lauren placed her hand over Athon's and gave it a squeeze. "So now you're all alone to do whatever you want."

"Pretty much. There's still Bridget. She treated me better than my parents."

"You mean you've never found anyone you wanted to be with in all these years?" Lauren asked. "I can't believe that, Athon."

"Sad, but true,' Athon said, dramatically faking being upset. "That's not to say I haven't played around a little though," Athon said as she cut a piece of steak and shoved it in her mouth. "The uniform helps."

"You look amazing in it, by the way. Very sexy and commanding."

"I'm sure the Army didn't have the sexy part in mind when it was designed."

"It suits you," Lauren said.

"I wasn't exactly officer material for quite a while. I went through basic without learning to keep my mouth shut." Athon laughed. "Dropping and doing twenty every time I opened my mouth finally taught me to control it."

They ate silently and although Lauren was happy to see Athon again, she felt uneasy.

"I had a good time, Athon," Lauren said when Athon pulled her rental car to the curb in front of her modest home. "But I didn't expect you to pay for dinner."

"Having the chance to catch up was worth it. It's been wonderful seeing you again, Lauren."

She rested her arm along the back of Lauren's seat and without thinking her fingers played with strands of Lauren's hair along her neckline just as she had when they were teenagers.

Lauren turned her body to face Athon while they talked. The light from a streetlight sparkled against a gold necklace around Lauren's neck. Athon touched it with her finger and brought it up far enough to see the heart-shaped gold piece dangling on the chain. Their birthstones, a blue topaz and an amethyst, were set, along with diamond chips, in the heart. Athon ran her thumb over the piece, remembering the delight in Lauren's eyes when she'd opened the small box so many years before.

"I never take it off," Lauren whispered.

"I read your letters," Athon said, releasing the necklace.

"Really?" Lauren said, her voice turning harsh.

"I found them when we were cleaning out the attic after Pudge's funeral. I read them for the first time a couple of days ago. I'm sorry I missed so much of your life. It wasn't my choice."

"I need to go inside," Lauren said, her voice cracking.

Athon escorted Lauren to her front door. "It was good to see you again." Athon hugged her quickly before retreating down the steps.

ATHON CHANGED FROM her uniform into comfortable jeans and a t-shirt. It was still early in the evening and she left the house to wander through the old junk yard. Perhaps one day she would return to Duvalle to stay. Pudge's house was on a nice piece of property if it was cleaned up and the remaining junk cars removed. She could plant a little vegetable garden and learn how to can some of it.

Athon stopped and couldn't resist a smile when she saw the outline of the old camper she had once called home. In fact, it was a peaceful place where she could go to be alone with her thoughts. She remembered the first time she had been there alone with Lauren. She had trembled with desire and need then, but had done the right thing, the honorable thing. Now she wished she hadn't. She hadn't made it to thirty-eight without knowing another woman's body. Best guess was, neither had Lauren. Yet they were both still alone. Athon had discovered it was possible to share her body without actually giving herself to anyone. She shook her head and chuckled to herself. Was she still looking for forever? Did it even exist? How would she know if she found it? There were too many questions and for now her life was too uncertain to ask for forever. Maybe the best she could look forward to was seeing Lauren once every few years and take what she wanted, hoping it left her satisfied between visits. She sat outside the camper and watched the stars overhead.

The sound of a twig snapping brought her attention back to the land around her and her eyes scanned the darkness that surrounded her.

"Athon? Are you out here?" Lauren's voice called out tentatively.

"Over here. By the camper."

Athon stood, but didn't see Lauren until she was only a few feet away. "What are you doing here?"

"When you didn't answer the door, I figured you'd be out here somewhere."

"Pull up a log," Athon offered.

"Tonight didn't go exactly the way I had planned," Lauren said.

Athon couldn't see her eyes in the dark. "What did you have planned?"

"This," Lauren said as she moved closer and found Athon's lips. The years fell away and Athon pulled Lauren deeper into a kiss and wrapped her arms around her.

When the kiss ended, Lauren rested her chin on Athon's shoulder. "The last time we were here I wanted you so much." She moved her forehead to rest against Athon's. "That was twenty years ago, Athon, and I'm tired of waiting."

Athon brought her mouth to cover Lauren's and was happy with the response she felt.

"Please, baby, don't ever leave me again," Athon whispered. She pulled Lauren into her arms and held her. "I was sure you'd found someone better than me."

"There's never been anyone better for me than you," Lauren said softly.

Athon led Lauren back into the house and into the downstairs bedroom as they kissed and touched. They stood close together as Athon closed her eyes and let her fingers take in the features of Lauren's beautiful face. She explored all of the curves of Lauren's still youthful body. She drew Lauren's pullover over her head and tenderly kissed her neck and shoulders. Her thumbs caught in the waistband of Lauren's slacks and she followed them down, kneeling in front of her, caressing her ass and letting her hands stroke along the backs of her thighs as she lavished soft kisses on her abdomen.

"Please, baby," Lauren murmured as her hands ran through Athon's hair. "Let me see you. Let me love you the way I've always wanted to."

Athon lifted Lauren and laid her on the bed before stripping from her own clothes and settling next to her. She propped her body up on one elbow and let her eyes wander the length of Lauren's body, touching her periodically along her journey. "You're everything I thought you'd be," she said as her hand slid up Lauren's thigh and over her hip. She leaned down to press her lips against Lauren's hip.

Lauren's hand ran through Athon's hair. "I remember how your mouth felt on me when I was a teenager. When I think about it I still get wet."

"Tell me what you want, baby," Athon said as she brought her lips to Lauren's.

"You," Lauren murmured between frantic kisses. "I want you."

"Where?"

"Everywhere. Now."

Athon had dreamed about being with Lauren, longed for it for twenty years. Suddenly she was afraid she wouldn't be what Lauren wanted. She rested on her knees and pulled Lauren's body up to straddle her thighs. Lauren rubbed her body slowly up and down Athon's, brushing their nipples together.

"Take me, Athon. Take me like you wanted to twenty years ago," Lauren demanded. "Show me you still want me."

"I've always wanted you," Athon said as she took Lauren's wrists and pinned them behind her. She kissed the valley between Lauren's breasts and let the warmth of her mouth settle over a dark hardened nipple, forcing Lauren to arch her back. She moaned as Athon's tongue circled the nipple and her teeth nipped at it. A long stroke of her tongue combined with the sucking movement of her lips caused Lauren's breathing to quicken.

"Yes, yes, yes. More, baby," Lauren gasped. When Athon slid her mouth to the other breast, Lauren came off the bed slightly and her hips began moving in unison to the sucking motion of Athon's mouth. When Athon released her hands, Lauren drew Athon's mouth up to hers in a frantic devouring kiss, her tongue entering Athon's mouth in rhythm with the movement of her hips as her legs opened to invite her in. "I don't know how much longer I can wait," she said in a raspy voice.

Athon lowered Lauren onto the bed and slid down her body, stopping to lavish more attention on the swollen nipples, before resting her forehead on Lauren's mound and taking a deep breath. "Home," she said as the tip of her tongue flicked out and teased Lauren's clit. When Lauren's hips jerked up, Athon's mouth attached to the slickened lips, her tongue deftly separating them. She found the sweet spot and sucked in the wetness, plunging her tongue inside. She tightened her grip on Lauren's thighs as her tongue moved in and out. Finally she slid two fingers inside and withdrew her tongue to pleasure Lauren's swollen clit by sucking it rapidly in and out of her mouth.

Lauren screamed out her pleasure and Athon held her tightly. Lauren's hands flew up to cover her eyes.

"Come for me, baby," Athon finally said as the movement of her fingers came deeper and harder and the pressure of her thumb against Lauren's clit increased. It seemed as if Lauren had lost control of every muscle in her body as she rode Athon's fingers. She savored the release gathering in her abdomen, moving like a tidal wave. It was over the moment Athon curled her fingers and stroked the roughened skin deep inside. Lauren's body arched and stiffened as her release flowed through her. Her body jerked involuntarily when Athon slowed the movement of her fingers and held her exhausted body close. Athon whispered, "I never stopped loving you."

Chapter Twenty

ATHON WAS AS nervous as a cat. Everything she had hoped for and dreamed of for twenty years was finally happening. She leaned against a mop as she gazed at the shiny hardwood floors. She was glad her unit was in stand down. She had been up almost twenty-four hours a day since Lauren called with the news she'd been hired for a teaching position at the Department of Defense high school serving American dependents in Kaiserslautern. All they had been waiting for was her passport and a few other papers required by her contract. That had been a month ago and Athon had been on pins and needles waiting for the call that Lauren's flight was finally scheduled and confirmed.

Athon had searched the area for an apartment or home to lease and found a place she hoped Lauren would love. It was a small cottage near the outskirts of town, but about halfway between their jobs. It was an understatement that the place needed some work done before anyone would be willing to call it a home. Athon cajoled Frank and a few members of her crew to give up their weekends off for a month. The cottage was soundly built though rustic. Prior to her departure for Europe Lauren shipped a few household goods from her home and gave Athon *carte blanche* to purchase anything else they would need. The household goods arrived four days before Lauren's scheduled arrival and Athon borrowed a deuce-and-a-half to transport them to their new home. Home, she thought. She and Lauren would finally have a home to call their own. A shiver of excitement ran down her spine. She had just put a final coat of wax on the worn, but still beautiful floors. She looked at her wristwatch and was startled at the time. Only four more hours until Lauren's plane landed and Athon still needed to shower and change before beginning the ninety minute drive to the airport in Frankfurt.

As she trotted down the walkway to her vehicle her phone beeped indicating an incoming text message. She pulled the cell from her coat pocket and glanced at it. She stopped and turned back to the house. "Weather delay" anywhere wasn't what she hoped to see, but over the winter months, flying weather could be a little iffy. She pressed another number and waited for someone to answer.

"Hardesty," a voice answered crisply.

"The flight's been delayed because of weather, Frank. I'll go to Frankfurt and just wait until it gets in."

"Give us a call before you leave Frankfurt. Sorry A," her wingman said.

"I will, but if it gets too late, don't wait up for us."

"We can put the food in the fridge if we have to. Be careful. Her flight might get in not far ahead of a major front moving in from the north Atlantic."

Athon disconnected and returned to her vehicle. She could smell the moisture in the air and could only hope they could make it back to Kaiserslautern before a ton of snow dropped from the sky. There was already a nice layer of dry snow covering everything, adding to the Christmas season three weeks away. The weather had turned unseasonably warm the previous day. If the new weather system moving toward them re-froze the slushy wet stuff, the roads would become treacherous at best.

The trip to Frankfurt, while only about seventy-five miles, took longer than Athon expected and the temperature when she stepped out of her car to hike to the terminal nearly took her breath away. She hurried to the main terminal and found the arrival and departure board. Apparently the delay in London had been shorter than anticipated and the flight was now scheduled to arrive only fifteen minutes later than originally posted. Athon found a coffee shop and grabbed a cup to warm up. If the storm was moving quickly, it was possible the flight would gain a little time aided by a favorable tailwind.

ATHON STOOD IN front of a floor-to-ceiling window and watched airplanes take-off and land. There was something majestic about watching them lumber down the long runways, seemingly bound to the earth by their enormous weight, only to lift effortlessly into the darkening sky. Others appeared to float back to the ground as if they were feathers on a breeze. Dark, angry looking clouds on the distant horizon loomed closer and larger as she watched. She glanced at a clock hanging near a terminal entrance. The flight she was waiting for should be coming into sight at any time. She felt her breathing and heart beat increase when she saw the runway lights of three or four aircraft lined up to begin their descent into Frankfurt.

She could barely contain her excitement. They had waited so long and now the moment she had longed for was there. No more waiting for a visit to Duvalle every ten or twelve months. No more nights in Lauren's arms knowing they would end too soon, trying to love her enough until her next visit. She wasn't sure she would be able to accept the idea of no more separation from the woman she had loved since high school. When the arrival board announced that Lauren's flight was at its gate, Athon walked quickly to the area deplaning passengers would pass through on their way to baggage claims. Soldiers weren't allowed to wear their uniforms when they traveled to avoid being targeted by terrorists and Athon hoped Lauren would recognize her in the large crowd. She wondered how many others were there to greet relatives or loved ones who would be joining them for the holiday. Lauren's principal wanted her to wait and leave after the Christmas holiday, but Lauren would begin teaching at the DOD school in Kaiserslautern after the New Year and wanted to spend time alone with Athon before starting work.

A thousand thoughts ran through Athon's mind as she waited. In the middle of a group making its way toward the main terminal she spotted a familiar head. She eased her way around and between the others waiting, getting as close to the entrance as she could. Her efforts were rewarded when Lauren's beautiful cinnamon eyes locked with her own. As she drew closer Athon backed into a small niche in the partition for a little more space. There was no hesitation as Lauren leaped into her arms and hugged her fiercely.

"I made it, baby," Lauren whispered. "I finally made it."

Athon held her tightly. "You feel incredible. Let's get your luggage and get out of here."

They each pulled one large rolling suitcase as they walked closely together, huddled against the freezing wind. Athon was parked in an enclosed parking garage, but it wasn't much warmer than outside. She started her car to warm it up before she met Lauren at the rear of the vehicle and loaded her suitcases. She hustled Lauren to the passenger side before making her way to the driver's side and jumping in. She didn't bother to buckle up and slid closer to Lauren, who met her in the middle. A frenzied kiss served as a testament to their long wait. Lauren's fingers twisted in Athon's hair refusing to let her go. Athon's lips moved to Lauren's neck and ear, their rising body heat fogging the windows.

"If it wasn't so damn cold, I'd rip your clothes off right here," Lauren breathed.

"I know, baby," Athon panted. "I've waited a lifetime to say this to you. Let's go home."

Athon scooted back under the steering wheel. Lauren took her hand and kissed it before buckling into the center portion of the seat. She leaned her head against Athon's shoulder. "Take me to *our* home, my love," she said with a delighted laugh.

Before she backed out of the parking space Athon pulled her

cell from her pocket and hit a speed dial number. She waited a moment, looked down at Lauren, and smiled. "We'll be there in two," she said without further conversation and drove out of the parking garage.

They chatted on the drive back to Kaiserlautern, but Lauren didn't want to know anything about their new home. She wanted to be surprised and discover everything about it on her own. Athon admitted she hadn't done much decorating. She wanted Lauren to make it special. Since Christmas would be coming up soon, they could find a tree and begin Christmas traditions that would be their own. They sounded like a couple of teenagers again, making imaginary plans for a future that might never be. Except their future had finally arrived.

ATHON SWUNG HER vehicle into its parking space not far from the cottage and unloaded Lauren's suitcases. She stuck her hand in her pocket and took out a key, handing it to Lauren.

"Two doors down on the right," Athon said. "Watch out for ice on the walkway. I'll clean it off tomorrow."

Lauren walked carefully and turned onto a shorter walk that led to a heavy looking front door. A portion of the cottage front was covered by evidence of ivy. She turned the key in the lock and started to push the door open. Athon stopped her and leaned over to lift her into her arms. "Welcome home, baby," she said as she kissed her lightly and stepped through the opening. Muted lighting in the front room and hallway allowed a subdued view of the area.

"Oh, my God! Athon, this looks like something out of a fairy tale," Lauren said as she hugged her lover's neck.

Athon set her down to explore further and stepped outside to bring in the suitcases. She left them in the entry and took Lauren's hand, leading her into another room to see if Frank had done his job. She was relieved to see that he hadn't let her down. A table for two, illuminated by red, medium tapered candles, took up most of a small dining area. Plates filled with steaming food, accompanied by a chilling bottle of wine, greeted them.

"Welcome home," Athon said as she smiled down at Lauren.

ATHON LEANED BACK in her chair and patted her full stomach. Lauren sighed and pushed her plate away. She reached out and took Athon's hand.

"That was delicious and I was starving," she said. "Airline meals and snacks are pathetic."

"I'll introduce you to the chef tomorrow," Athon said, running her thumb over Lauren's knuckles. "Her husband is my wingman. My protector, so to speak."

"What does that mean?"

"Medevacs don't carry any weapons other than sidearms. Frank pilots a bad ass, fully armed Blackhawk in case we run into trouble."

"What kind of trouble?" Lauren said with a scowl.

"It's a combat zone, honey. Sometimes the bad guys shoot back. If they do Frank sends them to greet Allah, or whoever they believe in. He must be doing a good job. No one in my crew has ever received a scratch."

"If I don't move pretty soon, I'll fall asleep with my head on this table," Lauren said, abruptly changing the subject.

"Then let me give you the grand tour," Athon said as she stood up and held out her hand. "It's been a long day and you're probably exhausted."

Athon became suddenly quiet as she showed Lauren the rest of the quaint cottage. She returned to the front room for Lauren's suitcases and rolled them into the bedroom. She hoisted them onto the king-size bed she and Frank had managed to wrangle into the largest bedroom. Nothing short of dynamite would be able to remove it again.

"Think you'll be happy here?" Athon asked as she handed clothing to Lauren.

"I'd be happy living in a mud hut as long as I'm with you."

"I hope so."

"What's wrong, baby?"

"Nothin'."

"We promised never to lie to one another, Athon. Don't start on our first day together."

Athon sat on the edge of the bed and stared at her hands. "We've waited so long. First that moving stunt your dad pulled. Then waiting while I was gone for months at a time. All we ever wanted was to be together. We've never been together for more than a few days at a time. What if it turns out that being together every day isn't enough?"

"Are you having second thoughts?"

"I'm not. But what if it doesn't turn out the way you want?"

Lauren shrugged. "Then it won't, but at least we gave ourselves the chance to be happy." She climbed on the bed and knelt in front of Athon. "Look at me, Athon." She waited for Athon's eyes to meet hers. "I love you, baby. When you weren't with me, I thought I'd get over it. But I never did. The moment I saw you again I knew there was no one else who could ever give me what I needed. No one else could fulfill my every dream. You're the only one who can. The only one who ever will. If you want me to go away, I will, if that is what would make you happy. I couldn't stand to see you unhappy."

Athon pulled Lauren up into her lap. "You're all I wanted then. You're all I want now. You're all I'll ever want."

Lauren shoved her back. "Then stop with all the doubtin' shit." She giggled when Athon pulled her down on top of her, then flipped her onto her back.

"You're way too overdressed, woman," Athon whispered as she kissed along her neck. When Lauren wrapped her arms around her, she whispered, "You're my home."

OVER THE NEXT five months Lauren couldn't remember being happier. She and Athon took short trips together, with Athon showing her all the castles and historical sites she had described to her in daily e-mails. She had sent pictures, but in person everything seemed so much more alive. They felt safe walking down ancient streets hand-in-hand, wandering into unique small stores, amazed at the variety of foods available in grocery stores. They spent time going to dinner with Frank and his wife, Amanda. Mandy Hardesty was an excellent cook and was determined to become proficient at European cooking before they rotated home. She convinced Lauren to learn German with her so they wouldn't feel like tourists. Lauren loved her job teaching at the American high school in Kaiserslautern and, as far as anyone could tell, her students liked their new teacher. She became involved with a variety of groups at school and volunteered to take classes on field trips to historical sites. For the first time in their lives they prepared meals together, occasionally argued, only to spend most of the night making up, slept in one another's arms, and woke up together.

It hadn't taken long for them to fall into a routine. Athon was out of bed every morning by five, dressed, and off to PT. Lauren had breakfast on the table by the time Athon returned from physical training at six-thirty. They chatted as food and coffee fully awakened them. While Lauren cleaned up the kitchen, Athon jumped in the shower. Lauren drove Athon to her office before heading to school and picked her up again about five. Over the weekends, they prepared their meals for the next week together. There was something reassuring about the sameness of their routines neither had had in the past. Because they had no weekend PT, Athon and Frank usually met early in the mornings for a three to five mile run before their spouses were awake. It gave them a chance to discuss what the unit was doing, discuss how they could improve their response time, or what they should do about a crewman who'd fucked up one too many times.

Lauren soon discovered that Athon loved her job, was dedicated almost to a fault and worked impossibly long hours. She told Lauren about her plans once she retired from the service. She had already been contacted about continuing to fly for a private corporation working with large trauma centers in the southwestern area. Her pay would rise significantly. However, she wasn't sure if she wanted to continue what she was doing. But she still had three years left on her current enlistment and was in the final eighteen months of her tour in Germany. Unless she was extended, they would be rotating home in less than two years.

As part of the Armed Forces Day celebration in May, Lauren made arrangements for her students to observe some of the units stationed in the Kaiserslautern region perform simulated duties. It was a chilly day as the students huddled together to watch a simulated battlefield rescue. Mandy tagged along as a chaperone to keep an eye on the students. Soldiers in full battle gear spent nearly an hour showing and explaining the various weapons at their disposal as well as the communication apparatus used to keep in contact with other units. When Lauren and the other teachers began herding the students back toward the bleachers, they could hear the distance thudding sound of helicopters approaching. Mandy smiled and pointed into the sky as two Blackhawks skimmed across the area firing blank rounds, presumably clearing it of hostiles before the medevac teams swung into action. Two at a time, in a well-synchronized maneuver, helicopters touched down. Crewmen jumped from the loading doors and volunteers acting as casualties were loaded. The first group departed, making room for the last two choppers. Lauren pulled a pair of binoculars from her shoulder bag and scanned the idling machines. She poked Mandy in the shoulder and handed her the binoculars. Lauren could tell that one of the pilots was Athon, even with her helmet on. She took a deep breath. Athon looked so in charge, so commanding, that Lauren wanted to break down and cry with pride. After the demonstration ended, all of the choppers landed and shut down their engines so the students could get a closer look inside.

"God, she's so handsome," Lauren sighed as Athon removed her helmet and swung out of the pilot's seat.

"Don't you think for a Minnesota minute they don't know that," Mandy said. "I want to tear Frank's clothes off when I see him like this."

Athon waved when she saw Lauren and walked toward her, her hips swaying in that leisurely way Lauren always noticed. Tonight would be a night to remember, Lauren thought with a smile. She was jealous she couldn't greet Athon the way Frank greeted Mandy. She would have been happier if 'don't ask, don't tell' was changed to 'Don't ask because nobody cares'. There had been talk that the policy might be repealed, but for now it was still in effect. Despite everything, Athon found a way to touch Lauren before the students moved away and the crewmen jumped back on their helicopters to return to their unit landing area for the day.

Chapter Twenty-one

Kaiserslautern, Germany
June 2008

ATHON HAD A ton of paperwork sitting on the old chipped wooden desk in her office, which was located near the rear of the hangar where her helicopter was undergoing its scheduled engine maintenance. The dog-and-pony show they'd put on for Armed Forces Day had put them a little behind schedule. She should get busy making the pile smaller, especially the personnel reports. In her opinion every member of her crew worked well together and their heads were fully into their mission. Partially because of her crew, she was the envy of their unit. She leaned her long body into the engine compartment before reaching back and patting the back pocket of her work coveralls. "Goddamn it," she muttered. "Somebody hand me a quarter-inch socket." Her hand fluttered around behind her waiting for one of the mechanics to drop the wrench in her hand, but after about a minute she pressed her middle finger against the bolt she had finally located and raised her head far enough to look outside the compartment. "Jacobsen! Where's the quarter-inch socket?" she called out.

"In your other back pocket!" the man called back.

"Attention in the bay!" another voice said loudly.

Athon strained to turn her neck and look behind her while still holding onto the bolt. It had taken her half an hour to locate it and she wasn't going to let go until it was tightened. A dark-skinned man with short black hair and a pair of aviator sunglasses hiding his eyes stared back at her. She hadn't seen anyone who looked so stereotypically like a pilot in years and had to smile. She recognized the cocky way he walked and carried himself. She had carried herself the same way as soon as she completed flight school. It hadn't taken long for a seasoned warrant officer to teach her she wasn't the hot shit she believed she was. Now she might get stuck teaching the same lessons.

She missed her former co-pilot. Captain Allison Struthers personified laid-back California beach girls. They had worked together well and the men in her crew thought they'd died and gone to helicopter heaven. Athon had to admit that Alli had been magnetically attractive with her long blonde hair and sky blue eyes. If she'd been single, she might have given her a whirl herself. But like everyone in the Army who was worth a shit, Alli earned a promotion and was shipped off to a new assignment teaching at the army flight school.

"Listen, buddy," Athon said. "There's a wrench in my left back pocket. Hand it to me, will ya." She didn't feel it being removed from her pocket, but it suddenly appeared in her hand. "Thanks. You must have been a pick-pocket or something in another life. Never felt you removing it." With a couple of quick turns, the bolt seated into place. She pushed onto her toes and felt the locking nut behind the bolt to make sure it was in place. She pulled her head out of the compartment and picked up a cloth from the housing to wipe her hands. "You new?" she asked the stranger.

"Yeah. I'm looking for Major Dailey. I'm his new co-pilot on this bird."

"That right? How long you been a real, live pilot?"

"Just direct me to Dailey's office so I can report in." He removed his sunglasses and let his eyes scan Athon from head to toe. "You might be kind of cute without the layers of grease."

Athon smiled. "A dirty mechanic is a good mechanic."

"I wouldn't know, blondie," he said.

"The major's office is over in that corner. Should be back in a minute." She glanced at the rank on the collar of his shirt and his name tag. "Chief Warrant Officer Ortega."

Ortega strolled toward Athon's office. "Now I really miss Alli," she said to herself.

"Who's that?" Jacobsen asked as he bent over to find the wrench he needed in the large rolling tool chest.

"New co-pilot," she answered. "Should be fun."

Athon cleaned her hands with a mechanic's abrasive gel and removed her coveralls, revealing her rank insignia. She took a deep breath and walked toward her office. She sat down heavily behind her desk. "You're indoors, Ortega. Remove the shades," she ordered sharply.

Ortega jumped up so fast he knocked his chair over. It clattered on the concrete floor as he jerked his sunglasses off and saluted her crisply.

"I wasn't told you were a woman, sir...er...ma'am," Ortega stammered, his eyes shifting around as if searching for words.

"At ease, Chief," she said, returning the salute and holding her hand out. "And look at me when I'm talking to you."

"Yes, ma'am," he said, handing her his orders.

She thumbed through the paperwork while he continued to stand in front of her, his legs spread slightly and hand behind his back.

"First, never assume," she said as she leaned back in her chair. "I began my career as a helicopter mechanic and then decided I'd like to fly them. Fortune smiled on me and here I am. Second, you will never treat the people who make sure we don't crash and burn with anything other than the utmost respect. Third, if you ever call me 'blondie' again, I'll make it my goal in life to bust you down to the enlisted ranks again. Are we clear, Chief?"

"Crystal, ma'am."

"You already checked into your quarters?"

"Yes, ma'am."

"Good. Married?"

"No, ma'am."

"Where you from?"

"Texas, ma'am. San Antonio."

"We're scheduled for a night flight at zero one hundred tonight. I assume you're experienced with night vision goggles."

"I've used them, ma'am."

"Have you flown in a real desert while wearing them?"

"Two practice missions at NTC, ma'am."

"I'll schedule more night flights. We're next on the rotation schedule so you'll need to learn quickly."

"Where are we going, if I might ask, ma'am?"

"Someplace unpronounceable in Afghanistan. Any other questions?"

"Not at the moment, ma'am."

"I don't deal with crap on my chopper, Chief. Stow any you brought and don't ever bring it onto the bird with you. I have a good team, the best in the unit. Anything or anyone that disrupts that won't be here long. Never doubt that I'm in charge of this crew. If you have a problem taking orders from a woman, request a transfer and I'll sign it. Bullshit macho complexes don't have a place on my crew, so if you have it, lose it. When we're working there are no ranks. Listen to what the crew tells you. They've been with me a long time and I trust them with my life every time we leave the ground. They're all professionals and know what they're doing. They expect us to get them to a site unharmed and return them the same way. Report to the pad at midnight to go through pre-flight. That's all," she said dismissively as she pulled the first papers in the stack on her desk in front of her. Without looking up again, she added, "I suggest you spend a little time getting acquainted with our crew." Giving the usual lecture to Ortega turned out to be the first in a series of events that shot the day to hell.

LAUREN HAD DINNER simmering on the stove and was grading papers at the kitchen table when she heard the front door open and slam shut again hard enough to jar pictures on the walls. The sound of Athon's boots retreated to the small room they had converted into a study and computer room. She hadn't paused to greet Lauren, which was usually a sign that something was wrong or it had been a bitchin' FUBAR day, as Athon called it. Nearly an hour later Athon reappeared, still in her uniform, but only her BDU pants and a white t-shirt. She followed her nose into the kitchen. Lauren was putting the finishing touches on something on the stove. Athon walked up behind her and slowly slid her arms around her, pulling her tightly against her.

"Whatcha makin'?" she asked.

"Mandy gave me this recipe for beef and vegetable soup with barley. As soon as the cornbread's done we can eat."

"Smells good," Athon said as she lowered her lips to the back of Lauren's neck. She took a deep breath. "But not as good as you."

Lauren backed up enough to open the oven door and wiggled her butt playfully against Athon's crotch as she slid the skillet inside. Athon ran her hands over Lauren's ass. "I love cornbread," she rasped.

Lauren set her spoon down and turned in Athon's arms. "Is something wrong, honey? You look like you lost your dog."

Athon smiled. "We don't have a dog. Maybe someday when we settle someplace permanently."

"What's wrong?"

"Orders came down today. We're rotating to Afghanistan in November."

Lauren's eyes widened. "That's in six months! I thought—"

"They changed the rotation order," Athon interrupted. "One of our units is being diverted to Iraq and we have to cover part of their rotation. As a result, we've been extended."

"What does that mean, honey? I'm new to the Army."

Athon frowned and tried not to let her anger show in her voice. "It means we'll do our regular rotation, plus eight additional months."

"You'll be gone over a year," Lauren said, shaking her head.

"About fifteen months probably. We'll spend most of October getting our equipment ready. The week we leave we'll be on lockdown in barracks at Ramstein."

When she saw the look on Lauren's face she took her in her arms. "I'm sorry I'll have to leave you here alone so soon, honey," she said, resting her chin on Lauren's shoulder.

"Mandy's staying, isn't she?"

"Yeah. Command will set up satellite conferences for spouses once a month, or so, on base. I won't be able to call you using my satellite phone. The enemy might be smart enough to intercept it and pinpoint our location."

Lauren's eyes sparkled with moisture. "I'm not your spouse, sweetie."

"Command knows I'm not married and don't have any family. I put your name on the contact list. I listed you as my beneficiary and before we leave I'll give you my power of attorney. It's just in case—"

Lauren jerked herself out of Athon's arms. "Nothing's going to happen to you. Do you understand me, Major?"

Athon playfully saluted. "Yes, ma'am!"

Chapter Twenty-two

LAUREN FELT SURPRISINGLY refreshed as she gathered her things from around and under her seat on the commercial flight from Frankfurt to Washington, D.C. She had fallen asleep not long after take-off and slept until the stewardess awakened her to tell her the plane would be landing within the hour. It was the first time she had slept more than three or four hours since Athon's last mission. Four days of emotional and mental hell, accompanied by prayers that begged, pleaded, demanded her lover's safe return. As she watched the ground grow closer, she wondered where Athon and the other injured soldiers were, whether they had already departed from Greenland.

She waited until the line of passengers finally began moving down the aisle of the plane before standing up. She had gone online before she left Frankfurt and made a reservation at a hotel close to Walter Reed. Once she was settled in she would make her way to the receiving hospital and attempt to locate Colonel Beverly Campbell. After Mandy reminded her about the paperwork Athon had signed giving Lauren both a medical and financial power of attorney before her deployment, she was certain she wouldn't have a problem. She rented a car at the airport and thanks to the GPS included in the vehicle she found her hotel within a relatively short time. She was certain she'd driven within viewing distance of the Capitol Building and other famous landmarks, but she wasn't in the nation's capital as a tourist.

She checked in and tried to settle into her new home away from home. She called the information officer at Walter Reed and was transferred five times before losing her temper with a man who sounded like a teenager. She knew the length of the red tape the government spun was unwieldy and implacable. She took a deep breath to calm her nerves and waited until the young man returned to the phone. The best he could do was tell her that the medical flight had left Greenland at the designated departure time and was en route to Andrews Air Force Base. Since she didn't know the designated flight departure time, she grabbed the keys to her vehicle and decided to drive to the air force base in Maryland and wait. The drive was relatively short, but the wait would be much longer. It took her half an hour to get through the main gate of the base after producing every possible piece of paper she had in her possession. She was able to acquire a temporary visitor's pass for the car and followed the gate guard's directions to the main terminal. She stopped military personnel in various areas to inquire about the arrival time of the flight. She knew she wouldn't be able to see Athon, but knowing she was safely back in the United States would make her feel better. There was nothing for her to do but find a place to watch incoming flights descend onto the tarmac.

She located a seat that gave her a relatively unobstructed view of the runways and sat down. She rubbed her eyes. Even though she had slept well on the plane they felt like someone had poured sand behind her eyelids.

"Ma'am? Can I assist you?" a young woman in uniform asked.

"I'm waiting for a flight to arrive," Lauren answered.

"Which flight are you here for? There are two scheduled to arrive in about twenty minutes."

"Is one of them coming in from Greenland?"

The woman flipped through the pages on her clipboard and nodded. "That flight will land immediately after a flight from Dover. This is as good a place as any to see them. You know, of course, that you won't be allowed near them. Do you have a loved one on the Greenland flight?"

"Yes. I plan to drive to Walter Reed as soon as I know it has arrived."

"Would it be all right if I waited here with you, ma'am?"

"Of course. My name is Lauren Shelton," she answered as she offered her hand.

"Airman Gail Connors, ma'am," the woman said as she took Lauren's hand. "I hope your loved one will be okay."

"I'm sure she will be, Airman Connors."

Connors squinted into the sky and pointed. "There they are. It won't be long now."

Lauren stood and watched two large cargo transports touch down. A flurry of activity followed on the ground as ambulances prepared to make their way to the cargo ramp behind the second plane and three shiny black hearses awaited the first. Lauren's hand went to her mouth as she watched uniformed personnel march toward the black vehicles. When both planes were completely stopped, the back cargo doors lowered to the ground. Medics came quickly down the ramp of one plane, bringing their patients with them. A line of men and women walked up the second ramp and slowly began carrying a flag-draped coffin back down and toward the open back doors of the first hearse. Lauren was momentarily startled when Airman Connors snapped to attention and brought her hand up slowly in a salute to a fallen comrade being brought home to his or her family. The dichotomy of the scene was heart-wrenching as the fallen who had not survived were removed in such close proximity to those still fighting to live. She felt a tear trickle down her cheek as the last of the injured troops was placed in an ambulance. She turned and hugged Connors before walking back toward her car, hoping she would see Athon again soon.

THE WAITING AREA at Walter Reed was much busier than the airport had been. In fact, to Lauren it bordered on chaotic. She asked at the information desk if Athon had arrived and was met with a chilly response. Once again she pulled out the paperwork she hoped would manage to work a miracle. Finally, she asked to speak to Colonel Beverly Campbell. That anyone even knew the name of the doctor who was the head of the Emergency Department seemed to surprise the civilian seated at the reception desk. After a lengthy telephone conversation, the woman at the desk explained that casualties from a war zone had only arrived recently and that Colonel Campbell was extremely busy.

"I'll wait," Lauren said as she gathered her papers.

"It could be a very long one," the woman said. "Perhaps if you left a phone number..."

"I'll wait."

Nearly two hours later a dignified woman with short graying hair stepped up to the reception desk. Lauren saw the receptionist point in her direction and stood. The older woman looked exhausted as she approached Lauren.

"Lauren Shelton?" she asked.

"Colonel Campbell?"

"I am," Campbell nodded. "My feet are killing me. Would you mind if we sat?" she asked with a smile.

"Of course. I'm sorry to bother you."

Campbell reached into the pocket of her lab coat and pulled out a small piece of paper. "You're here about Major Dailey, is that correct?"

"Yes. Can you tell me anything about her condition? I have a medical power of attorney if you need to see it."

"I have better than that. I have a directive from Doctor Stephens at Landstuhl. Wouldn't want to make Karen mad or she'll never speak to me again. Okay, I've examined Major Dailey and have scheduled a series of tests. At the very least she has suffered multiple serious head traumas. From what the people at Landstuhl were able to piece together, it's probably one concussion on top of another one. We won't know the extent of the damage caused by that until we run more tests."

"Is she conscious?"

"Not at the moment. She suffered a seizure before being transported here and they gave her enough medication to hopefully prevent a reoccurrence. She suffered a gunshot wound to her left side that was left untreated a number of days, but while she does have an infection it didn't appear to damage anything vital. When I know she's fully stabilized, I'll deal with an assortment of painful, but relatively minor injuries, specifically to her feet. They were exposed to very low temperatures. At this time I don't believe any of her toes will need to be amputated, but we'll keep an eye on them to make sure her circulation wasn't compromised." Campbell cleared her throat. "When you see her, don't be shocked. They didn't take it easy on her, Ms. Shelton. There may not be more than an inch of her body that isn't bruised and damaged. The bruises on her back and abdomen are quite severe, but it's her head injuries I'm most concerned about. From the report that came with her, she may have suffered a minor concussion from exploding ordnance. At some time, subsequent to that, it appears her head suffered additional blows that may have been severe enough to renderd her unconscious for a period of time. She was awake and listed as semi-alert when she was taken to the hospital in Kandahar. She apparently told the staff there that she had drowned. She may be able to clarify that once she's awake." Campbell shrugged. "Or it could have referred to something totally unrelated to her capture. I don't want to frighten you, but we'll be watching her very closely while we gradually wean her off the medication she's receiving. For now she's essentially in an induced coma. We need to bring her out of that before we can attempt anything else. Until she's fully awake it's difficult to give you a long-term prognosis. At the moment her condition is listed as guarded."

"Could she—"

"We'll do everything we can for her," Campbell said as she patted Lauren's arm. "We've placed her in ICU for tonight. Would you like to see her?"

"Can I?"

"For a few minutes."

Lauren drew a hospital gown over her clothes and placed a mask over her mouth and nose before being led into the ICU. She could feel tears beginning to form in her eyes and blinked them away as she followed a nurse inside. Athon lay on a hospital bed near the back of the large room. The bandages on her head had been changed and a shiny substance almost glowed on the bruised skin of her face. Round gauze pads covered her eyes and IV lines ran into both arms. As Campbell had warned her, bruises covered her arms and legs, the red and angry looking marks around her raw wrists and ankles clearly showing she had been restrained. The sheeting over the lower portion of Athon's body was raised to prevent it from chafing against her damaged feet.

"Can she hear me?" Lauren asked quietly.

"We don't really know," the nurse answered. "We'd like to think so on some level."

"The bandages over her eyes?"

"They keep her eyes moist and block out the fluorescents in here."

"May I touch her?"

"Very gently. You only have fifteen minutes. I'll be back," the nurse said.

When Lauren was finally alone with Athon, she took her hand and squeezed it lightly. She leaned down close to Athon's ear and whispered. "I'm here, baby. I promised I would be. You need to fight to come back to me. I want to hear your voice and see those beautiful blue eyes again." Lauren covered her face with her free hand to stifle a sob. "I miss you so much. I love you more than you will ever know. I'll be here to pester you until you come back."

In all too short a time the nurse told Lauren her time was up. "Get some sleep tonight if you can. We wouldn't want another patient on our hands."

THE NEXT SIX days were agonizingly long and slow for Lauren. She was allowed to see Athon for no more than fifteen minutes each hour and began to develop a routine. She spent her first visit telling Athon how much she loved and missed her. Occasionally she expressed her desires for the future once Athon was awake. She read newspaper articles she thought Athon would be interested in. She read cards Athon received, especially from Frank, who also sent a recorded message telling her the trials and tribulations of being waited on hand and foot by his wife and suggesting she try for the same treatment from Lauren.

As Lauren prepared to re-enter the ICU for her next fifteen minute visit, she saw Colonel Campbell stepping off the elevator.

"Could I speak to you for a minute, Colonel Campbell?"

"Certainly, Ms. Shelton. What can I do for you?"

"I know you ran tests on Athon after she arrived and I was wondering whether you had received the results yet."

"Have a seat, Ms. Shelton." Campbell rubbed her forehead with her thumb and forefinger as if gathering her thoughts before speaking. "From the MRI we believe Major Dailey may have suffered a stroke at some time following one of her concussive injuries."

"How serious was it?"

"It was a significant event, but until she wakes up we simply don't know what systems of her body, if any, may have been affected." Campbell paused for a moment. "I wish I had better news for you, Lauren, but there is a possibility Athon may never wake up," she said in a soft voice.

"She will!" Lauren insisted. "She would never leave me like this and she wouldn't want to exist like *that*," she said jabbing a finger toward the ICU.

"She's breathing on her own and that's always a good sign. Her EEG shows brain activity, so I'm hoping for the best. You need to be aware of the possible outcomes. You need to be prepared in case it's less than optimal. That's assuming you plan to stick with her, of course."

Lauren sprang from her chair and glared down at Campbell. "How dare you! Nothing, nothing would make me abandon Athon!"

"It could be a long road back for her." Campbell studied her hands before meeting her eyes solemnly. "No matter how much you love the warrior who left to do her duty, most families aren't prepared for how they've changed when they come home, especially if they've been badly injured."

"I don't care. I promised I'd be there when she woke up. I lost her once and won't do it again."

For the next month Lauren was a daily presence at the hospital. Athon was stable enough to be transferred out of ICU and put into a private room, which allowed Lauren to be with her all day. Campbell arranged for a recliner and gave permission for her to remain at night as well. She held Athon's hand and continued reading to her. Gradually, the bruises covering her body began to fade and her feet and toes had pinked up as the badly lacerated tissue healed. A physical therapist appeared twice a day to prevent Athon's arm and leg muscles from atrophying and a feeding tube was placed in her abdomen for nutrition. Despite that Athon's weight steadily dropped. Lauren couldn't stand to watch as the slightly thickened liquid keeping her body alive was administered and oozed through the tube. Instead, she took the opportunity to go for short walks outside, stopping from time to time to soak up the sunshine and cold, fresh February air. She found a private place and called Bridget. It was the first time she'd spoken to anyone else close to Athon. Bridget offered to fly to Maryland to relieve Lauren, and while she appreciated the offer, she knew Athon wouldn't want anyone else to see her yet. Lauren promised to call every week to let her know if there was a change in her condition.

Lauren rode the elevator back to Athon's floor and stopped to get a cup of coffee. It seemed that she lived on the substance. When she returned to Athon's room she set the cup down and resumed her position next to the bed. She took Athon's hand and gave a light squeeze. "I'm back, baby," she said. "Did you enjoy that prime rib dinner with all the fixin's you had this evening?" She laughed. "It's still cold outside, but it will be spring soon. I called Bridget to let her know you're okay. Probably hot as hell down there already."

Lauren felt the hand in hers tighten, accompanied by a groan. She stood up quickly and stared down at Athon. With her free hand she stroked her cheek and forehead. The corner of Athon's mouth curled up slightly. "L–Lauren?"

"Oh my God! Athon! Open your eyes and look at me, baby. Please." Lauren grabbed the call button to summon the nurse.

"Can I help you?" came over the tinny sounding speaker over the bed.

"She's awake, she's awake," Lauren sobbed. "Call Colonel Campbell!"

"I've got a headache from hell," Athon said as she struggled to open her eyes and keep them open.

She tried to release Athon's hand as nurses entered the room, followed moments later by Colonel Campbell, but Athon refused to let her go. Campbell smiled and said, "I can work around it. It isn't much of an obstacle." She looked down at Athon. "Welcome back, Major. How do you feel?"

"Like a half-track backed over me," Athon croaked.

"Do you know where you are?"

"Hospital."

"That's right. You're in Maryland at Walter Reed Military Hospital."

"How long?"

"A little over a month. You had us worried for a while." Campbell smiled at Lauren. "Except for Lauren. What can you remember about what happened to you?"

"Frank found me." Athon frowned. Tears filled her eyes and spilled over. "Lost my crew."

Campbell proclaimed Athon on the road to recovery physically and made notations on her chart. "Are you hungry, Major?"

"A little."

"How about a milkshake?"

"Sounds good." Athon leaned her head back to look at Lauren. "Will you stay with me?"

"Wild horses couldn't drag me away."

The room seemed to empty as quickly as it had filled. Campbell gave orders to remove the feeding tube and ordered a liquid diet for the next twenty-four hours. If she tolerated it without difficulty she could be moved up to a soft diet. She also ordered more tests as well as additional therapy sessions. She motioned for Lauren to follow her into the hallway.

"She still has a long way to go, Lauren," Campbell said when they were alone. "She looks good enough, but we can't know her status until we know what the long-range effects of her brain injury might be. It was obviously a traumatic brain injury that was further exacerbated by seizures and a stroke. Fortunately, neither of those events affected vital systems like her respiratory or circulatory systems. It'll take a while to rebuild her muscles, but I'm sure she'll be fine there as well. I'd like you to keep a journal or diary or something like that."

"For what?"

"I want you to record what she tells you about what happened to her. It's possible she doesn't remember and it could be a permanent memory loss, which is not necessarily bad. Or it could come back in pieces that don't make sense to her. Considering what we know, it's also possible she will eventually show symptoms of post-traumatic stress disorder. If that's true, she will require counseling to deal with it. It's not something you can take care of at home. It's probable the Major Athon Dailey you knew is not the same Major Athon Dailey who just woke up."

"She knew who I was."

"And she knows who she is. But she might not be as sure about the relationship between the two of you right now."

"I need to do some research so I'll know what to expect," Lauren sighed.

"A wise decision. I'll schedule an appointment with a counselor who's dealt with many brain injuries. He can probably give you some useful information. Let me know if there's anything else I can do to assist you."

"Thank you for everything, Colonel. Dr. Stephens said you were the best."

Campbell laughed. "That's because she's been overly fond of me for the last seventeen years," she said with a wink.

Chapter Twenty-three

THAT NIGHT LAUREN held Athon's hand while she tried to go to sleep. Every time she glanced toward Athon she could see that her eyes were still open. She ran her thumb over the back of Athon's hand and sat up.

"Having trouble sleeping?" she asked.

"According to the doctor I've been asleep for a month. How tired could I be?"

"Good point." Suddenly Lauren felt uncomfortable. After so much time had passed she didn't know what to say the Athon.

"I'll never fly again," Athon said flatly. "Too damaged." She turned her head toward Lauren. "I love you."

"I love you, too, baby," Lauren said as she brought Athon's hand to her lips. "I've been so lonely without you."

"Sorry I worried you."

"It wasn't your fault. All that matters now is that you're home again."

"Once I get out of here I'll file my paperwork to retire. I've given my twenty."

"Where do you want to go then?"

"Back to Duvalle, I guess." She smiled. "I own a pretty nice house there," she said, as if Lauren was unaware of that.

Lauren ached to take Athon in her arms and tell her everything would be all right, but she couldn't. She closed her eyes for a few moments, remembering the last time they had been together. She felt the muscles in her abdomen clench as she remembered the touch of Athon's hands on her skin, pressing into her. Would she ever feel that again?

WHEN HER LESSER injuries were completely healed, Athon began re-training her brain to do things which had once come naturally. The physical therapist quickly discovered that because much of the damage done to her brain affected the left side, she had a tendency to list slightly to the right. Her balance and equilibrium had been compromised, which created problems walking. The stroke had left her with some weakness on her left side and difficulty swallowing which caused her to choke occasionally. Her eyesight had also been affected, requiring that she now wear corrective lenses.

While Athon went to her physical therapy sessions, Lauren met with a counselor who had spoken to Athon. Lauren had noticed some changes in Athon's behavior and was concerned about what she could expect.

The counselor, Leeanne Patterson, greeted Lauren at the door. After spending a few minutes chatting about the length of time Athon might need to recover, Leeanne finally got to the crux of their meeting.

"I've diagnosed Major Dailey with PTSD, Ms. Shelton. That, combined with her brain injury, will make her recovery time longer than normal. I, unfortunately, can't tell you what you can expect. Every case is different."

"We're returning to Texas as soon as she's released. She's been placed on terminal leave pending her retirement."

"Will she be retiring in San Antonio?"

"Not far from there. It's close to the medical facility at Fort Sam in case she needs it. Duvalle is only a few miles away."

"Have you noticed anything unusual about the major's demeanor?"

"What do you mean?"

"Does she act or speak any differently than she did prior to her injury?"

"From time to time. Sometimes she pauses when she talks as if she's searching for the right word. She doesn't remember much about what happened to her. I'm hoping that's a good thing."

"Eventually, she might remember. If she does, it may not be a happy memory. How long did you live together before she was hurt?"

"About a year. I arrived in Germany before last Christmas and she deployed the first of November this year. I've contacted some friends in Germany who will pack our household goods to ship home. Athon owns a house in Duvalle."

"Has she talked about any plans for the future?"

"She knows she'll never fly again. Otherwise, she doesn't have any plans beyond recovering as much as possible."

"Have you noticed any anger or irritation, impatience, anything like that?"

"I know she wishes her rehabilitation was going better."

"Do you go to the physical therapist with her?"

"Occasionally, but she doesn't like me to see her like that."

"Like what?"

"I don't know. She has always been strong and confident. She doesn't want me to see her as weak, I guess."

Leeanne leaned forward slightly. "She might never be like she was, Lauren."

"I know that."

"What about intimacy between you?"

"You know I can't discuss that."

"Anything you tell me is confidential, Lauren. It can't be used against either you or the Major. Have you kissed one another?"

"No, but she has told me she loves me."

"Has she tried to initiate physical contact with you?"

"No."

"How does that make you feel?"

"Why are you asking these questions?"

Leeanne leaned back in her chair. "It might not become a problem, but returning soldiers with PTSD or a traumatic brain injury, not to mention a combination of the two, sometimes have issues with intimacy. They also have anger management issues which seem to come on suddenly for no apparent reason." She smiled. "But since they have problems with short-term memory, they tend to forget why they were angry in the first place fairly quickly. That doesn't stop their outbursts from hurting though."

"Is it possible that Athon doesn't remember that we lived together or our relationship?"

Leeanne thought about the question for a few minutes. "I'm not sure I can answer that. Does she object if you touch her?"

"No." Lauren shook her head. "She almost seems ambivalent about it. I'm not sure what to do."

"Do you want her to touch you?"

"Of course I do."

"Have you told her that?"

"I don't want her to feel pressured. She has enough problems to deal with."

"Unfortunately, only time will tell. Until she's physically better, it's too early to treat her psychological problems. Are you keeping a journal?"

"I started a couple of weeks ago."

"Whoever is assigned to her case in Texas will want to read it before they meet to get an idea about how she reacts to various things, whether she has any flashbacks, that sort of thing."

"Would it be possible to take Athon out of the hospital for the night sometime? Just to start getting her accustomed to being away from this place."

"I can recommend it, but that would be up to her primary physician."

By Friday, Colonel Campbell had agreed to give Athon a weekend pass. Lauren bought her a t-shirt and cargo pants, along with new underwear, socks and sneakers. When Athon complained about the length of her hair, Lauren arranged an appointment for a haircut. She gave a picture of Athon to the stylist to show her what Athon's hair had looked like. They spent the better part of the afternoon doing light shopping and sightseeing before locating a restaurant close to the hotel. A slow stroll after dinner to help their food settle ended the evening.

"I'm going to take a quick shower," Lauren said as Athon stretched out on the king-size bed. She pulled her top over her head and sat on the edge of the bed to remove her shoes. She felt movement behind her and her breath caught when Athon's hand touched her back. Goosebumps prickled over her skin.

"I remember the feel of you," Athon said, drawing her fingers slowly along Lauren's spine.

Lauren turned and wrapped her arms around Athon. She felt Athon stiffen slightly as their lips brushed together for the first time in months. She leaned back and swept her hand through Athon's newly cut hair before standing and walking into the bathroom. When she returned Athon was curled into a ball and sound asleep.

Chapter Twenty-four

Duvalle, Texas
May 2010

LAUREN WAS RELIEVED as their plane descended toward the San Antonio International Airport. The stay at Walter Reed seemed to linger forever, followed by almost a month of intense rehabilitation. Athon still had occasional balance problems, but nothing that would prevent her from leading a reasonably normal life. Lauren had caught Athon looking at her, but she didn't recognize what she saw in her partner's blue eyes. Athon would return a hug when Lauren initiated it and hadn't seemed uncomfortable or distant if Lauren held her hand and leaned against her to whisper words of encouragement or endearment. They talked about their life together in Germany and the friends they had made. Athon had seemed excited when she spoke to Frank. He had been promoted and, due to his leg injury, was also removed from active flight status. The good news was he was being transferred to the Pentagon and he and Mandy would be returning home. He promised they would attend Athon's retirement ceremony scheduled for mid-July at Fort Sam.

Lauren rented a vehicle at the San Antonio airport and was soon negotiating their way through noon rush hour. Athon watched everything they passed with interest.

"Everything looks so different," Athon said.

"It's because you haven't lived here in twenty years."

"I came back to visit," Athon said, looking insulted. "It's your fault I never got out of my hotel room."

"And I suppose you were completely innocent."

"I was an officer and a lady despite your blatant sexual advances," Athon said with a smile.

"Yeah, for five whole seconds." Lauren laughed. For a few seconds she caught a glimpse of her lover as she had been.

When they reached the turn-off to Pudge's house, Lauren signaled and waited for an opening in the traffic. "I called to tell Bridget when we would be here. She promised to get the house cleaned up a little and stock a few things in the kitchen."

"Probably bought enough food to feed a platoon."

The house was located at the rear of the property and the drive curled around toward a large two car carport.

"My Jeep is here!" Athon exclaimed.

"That's faster than normal, isn't it?" Lauren asked as she stopped the rental and stepped out.

Athon waited for her before starting toward the front door. "Wonder if our household goods are here too," she said as she used her cane to steady herself on the uneven drive.

Lauren moved to Athon's side and wrapped an arm around her waist with an affectionate squeeze. She knew Athon hated the idea of anyone helping her. Lauren kissed her lightly on the cheek and released her. "It'll be fun setting up another house together," she said.

Bridget exploded through the front door and ran down the porch steps. She collided with Athon, wrapping her in a tight embrace. Tears streamed down her face as she released Athon and held her at arm's length to examine her.

"Ohmygod, ohmygod!" she said. "You're so damn skinny! Didn't they feed you in that damn hospital? That uniform is practically hangin' off your body."

"Nothing memorable," Athon said with a laugh.

When Bridget finally removed her hands, Athon leaned against the cane she held in her left hand. Bridget stared at it and then at Athon's face. She turned to Lauren and frowned.

"I told you she had an injury," Lauren said. "The cane's only until she's back to normal again."

"Your furniture arrived yesterday. I'll get it all settled for you."

"We'll do it," Athon said.

"You need to rest, woman, and eat. I could shake you around like a used rubber," Bridget huffed. "Right now let's get some real food in you."

Lauren slipped Athon's hand into hers and followed Bridget into the house. "At least let us set up the bedroom," she said.

"Just the bedroom," Bridget said over her shoulder.

After a more than filling lunch, Athon changed into baggy shorts, a white t-shirt, and sneakers. She paused when she returned to the dining room to kiss Lauren on the forehead.

"I think I'm going to try and walk off some of those calories Bridget force-fed me," she said.

Lauren patted her lightly on the butt and smiled. "Leaving us on KP, huh?" she asked.

"I was hoping you'd miss that," Athon said, returning the smile.

Bridget and Lauren watched as Athon made her way to the back door and down the steps.

"How is she, really?" Bridget asked, her voice more subdued than usual.

Lauren picked up her glass of iced tea and finished it off in two swallows. "She's going to be fine," she answered.

"Do you know how she was injured?"

Lauren shook her head. "I haven't asked. I'm not sure I want to know." She cleared her throat to stave off her emotions. "If she wants me to know, she'll tell me when she's ready."

Bridget placed her hand on Lauren's forearm. "If either of you ever need anything all you have to do is call, day or night." She patted the forearm and took a deep breath. "Now you go change out of those clothes into something more comfortable while I put this food away."

"I'll help you first," Lauren said as she stood up.

"Nonsense. You look as uncomfortable as a whore in church," Bridget blustered.

Lauren laughed and wandered into the downstairs room that would be their bedroom. Their furniture was pushed haphazardly against the walls. Lauren squatted down and opened her suitcase, rummaging through it for something lightweight enough for the already hot Texas weather. She was grateful she had pulled a few summer things from the clothing they had packed away for winter and began stripping off the suit she'd worn on the plane. She pulled a chair away from the wall and placed her skirt and jacket over the back before stepping into a pair of khaki cargo shorts and tugging a t-shirt over her head. She dug a pair of sandals from along the side of her suitcase and wiggled her toes into them. She took a deep breath and ran a hand over the fabric of Athon's uniform. Lauren loved her in it, but wouldn't miss seeing it every day.

Bridget was wiping down the kitchen counters when Lauren walked back into the room.

"I'm going to check on Athon," Lauren said. "Want to join me?"

Bridget threw the sponge she was using into the sink and dried her hands. "You know where we'll find her, of course," Bridget said.

"Pretty sure," Lauren said with a nod as she stepped out the back door.

"What are you planning to do now that you're back home?" Bridget asked.

"I've applied for a few positions with local school districts," Lauren answered while they strolled across the property. "I miss my job in Germany and considering that I had to leave it so suddenly, I hope they don't hold that against me."

Bridget stopped and her hand flew to her forehead. "Oh, shit! I almost forgot," she said, digging in her pocket. "I guess you gave them my phone number or something."

"I listed you as a local reference on my resume," Lauren said.

Bridget pulled a piece of paper from her back pocket. "I wrote this down, but was so excited to see Athon again I forgot to give it to you sooner."

Lauren took the paper and read the information on it, which was only a name and a contact number. She re-folded it and placed in the pocket of her shorts. "I'll call this afternoon," she said. She glanced at Bridget. "Be patient with Athon," she said. "Whatever happened to her over there affected her memory."

Bridget stepped out of the bright sun and into the shade of a nearby tree. "What else do you know, honey?"

"She suffered a very severe concussion and they believe she also had a stroke while she was in the coma." Lauren took a deep breath, not wanting to think about everything Athon had been subjected to during her capture. "Her feet were badly injured and she had bruises in places I didn't know could be bruised. Her crew was killed and she was captured. It was four days before she was located and rescued." Lauren shook her head and wiped away the tears that fell down her cheeks. "She was shot twice, but fortunately they were both grazes. The doctors believe her brain was deprived of oxygen for a time, but not long enough to — to — "

Bridget pulled Lauren into her arms and held her, rocking back and forth until Lauren indicated she was once again in control of her emotions.

"I'm sorry," Lauren said softly as she collected herself and wiped away her newest tears. "God! I promised myself I wouldn't do this," she exhaled.

"You gotta let it out sooner or later, sweetie," Bridget said. "She's always been a tough nut. She'll be okay."

"I hope you're right, Bridget."

They found Athon resting in the shade of her old camper home. Lauren offered her a hand to stand once again, but Athon shook her head without meeting Lauren's concerned eyes. Using whatever was available, Athon managed to stand and stabilize her body.

"Feeling okay now?" Bridget asked.

"Never better," Athon answered, squinting into the afternoon sun and flashing a dazzling smile. She looked at Lauren. "I was thinking we could use one of the rooms as a workout room. Maybe get a treadmill and a few weights. Something we could both use. What do you think?"

Lauren pursed her lips and nodded. She patted her stomach. "If we continue eating like we have today, we'll both need it," she said. "That reminds me. When we get back to the house I need to call the hospital and see if they've received your records yet so we can schedule your physical therapy appointments."

"Bridget can help me get the furniture in place while you do that," Athon said.

IT WAS A little before one the next afternoon when Lauren stepped out of her rental vehicle and adjusted her skirt and blouse before slipping into the pale yellow jacket that matched her skirt. She closed her eyes and took a calming breath. She stepped onto the sidewalk in front of Cisneros Middle School, gripping her briefcase in her right hand. Middle school would be something different for her, but she was confident she could handle the position she would be interviewing for. She had applied for a high school position, but when none were available she had been asked if she would consider a middle school administrative position. She needed and wanted to return to teaching. She and Athon could use the money to begin the next phase of their lives. Until after Athon's official retirement, she would continue to draw her military pay. Due to her injuries she would continue on medical leave. She would receive a disability in addition to her retirement benefits, but the percentage had yet to be determined. A series of appointments for physical therapy had been scheduled as well as an appointment with a psychologist to assess the severity of her TBI and PTSD diagnoses from Walter Reed.

Lauren found the front office of the middle school and opened the glass door.

"May I help you?" a middle-aged woman at the desk asked.

"My name is Lauren Shelton. I have an appointment with Patrice Stanton."

"I'll let her know you're here Ms. Shelton. She's in a meeting with our counselors and it's run a little longer than expected."

"Thank you," Lauren said with a smile. She located a chair and sat down, crossing her legs, while trying to think about answers to possible questions about her educational philosophy. There were always questions that had nothing to do with handling everyday problems.

Fifteen minutes later a tall woman in a light gray tailored slack suit swept into the main office. Lauren couldn't help but notice the thick, straight blue-black hair that fell down the woman's back as she spoke to the secretary behind the desk. She turned toward Lauren and smiled. Perfect white teeth stood out against her deeply tanned skin, making her high cheek bones seem even higher. Her thin lips had just a touch of color. Lauren stood and took the large hand the woman offered in a warm greeting.

"Ms. Shelton? Pat Stanton. I'm sorry to keep you waiting," she said. She leaned forward slightly as she held Lauren's hand and lowered her voice. "Scheduling can be a bitch," she said with a light laugh. "You can leave your briefcase with Lucinda," she added, motioning toward the woman behind the desk. "We can talk while I show you our school."

Pat held the door while Lauren gave her briefcase to the secretary. As they started down the hall, Pat said, "Aren't these floors beautiful? Too bad they won't look like this after one day of the thundering herd."

Lauren wasn't sure what to say as they walked casually down the hallway. "I have the same problem at home," she finally said. "Sometimes I don't know why I bother."

Pat laughed. "Same here and I don't even have kids at home. Anyway CMS has approximately six hundred students, depending on whether or not the boundary lines for our zone are changed. We aren't expecting a change this year, thank God. Demographically, the student body is about sixty-five percent Hispanic. Do you speak Spanish?"

"No."

"The district has a decent bilingual training program. I took it when I was hired and recommend it to all new teachers and administrators. Essential for keeping in contact with our parents and they seem to appreciate the effort."

"Do you offer any special programs here?"

"We have the usual, special education and talented and gifted," Pat said with a shrug. "The high school in this section of town has recently become an International Baccalaureate school. So this year we will become a feeder school for that program. It's driving me crazy with scheduling."

"So you'll have the Middle Years Programme?"

Pat stopped. "You know about that?"

"My last teaching position was with a Department of Defense school in Germany that offered the International Baccalaureate Programme. I'm vaguely familiar with MYP."

"You're hired! I don't even know what MYP stands for yet. It's going to be a steep learning curve."

Lauren laughed. "It's the Middle Years Programme and usually feeds students into IB. It doesn't have a secret handshake or anything mysterious like that. Have your faculty members been trained?"

"Even as we speak. Let me show you to your office," Pat said as she started walking.

"Wait. I thought you were only kidding."

"You don't want this position? I know your background is at

the high school level and that middle school is generally seen as a vast educational wasteland, but it plays an important role in preparing our kids for the future."

"You haven't asked me a single question about my qualifications or educational philosophy."

"I assume personnel wouldn't have sent you unless you were qualified and we all know that educational philosophy thing is total bullshit. This is a tough area, a poor area, and I need someone who is willing to take on that challenge. If you are that person, and I think you are, then I want you on my team at Cisneros. Our scores on the new state tests were acceptable, but I want them to be exceptional. Quite honestly, I don't believe central administration thinks these kids can pull it off and I want to prove them wrong. This won't be an easy gig because I can be very demanding, but I promise it won't be boring."

Lauren liked the passion she heard from Pat Stanton. She stuck her hand out and said, "I accept."

Pat grinned. "I knew you would. Now let me show you your office. I should warn you in advance that it's a bit of a mess. Nothing a little paint won't take care of. I'll notify personnel that the opening has been filled."

Pat showed Lauren where her office would be located. It basically was next door to Pat's and there was a connecting door between them. Lauren looked at the institutional green walls and quickly came up with some ideas she thought would make it more welcoming to students and parents. Pat informed her that she would be receiving a phone call from the personnel office within a day or two. Once Lauren signed her contract, Pat would see that she received keys to the building and her school identification.

Although she didn't like the length of the drive from the middle school to Duvalle, Lauren couldn't wait to get home and tell Athon the news. She almost ran into the house. She quickly looked through the front rooms before finding her lover in the new workout room, putting together an exercise machine. Lauren flew across the room and wrapped her arms around Athon, so excited she managed to lift her a few inches off the floor. She set her down and pulled her into a passionate, hungry kiss.

Athon chuckled as she broke the kiss. "You must have had a very good day," she said.

"You're looking at the new assistant principal of Cisneros Middle School. Well, I will be as soon as personnel calls and officially offers it to me."

"I'm proud of you, honey," Athon said and turned back to the machine.

Lauren watched the muscles in Athon's arms and down her

back flex as she tightened a nut holding a bolt in place. It had been six long, frustrating months since she'd felt Athon's hands stroke her body intimately. She stepped closer to Athon and ran her hands up her arms and back down as she kissed her shoulder.

"I want you, baby," she breathed close to Athon's ear and pressed against her back as her hands slipped under Athon's t-shirt and over her abdomen. "I hunger for your touch. I need to feel you."

Athon's chin fell to her chest. "Lauren, I—I—"

Lauren made Athon turn to face her. "I love you, Athon Dailey." She rested her head against Athon's chest before looking up at her. She stepped closer and began kissing her neck, pausing to kiss and suck the pulse point on the side of her neck. She heard the hitch in Athon's breathing and ran her fingers over her nipples, feeling them harden. "I want you," she whispered again. She pinched Athon's nipple and grinned when she grunted. "Take me, baby. I'm yours...forever and always."

Lauren sucked in a breath when Athon's mouth covered hers with a demanding kiss. Athon's hand slid over Lauren's hip and onto her upper thigh, pushing her skirt up as her hand drew Lauren's leg up and slipped her fingertips beneath Lauren's underwear. Athon pulled her lips away and lifted Lauren to lower her onto the new foam-covered floor. She knelt beside her and yanked Lauren's blouse open. She slid her hands beneath her and unclasped the lacy white bra. She pulled Lauren up to slide the blouse and bra from the treasures they covered. She leaned down and filled her mouth with soft skin while drawing her tongue over a rock hard dark nipple. She straddled Lauren and lifted her upper body off the floor to suck at the tender flesh. Lauren's hands found their way into Athon's hair and held her to her breast.

"Oh God, yes!" Lauren panted. She sat up farther and forced Athon back, reversing their positions on the floor.

Lauren's full breasts hovered tantalizingly over Athon's mouth as she reached down to hook her thumbs in the elastic of Lauren's panties and pulled them down over her full hips. Athon raised her head far enough to take a breast into her mouth once again and held Lauren tightly against her as she flipped her onto her back. Her hand drifted along the toned abdomen until it slipped easily into hot, slick wetness. Athon settled over Lauren on her elbow and kissed her as her fingers fell into the smooth, soft entrance to heaven. Moving her mouth to Lauren's neck and shoulders, Athon rocked their bodies together as she drove into Lauren. With each rise of Lauren's hips to meet her hand Athon increased the pressure of her thumb against her clitoris until Lauren grabbed her head and pressed it onto her breast as she cried out Athon's name.

Lauren didn't know how many times Athon had taken her over the edge, but her voice was hoarse from crying out her pleasure. "Athon, baby," she managed to gasp. "I can't...again. Need to rest."

Athon gazed down and laid her head on Lauren's heaving chest. Lauren ran her fingers through the blonde sweat-soaked hair and took deep breaths. She gasped as Athon withdrew her fingers slowly, ending with them lazily drifting over Lauren's swollen clit one finger at a time, eliciting more small gasps. Athon lifted her head and pulled her body up to find Lauren's lips.

"Did I please you?" Athon asked.

Lauren grabbed Athon's head as they kissed. "You have always pleased me, love." She wrapped her arms around Athon's body and held her. "I've missed you so much."

When Lauren finally released her, Athon rocked back onto her knees and stood, offering Lauren her hand. "Sorry about your blouse," she said.

"I needed to change anyway," Lauren said with a husky laugh. She looked at Athon. "Tonight you're mine."

Chapter Twenty-five

Duvalle, Texas
June 2010

TWO WEEKS PASSED and Athon seemed to be happy and settling into the house in Duvalle. Lauren signed a contract and was occupied taking classes in Spanish and what seemed like an unending number of training classes to prepare her for her new job. She had established a good working relationship with Pat and already been introduced to over half the faculty. Lauren began to feel like she was neglecting Athon, especially when she came home in the afternoons and found notes and lists stuck on the refrigerator and bathroom cabinet. Athon was still having difficulty with her memory and used the notes to remind her of appointments, when to take her medication, or where things were located around the house.

After what seemed like the longest day she'd ever had, Lauren got out of her car and dragged into the house. She didn't find Athon in any of her usual spots and went into their bedroom to change into comfortable clothes. She stopped by the refrigerator and picked up a bottle of water before heading out the back door. Tall grass, despite the lack of water, had sprouted up around the remaining old cars. Lauren heard a sputtering sound and was halfway around a bush when she saw Athon. She was holding a gas-powered grass trimmer in her hands and pulling the cord to start it. The back of her t-shirt was soaked with perspiration. She pulled the cord again and it sounded as if it would start, but then stopped. Lauren watched as Athon fiddled with it and tried again. She pulled the cord five more times, but the motor refused to catch. Lauren could tell that Athon was growing frustrated by the way her shoulders rose and seemed to tighten. She had seen the same reaction due to frustration a few times before and knew that eventually Athon would explode in anger. Maybe she needed a few minutes to cool off. Lauren stepped around the bush and stopped next to Athon, running her hand lightly down her arm.

"Get away from me," Athon growled, her voice and body vibrating with anger.

"Is taco salad all right for dinner?" Lauren asked calmly.

"Fine," Athon snapped.

Before Lauren made it back to the house she heard loud yelling and cursing, along with the sound of something being beaten against the ground. She shook her head. They would need to purchase a new grass trimmer.

A few minutes later, Athon stomped into the house, letting the back door slam behind her. Lauren was at the counter chopping up ingredients for their salads while the ground beef simmered on the stove. "This will be ready in about fifteen minutes if you want to grab a quick shower," she said with a smile.

"Don't tell me what the fuck to do!" Athon stormed as she walked purposefully down the hallway toward their bedroom.

By the time Lauren set two plates on the table and was pouring iced tea into glasses, Athon had returned. She paused long enough to kiss Lauren on the cheek and pat her lightly on the rear.

"Smells great," Athon said cheerfully, taking a long swallow of tea.

Lauren pulled a chair from the table and sighed as she sat. "Feels good to take a load off my feet for a while," she said as she brought her fork to her mouth. "Did you have a good day?"

Athon nodded as she chewed. "Frank called," she said around a mouthful of food.

"Are they back in the States?"

Athon laughed. "Mandy's dragging his ass all over the place looking for a house. They'll be here in a couple of weeks."

"It'll be good to see them again."

"Frank gave me the name of a friend, some contractor he met in D.C. He's looking for an analyst to go over data at Randolph. Thought I might be interested once I become a civilian again."

"Are you interested?"

Athon shrugged. "I might be." She laughed. "I can only cut the grass so many times."

ATHON SAT UP in bed, gasping for air. She brought her hands to her face and ran them through her hair. She shivered slightly as her wet clothing stuck to her body. *No!* her mind screamed as she threw the covers back and stood to rip the t-shirt away from her skin. She looked down at Lauren, who was soundly sleeping. After pulling on a dry t-shirt, she tried to settle back into bed. She was still shivering and moved closer to Lauren, sliding an arm over her side to absorb the warmth of her body. Lauren rolled toward Athon in her sleep and cuddled closer.

Athon closed her eyes, but could still see the laughing, bearded faces. She raised her head and glanced at the clock on the nightstand. Nearly an hour had passed. She carefully extracted her body from Lauren's arms and slid out of bed. She picked up her clothes and walked quietly down the hall into the bathroom. After closing the door, she stared at herself in the mirror over the sink as she splashed cold water on her face and dried it. There had been times since her return home when she didn't recognize the face looking back at her. She wondered what Lauren saw. She jerked her eyes away from the mirror and pulled on her socks and jeans before slipping her feet into her sneakers. She pulled a shirt over her t-shirt and left it unbuttoned. She flipped off the bathroom light and let her eyes adjust to the darkness. She grabbed to keys to her Jeep and walked outside. Hoping the sound of the engine wouldn't awaken Lauren, Athon drove slowly down the drive and turned onto the highway. She didn't have a destination in mind. Fresh air blowing in the driver's side window felt good and she inhaled it deeply, no longer feeling as if she was suffocating.

She rubbed a hand through her short hair, letting her mind wander wherever it wanted to. There were times when she didn't know who she was anymore. She needed to ground herself some way. She needed to find the woman she thought she had been. Words seeped into her consciousness. Confident, commanding, loving. Had she been those things? She saw Lauren's smiling face float in front of her causing her abdomen to flutter. The beautiful mocha-skinned woman told her she loved her and everything she did seemed to confirm that. Lauren made her laugh and want to cry at the depth of her desire for Athon, her desire for the other Athon, the one who hadn't come home broken and lost.

The outline of a vaguely familiar sign loomed on the left-hand side of the highway and for reasons she didn't understand, Athon turned onto a long neglected road. The asphalt was cracked and tall grass grew stubbornly through them. She slowed the Jeep and followed the road. At the end of it her headlights swept across the side of a long abandoned mobile home, the roof long since collapsed into the interior. She stopped and shifted the Jeep into park, staring at the mobile home. She left her headlights on and eased out of the Jeep. Flashes of pictures seemed to strobe through her mind. She knew this place. She carefully walked up what remained of concrete steps to a door. The knob turned when she twisted it, but it didn't open. Flooded with frustration and sudden rising anger, she clasped the knob tightly and slammed her shoulder into the flimsy looking aluminum door. Whatever held the door in place relinquished its hold and Athon flew into the blackness inside the mobile home, landing in a stinking pile of damp insulation and other debris. She found something stable enough to hold her weight as she pulled her body up. She could see stars overhead when she looked up and dusted her jeans off. The Jeep's headlights were on high beam and cast an eerie light into the interior. She climbed over a broken section of the rusted-out roof.

As she stepped off the collapsed section she caught her foot on a piece of wiring and fell again. When she rolled onto her back and pulled the wire away, the breath seemed to leave her lungs as Hank's sneering, filthy face glared down at her. *You ain't got what it takes, kid,* he said as he threw his head back and laughed.

Athon scrambled to her feet as quickly as possible and pressed her body against the rusted remains of a refrigerator, afraid to open her eyes. When her breathing was under control again and she felt her heart stop thumping against her chest, she opened her eyes defiantly and saw nothing. The unhappy yowling of a cat as it dove through an opening in the hallway startled her and she shook her head. Why the hell was she prowling through an abandoned old mobile home? What had drawn her inside this shithole?

She saw an opening on the other side of the hole and stepped inside. Light from her headlights was weaker here, but she could still see an old mattress on the floor. Screaming and laughter assaulted her ears and her hands flew up to cover them as her eyes slammed shut. Small, flailing arms and legs, grunting sounds, and the hollow-looking eyes of a woman leaning against the opening into the room made Athon bend over in pain and sent her racing to the front door of the mobile home. Not stopping to go down the concrete steps, she jumped to the ground and fled to the safety of the Jeep. She stomped on the accelerator and swung the vehicle into a half circle before speeding away.

She was breathing fast and didn't bother to slow down as the Jeep careened back onto the highway as she fought to escape and maintain control of the vehicle. She hadn't gone far when blue and red lights swept across the rearview mirror. She had to get away and increased her speed. The lights followed her and a voice ordered, "Police! Pull off the road!" Was it a trick? She locked the doors and brought the Jeep to a halt along the shoulder of the highway. Her hands shook as she looked around for something she could use to defend herself. She had been helpless then and felt helpless now. She felt a stabbing pain low in her abdomen and leaned forward to make it go away. Pounding on the driver's window drew her attention and she turned her head to stare into the muzzle of a weapon held by a man with a beard. Adrenalin flooded her body and she blinked at the bearded faces that surrounded the Jeep.

"Get out of the vehicle slowly, hands first!" a voice commanded as a man motioned with the weapon. The pain in her abdomen disappeared as she reached for the door handle and pulled on it. She needed to be calm and find an avenue of escape. Frank would come for her soon.

The man backed away and watched her nervously as a smile

crossed her face. She was certain she had seen a slight waver in the hands holding the gun. "Move to the front of the vehicle and spread your arms on the hood," the officer ordered.

Athon closed the door and backed toward the front of the Jeep, her hands clasped behind her head. The officer grabbed her arm and spun her around, forcing her to bend over the hood. He kicked her legs slightly apart and re-holstered his weapon as he began running his hands over her body searching for hidden weapons. *I know what tough women like you fear most,* she heard as a body pressed against hers.

The officer started to back away, leaving Athon an opening, although a small one, to make her escape. She turned before the officer could react and brought her hand up quickly using the heel of her hand to break the man's nose. She watched as blood poured from his nose and tears blinded him temporarily. She moved behind him and wrapped her arm around his throat as she relieved him of his weapon. He grabbed at her arm to dislodge it, but she held on.

"Let him go, Athon!" a voice yelled.

Athon looked up and saw a semi-crouched figure approaching quickly, their weapon drawn and pointed steadily at the pair.

"Frank?" Athon called out.

"I gotcha Major. You can lower the weapon now."

Athon breathed heavily and shoved the man away from her. She flipped the weapon around and held it out butt first.

Sheriff Raynelle Cosper took the sidearm and shoved it into her belt. She dropped a hand on her deputy's shoulder. "You okay?" she asked.

"She broke my node," he answered.

"So it seems. Medics will be here soon. I've got it from here," she said.

"You're bleedin' a little," Cosper said when she walked up to Athon.

Athon hadn't seemed to notice and brushed her fingers across her forehead, staring at the blood on her fingers. "Not too bad," she mumbled.

"How do you feel?" Cosper asked, tapping her head with her index finger. "You know. Inside."

"You think I'm fucked up too?" Athon asked with a frown.

"Don't know. Where were you?"

The deputy held a handkerchief to his nose. "When I stopped her she was coming out of the drive at that old abandoned trailer park," he said, his nose obvious badly stuffed up.

Cosper looked back at Athon. Her eyes seemed unfocused. "How're you doin'? Really?"

Athon shrugged. "Some days are better than others."

"And Lauren?"

"Don't know why she sticks around. I treat her like shit."

"Guess maybe because she loves you, girl," the sheriff said.

Athon looked at Cosper and shook her head. "She loves who I was, Sheriff, not so much who I am now."

Cosper squinted at her. "Then maybe you should clean up your act, Dailey."

"I can't change who I am."

"Lauren deserves better and you know it. If you don't want to be with her then leave, but don't leave her hangin' in the wind."

Cosper escorted Athon to her patrol car and noticed she seemed off-balance. She eased an exhausted Athon into the back and she fell into the seat. Athon watched as an ambulance and two additional patrol cars arrived. Cosper removed her hat and sat behind the wheel of her car.

"What about my Jeep?" Athon asked, rubbing her forehead.

"A deputy will follow us back to your place," Cosper answered, craning her neck to look for oncoming traffic. "What were doin' out here anyway, Athon?"

"Don't know. Couldn't sleep," Athon mumbled.

"You assaulted my deputy."

"He touched me. I had to defend myself," Athon said, her voice stronger. She leaned her head back and stared at the headliner of the car. She scrunched her forehead as a headache beat a rhythm keeping time with her heartbeat. She looked down at her clothing and shook her head at the sight of blood on her shirt and took a deep breath. Lauren would be pissed.

By the time Cosper, followed by Athon's Jeep, pulled up next to the carport at Athon's house Lauren was waiting on the front porch, frowning. Cosper opened the back door of her car and helped Athon out.

"Sheriff Cosper called," Lauren said as her eyes drifted up and down Athon's body when she started up the steps to the porch. "Are you all right?"

"Just a bump on the head."

"Your head doesn't need any more bumps, Athon," Lauren said tersely.

"I know that, Lauren," Athon snapped. "It was just a misunderstanding."

"It's always a misunderstanding," Lauren said.

For the first time Athon clearly saw the look of profound disappointment in Lauren's eyes. She slowly made her way up the four steps to the porch and leaned against the railing. "I'm sorry, Lauren. I know I've hurt you, but I never meant to." She stepped forward and hesitated before wrapping her arms around Lauren, the muscles stiffening under her touch. She lowered her head to Lauren's shoulder and felt tears run from her eyes.

Chapter Twenty-six

LAUREN WAVED WHEN she saw Mandy and Frank Hardesty making their way down the concourse from the gates at the San Antonio International Airport. As soon as they left the security area. Lauren and Mandy rushed toward one another and chattered as they hugged. Then Lauren stepped back and stared at Mandy's bulging abdomen.

"Oh my God! When?"

Frank stopped next to his wife, shaking Athon's hand briskly and wrapping an arm around her shoulder. "You mean when did I knock her up or when is the kid supposed to arrive?"

"Congratulations, Frank," Athon said with a laugh. "Tell us when it's due and we can figure out the other part."

Frank grinned. "Four more months circling the field before landing. You should give it a try."

"I could try day and night, but it ain't gonna happen, buddy," Athon said shaking her head. "Let's get you someplace less hectic." She took Mandy's rolling suitcase and they followed Lauren and Mandy, who had linked arms, out of the terminal and across a street to the parking lot.

"How's your new job going?" Athon asked.

"I'm a paper pusher. The only flying I'll be doing is throwing paper airplanes across the office. You miss it?"

"Sometimes."

"You doing okay? Really?"

"Some days are better than others, but I have things to keep myself busy. Lauren found a position with a school in San Antonio, so she's happy. I spend most of my time cleaning house and getting dinner on the table when she comes home."

"I bet that hurts."

Athon shrugged. "Now I know how the other half lives, at least for now."

"What are you planning to do once you're officially out?"

"Haven't decided, but I'll find something."

On the drive home, Mandy and Lauren continued talking. Athon looked in the rearview mirror and smiled. "You two are going to run out of things to talk about before we get to the house."

"Never happen, Athon," Mandy said.

"Nothing short of lockjaw would be effective," Frank added.

"It's a wonder she stopped talking long enough to get pregnant," Athon quipped.

"I don't have a problem ignoring her when necessary," Frank said, looking over the back seat at his wife.

Mandy winked at him. She grabbed the back of the front seat and leaned forward. "I'm looking forward to seeing you in your dress blues, Athon," she said.

"You're looking forward to seeing me uncomfortable? Thanks a bunch," Athon said.

Mandy glanced at Lauren. "I want to see if Lauren's right."

Athon saw Lauren beginning to blush through the rearview mirror. "About what?"

"She's always told me you're so fucking hot in your dress blues that she practically has an orgasm just from looking at you."

"Is that right?" Athon said with a grin as she watched Lauren cover her face with her hand. "I'll get a chance to test that theory in a couple of days."

"Oh God," Lauren mumbled as she slid farther down into the back seat.

"In fact, I might have to try it on tonight to make sure it still fits," she added with a laugh. For the first time in a long time, Athon felt at ease and almost normal again.

TWO DAYS LATER, Athon stood nervously waiting for her retirement ceremony to begin. She knew it would be a lengthy, tedious process and she had suffered a few equilibrium problems that morning. She looked down at the cane Lauren had convinced her to use and tapped it against the side of her polished dress shoes.

Frank clapped her on the shoulder. "Nervous?" he asked.

"Tired of standing around and waiting for this damn circus to get under way," she groused.

Frank pointed to four officers who were assembling off-stage in the auditorium where the ceremony would take place. "At least it's indoors," he said.

"Thank God for that," Athon breathed. She looked at Frank. "You're not going to say anything that will embarrass me, are you?"

"Would I do something like that?" he answered, pressing a hand against his chest, feigning shock. "This is a dignified occasion."

"That's what I was afraid of," she groaned.

An officer stepped to the microphone on the stage and began.

Athon closed her eyes and took a deep breath. "Good afternoon, ladies and gentlemen. I am Captain Leonard Woolford. It is my honor and privilege to welcome all of you to Fort Sam Houston. Today we will celebrate the career accomplishments of Major Athon Michelle Dailey."

Frank and Athon joined the four other officers, shook hands, saluted, and waited.

"Ladies and Gentlemen, when the command party arrives, I will ask everyone to stand. During the ceremony, military and civilian guests should stand for the playing of Ruffles and Flourishes, the national anthem, and the Army Song. Military personnel should not salute during the playing of Ruffles and Flourishes and the national anthem. Civilians should place the right hand over the heart during the national anthem. For your convenience, I will announce the main events of the ceremony prior to their occurrence." A few moments passed before the narrator for the ceremony saw the signal to begin and spoke again. "Ladies and gentlemen, please rise for the arrival of the reviewing party."

Amid the shuffling of seats, the six officers made their way to the podium and assumed standing positions in front of a row of chairs. They stood at attention as four soldiers brought the colors to the stage and turned to face the audience as the national anthem was played. Crossing one another, the color guard posted the colors and left the stage. A moment later a chaplain stepped to the microphone to give the invocation. Athon stood tall and erect next to Frank. She watched as Lauren brought her small video camera up to record the event. She looked so proud of Athon. Bridget and Marty were standing behind Lauren, looking just as proud. The narrator stepped back to the microphone, asking everyone to be seated. He waited until the audience had adjusted themselves.

"Today we will be part of history as we witness an award and retirement ceremony honoring Major Athon Michelle Dailey for twenty years of outstanding service. We are pleased that you are with us to share this important event. Ladies and gentlemen, Major Franklin P. Hardesty, Pentagon Liaison Officer for the Twelfth Air Rescue, Second Medevac Unit, Ramstein Air Force Base, Germany."

Frank patted Athon's thigh and approached the microphone. For the next several minutes he recounted Athon's enlistment at eighteen, her service as a helicopter mechanic, eventually her selection to the Army's Officer Candidate School, and acceptance into pilot training. He listed the bases she had served at until her final assignment at Kandahar, Afghanistan. Athon thought Frank made her sound so good she was almost embarrassed by her own accomplishments. When he concluded his remarks, Frank stepped to center stage. An enlisted man took a medal from a nearby table and held it as the narrator returned to the microphone.

"Ladies and gentlemen, please rise for the reading of the citation to accompany the award of the Distinguished Service Medal to Major Athon Michelle Dailey." The narrator held the citation until everyone had risen, then read. "By the order of the President of the United States of America, authorized by Act of Congress July 9, 1918, the Distinguished Service Medal, First Oak Leaf Cluster, is awarded to Major Athon Michelle Dailey. The singularly distinctive accomplishments of Major Dailey culminate a long and distinguished career in the service of her country and reflect the highest credit upon herself and the United States Army."

The enlisted man took the medal to Frank and handed it to him, saluted, and returned to his position. Athon stood and moved crisply to stand in front of Frank. He pinned the DSM to her uniform and stepped back. They saluted, shook hands, and turned to face the audience. Athon watched Lauren snap a series of pictures. She felt relieved that the ceremony was almost over. She was more than ready to get out of the formal uniform. Her smile broadened as she thought maybe Lauren would rip it from her body as she had threatened to do earlier that morning.

"Ladies and gentlemen," the narrator resumed. "Please remain standing for the reading of the retirement orders. Attention to orders: Department of the Army, Washington, D.C. Special order number ACG010, dated 30 June 2010. Subject: Retirement of Major Athon Michelle Dailey, currently assigned to Fort Sam Houston, Texas, is relieved from active duty assignment effective 3 July 2010. Athon Michelle Dailey is retired in the grade of Major, effective 3 July 2010, by order of the Secretary of the Army." The narrator stepped forward and presented the retirement orders to Athon, then stepped away to salute her.

Athon sat through the remainder of the ceremony without paying a great deal of attention to what was going on. There were letters from several officers farther up the chain of command, most of whom she had never and would never meet. She had been surprised to receive a message from the commanding officer of her last helicopter unit in Kaiserslautern. Along with the letter he sent a picture of Athon with her crew standing, sitting, and kneeling by the bay door of their chopper. She smiled when she saw that included in the picture were several members of her maintenance crew. Even though she had moved up to pilot, she always enjoyed being around and occasionally working with the unit's mechanics. She jumped when asked to rise for the Army Song. As the voices died away she executed a left turn and exited the stage, followed by the other members of the reviewing party. It was finally over, she thought as she looked around for Lauren. When she finally saw her working her way toward her, Athon wanted to sweep her into her arms and kiss her, but that would have to wait.

Lauren slid an arm around Athon's waist and hugged her long enough to whisper, "God, you're so damn hot I could eat you up right here."

Athon kissed the top of her head and said, "Later."

Accompanied by Frank, Mandy, Bridget, Marty, and, surprisingly, Raynelle Cosper, the group slowly made their way out of the auditorium. Athon and Frank put their hats on as they stepped outside. Suddenly a stout Hispanic woman wearing black stepped in front of Athon and stopped her.

"Major Dailey?" the woman asked.

"I'm Major Dailey," Athon answered with a smile.

Before anyone could react, the woman's hand slapped Athon's face with enough force to stagger her. As she touched her face and tried to recover, the woman moved toward her. "My son was Richard Ortega. He died because of your incompetence, while you came home."

Athon stood and rolled her head. "I'm sorry for your loss, Mrs. Ortega. If there was any way I could bring him back, I would. I would gladly exchange my life for his. Richie was a fine young man and an excellent pilot."

The grieving woman lunged at Athon, but was grabbed by Raynelle and held until the group made its way to their vehicles. Frank opened the door and ushered Athon and Lauren into the back seat before he slid into the driver's seat and waited for Mandy to snap her seat belt. He sped away from the area as quickly as possible. Lauren drew a sobbing Athon into her arms and held her, murmuring as she stroked a hand through the grieving woman's hair.

WHEN THEY ARRIVED back at the house in Duvalle, Athon was exhausted and went into the bedroom to change clothes and take a nap. Lauren placed the picture on the small mantel in the living room. "Which one was Ortega?" she asked as Frank stood beside her.

"He was her co-pilot," Frank said, pointing at a cocky-looking young man standing slightly apart from the others. "Only joined her crew a few weeks before they deployed. He was killed by enemy gunfire on the last mission. There wasn't anything Athon could have done."

"I know, but she'll always believe it was her fault."

"It's tough when you lose your whole crew and you're the only one who comes home. Athon was lucky to get that bird in the air."

"What happened?"

Frank unbuttoned his dress jacket and sat down. "It was only about sixty miles from Kandahar to the site about twenty miles from a shit town called Girishk. I didn't see everything when I swept the area, but the insurgents were waiting for us. Athon's crew did everything they could, but there was too much gunfire. It was intense. She ordered Junior out of there and waited to take on the last of the injured from the convoy. By the time I swung around to lay down cover, she'd already taken a lot of strikes. She banked away, but without Ortega to help hold the chopper steady, she couldn't gain much altitude. My co-pilot told me our fuel was low. As soon as I saw her put down safely a few clicks from the LZ, I..." he cleared his throat before continuing, "I had to return to base to refuel. I thought they'd be all right until I could return." Frank looked tired as he rubbed his face. "I didn't make it back until the next day. All that was left was a burning hulk." His voice cracked. "The last thing she said was for me to take care of you."

"How did you know she was still alive?" Lauren asked.

"We didn't find a...a body in the pilot's seat. There were a bunch of hoof prints and some drag marks. Just took a chance." He shrugged. "Or maybe I was only hoping."

Lauren knelt in front of him and embraced him tightly. "Thank you for hoping," she said softly.

Chapter Twenty-seven

Duvalle, Texas
September 2010

EARLY SATURDAY MORNING, a month after school started, Lauren unlocked the door to her office and flipped on the lights with her elbow before she set down the items in her arms. She had found a few things she thought would make her office look more inviting and warm. She had worked hard so far to improve the relations between the school administration and the community of parents and children they served. Between reaching out to parents and in-service classes, she hadn't had much time to do something as simple as paint. Her middle school was located in a low income zone. The students didn't believe anyone at the school genuinely cared about them and the parents had difficulty understanding many of the state laws regarding education. Lauren spent hours establishing at least a tentative trust factor. She made herself approachable to students and parents and listened to more heartbreaking stories than she ever imagined.

The building itself wasn't exactly inviting and Lauren finally received permission to repaint the office to alleviate the institutional feeling it engendered. She tried to convince Athon to accompany her. The two of them could knock it out in a few hours. But her pleading only led to a spat that could have escalated into a full-blown, and unnecessary, argument. That was all they seemed to do since Athon's retirement. Every day was becoming either a high or a low with nothing in-between. Today she had eventually received a promise that Athon would prepare dinner instead.

Due to the delay getting away from the house, it was a little before eleven that morning when Lauren began clearing things out of her office and draping plastic sheeting over the larger, heavier items. She had chosen a sand tinted paint that would match virtually anything and terra cotta and teal contrast trim. She had already made arrangements with one of the school's art teachers to have students design and paint scenes that depicted the school on one of her walls. It would be a little hectic, but worth it in the long run.

Lauren stopped to take a water break and look around the room, trying to get a view in her mind's eye as to what it would look like when finished. A noise behind her made her whirl around. No one, other than the weekend janitorial staff and herself, should have been in the building. She was surprised to see Pat Stanton, dressed in worn jeans and a faded orange University of Texas sweatshirt, leaning against the door frame. Her attire was so different and relaxed from what she usually wore that Lauren had to smile.

Pat pursed her lips together and nodded. Elegant, manicured fingernails showed on a hand resting on her hip. "Maybe I should hire you to paint my office," she said, a slow smile curving her lips.

"Well, I'd be glad to supervise while *you* paint," Lauren countered. "At least lend my moral support."

The way Pat's eyes scanned Lauren's body felt like a caress and Lauren set her water bottle down and picked up the paint roller again.

"I have a stack of reports in my office," Pat said as she looked at her wristwatch. "Why don't we both take a break around twelve-thirty or one and grab some lunch?"

"I...uh...brought lunch from home."

"Put it in the fridge in my office. You can eat it next week."

"I'll think about it. Depends on how much paint I manage to get on myself instead of the walls."

Pat squinted slightly and stepped closer. She pulled the rag Lauren had tucked into her waistband out and pressed it against Lauren's cheek. "Looks like you've already started self-decorating," she said with a soft chuckle. "But, as cute as it is, I think I like you better without the polka dots."

Lauren felt a blush rise up the skin on her throat and took the rag from Pat. She stepped away and looked around the walls of her office. "The color is cool and calming," she noted. "Think it'll seem that way to the first kid hauled to the office?"

"I'd call it a crap shoot, but can always hope for the best," Pat said. She took a deep breath and exhaled. "Well, the paperwork unfortunately won't fill itself out. I'll be in my office if you need any help or change your mind about lunch."

"Thanks, Pat."

Lauren watched the attractive woman walk away. She had been impressed by Pat Stanton since the day she interviewed for the assistant principal's vacancy. Her long black hair outlined strong facial features that, in some ways, reminded her of Athon, or at least the woman Athon had been. Tears formed in Lauren's eyes, a familiar sign of the grief she felt for the loss of the woman she loved and missed. Every day the shell of that woman walked through Lauren's life without actually being there. Lauren knew she would never return.

Pat had been warm and gracious when she interviewed for her current position and Lauren had been drawn to the friendly, athletic woman immediately, determined not to let her down. Since then Lauren had been placed in charge of a variety of projects aimed at the preparation for transition. What she missed the most was not having anyone she could discuss her ideas with. For her classroom lessons in Germany, she bounced ideas off Athon who had given her many insights into presentation. Now she was virtually alone.

Lauren stepped back and looked at her work. She glanced at her watch and was surprised at how much time had passed. She had been so absorbed by her thoughts that she hadn't realized how much she had accomplished. She wiped her hands on her rag and heard her stomach grumble. She unpacked her sandwich and chips and pulled a bottle of water from a small cooler before sitting on the floor in the middle of the room and stretching her legs out.

"Mind some company?" Pat asked, holding up a small lunch box.

"Pull up a piece of tile," Lauren said with a sweep of her hand.

Lauren watched as Pat lowered her body to the floor and folded her legs in front of her. Within a few minutes both women were chatting easily and eating at a leisurely pace. From time to time Lauren felt Pat looking at her.

"Is something wrong?" Lauren asked as she washed her last bite down.

"No. Why?"

Lauren shrugged. "You just look like you have something on your mind. Anything I can help you with?"

"No. It's sort of a personal thing," Pat said staring at her sandwich. "How's your partner, by the way? I should have asked sooner."

"Athon's fine," Lauren answered without elaborating.

Pat played with the bread of her sandwich and cleared her throat. "You know, I don't usually stick my nose into the personal lives of my co-workers."

"But you'll make an exception in my case," Lauren sighed.

"I'd like to help if I can."

"Athon was a medevac pilot in Afghanistan when she was injured." A tear escaped and ran slowly down Lauren's face. "Her chopper went down during a night mission. She was the only one who survived...sort of. She was captured. Her body survived, but her mind wasn't as fortunate. She looks the same, except for a couple of roguishly attractive scars, talks the same, walks the same..."

"But she isn't the same," Pat finished.

Lauren shook her head. "I don't know from day to day who will greet me when I come home. The wrong word, a strange noise, almost anything can be the trigger that sends her to a place I can't begin to imagine. She knows who I am and that I love her, so I should be grateful for that."

Lauren saw the question in Pat's eyes. "We haven't been— together in a while and I miss her. I was warned by her doctors it might happen, but that doesn't make it any easier. I don't know what to do any more except live one day at a time."

"I'm sorry, Lauren. If you ever need someone to talk to, please don't hesitate to let me know. You're a beautiful woman in the prime of your life. Your partner's a lucky woman, whether she realizes it or not."

Lauren watched as Pat threw her trash away. She looked so relaxed and sexy. Sexy! Shit! Lauren shook her head and returned to her painting.

She was surprised when her cell buzzed, but didn't recognize the number on the display. She pushed a button and said a confident hello.

"Lauren? This is Sheriff Cosper," the voice on the other end of the connection said. "I'm sorry to disturb you."

"Is something wrong, Sheriff?"

"I was called about a potential problem and–well–you might want to meet me at a bar called–um–The Down Under."

"Where is that? I'm not familiar with the local bars," Lauren said.

"Hasn't been open long. It's about a mile or so past Tiny's old place goin' toward Duvalle," Raynelle directed.

"I'll be there as soon as I can, Sheriff. And thanks for calling me."

NEARLY FORTY-FIVE minutes later Lauren pulled into the unpaved parking area in front of the bar and stepped from her vehicle. She glanced at Athon's Jeep as she strode toward a patrol car from the Sheriff's Department. Raynelle stood and rested against the open door of her car as she watched Lauren approach in paint spattered jeans and t-shirt. Lauren stopped when she reached the vehicle.

"Thanks again for calling me, Raynelle," Lauren said. She was embarrassed and couldn't meet the sheriff's eyes.

"Don't let her drive," Raynelle warned.

"She seemed fine when I left home this morning."

"Want me to wait around, just in case?"

"No, thanks. It's not that far to the house."

Raynelle nodded and got back into her car. Lauren waited until the sheriff drove away before walking to the bar entrance and taking a calming breath. She pushed the door open and stepped inside, moving to the rear wall to let her eyes and ears adjust. She coughed slightly from the haze of cigarette smoke drifting over everything. She let her eyes travel from left to right across the seating area and the dance floor. She hadn't known the lesbian bar had opened, but Athon obviously did. She hadn't said a word and Lauren wondered how often Athon patronized the establishment. On her first visual pass she hadn't seen Athon even though Raynelle said she was inside and hadn't left. Lauren pushed away from the wall and wandered slowly through the tables and booths, trying not to be too conspicuous. She was stopped when a huge woman blocked her path. She wasn't overweight, just extremely tall and as muscular as a weightlifter.

"Excuse me," Lauren said.

The woman took Lauren's upper arm, her grip surprisingly soft. "Wanna dance, sweet thing?"

"No, thank you."

When the woman moved away in search of another dance partner, Lauren breathed a sigh of relief. Then she saw Athon. She was on the dance floor, her body draped over a gum-smacking young woman with brassy blonde hair and wearing very few clothes. Their bodies were pressed so close against one another that no light could be seen when they turned to the side. Lauren shrank back into a shadow and watched as Athon kissed along the side of the woman's face while her hands groped along her waist before cupping her ass to hold her closer as her hips ground against the woman. Lauren watched the young blonde slip her hand down Athon's body toward her crotch and closed her eyes before they reached their destination. She wiped a tear from her cheek. As the music began to die down the woman took Athon's hand and started leading her from the floor toward a darkened booth. Athon gripped the railing surrounding the dance floor and negotiated the first step down. Lauren moved quickly to the bottom step.

"Athon," she said and waited until her partner's eyes met hers. "Come home, baby," she said, holding her hand out.

A stupid grin flashed at Lauren. She looked at the blonde. "This is Lauren," she said.

Lauren turned to the confused-looking woman. "I'm her wife," she said boldly.

Athon nodded briskly and slurred with a crooked smile, "That is correct."

"She must not be gettin' what she wants at home or she wouldn't be here," the woman snorted.

Lauren ignored the blonde and reached for Athon's hand. The woman shrugged and dropped it. "Next time," she said as she walked off in search of either another woman or another drink. Lauren shook her head. She wrapped her arm around Athon's waist as she guided her toward the entrance to the bar. They didn't speak as she got Athon in the car and drove home.

Lauren tossed her car keys and purse on the dining room table and helped Athon toward the bathroom. She pulled the shower curtain back and stepped in, encouraging Athon to follow. Lauren stepped out again, leaving Athon fully clothed and reached inside to turn on the cold water. She walked out of the bathroom and slammed the door behind her.

She changed into a pair of running shorts and a sleeveless shirt before leaving the house again, running at a slow pace. The more she ran the more she thought and the angrier she became. She increased her pace and ran full out until her legs screamed in pain and she thought her heart would burst from the punishment she was inflicting on it. Too late, she thought. She wanted to scream out her frustration and her heart was already shattered. Since that day on the floor of the exercise room, that day she had virtually seduced Athon into fucking her until she ached, there had been no real, honest intimacy between them. Tears ran down her cheeks as she willed her body forward. When she could no longer breathe easily she jogged off the shoulder of the road and collapsed onto a grassy patch. She could hear her heart beat in her ears and her chest heaved as she breathed through her mouth in sobbing gasps. Cramps attacked the muscles in the calves of her legs and she couldn't stand. Her body arched off the ground, forcing her head back as she fought to reach her legs and massage the cramps away. Tears rolled down the sides of her face as the painful knots pulled even tighter. She thought she would pass out from the constricting pain when she felt a hand on her shoulder. A teenaged boy knelt next to her. He pulled off his bicycle helmet and dropped it on the ground.

"Are you hurt? I can call an ambulance," he rasped.

"Cramp," Lauren managed.

"Where?"

"Calf," she said, breathing heavily.

He quickly grabbed the toe of her shoe and slowly forced it back. She screamed in relief as the muscle along the back of her calf released.

"Other leg," she begged.

A few minutes later the boy ran his arms under Lauren's arms and lifted her off the ground. He retreated to his bicycle, pulled off one of the water bottles mounted on the frame, and handed it to her. She drank greedily and the water ran down the sides of her mouth. She limped around while holding the boy's shoulder. She would be sore the next day, but it still wouldn't be as bad as the other invisible places where she ached. Assured she was all right, the boy pedaled away as she began walking back to the house.

Two hours later, Lauren forced her legs up the front steps of the house and sat down heavily on the couch in the living room. She needed a shower to cool her core down. After downing a glass of water, she reached in the freezer and took out a bag of frozen grapes, popping one in her mouth to begin the process of cooling her body. She was feeling better by the time she went into the bathroom and began stripping her clothes off. She let the tepid water run over her head and down her body. As she patted her skin dry she noticed her face was still flushed and hoped she didn't develop too bad a sunburn. She stepped out of the bathroom and looked into the master bedroom where Athon was sleeping it off. She pulled the door shut and went upstairs to the guest room and fell onto the bed.

A HAND RUNNING across her back woke Lauren up. She rubbed her face back and forth across a pillow and stretched, regretting it as her calf muscles twitched. She turned her head to the side when she felt warm lips between her shoulder blades and a hand on her bare ass. Memories of earlier that day rushed back.

"Don't touch me," she said, pushing her body off the bed.

Athon stood close to her and said quietly, "It's hard to resist a sight like that." Athon's hand slid around Lauren's waist.

Lauren slapped the hand away and glared at Athon. "I said don't touch me." Her eyes drifted up and down Athon's face. "Resisting me hasn't been a problem for you so far."

"Please, baby," Athon said.

"Please my ass," Lauren spat. She looked down at her naked body. "Oh hell! I cannot argue with you while I'm standing here butt naked." She turned and went quickly down the stairs toward their bedroom. She closed the door behind her and slipped into a soft pair of jeans and a thin long-sleeve pullover. When she opened the door Athon was standing there. Lauren pushed by her and retreated to the kitchen for a glass of tea. She leaned against the counter and drank slowly to calm down.

"Are you going to leave me?" Athon asked, resting her shoulder against the door frame.

Lauren barked a laugh. "Is that what you want?"

"I think you've been looking for a reason to leave," Athon said as she picked at her cuticles. "And now I've given you what you wanted, just like I always have."

"If I wanted to leave you I know where the fucking door is. I don't need your permission to leave." Lauren could feel her anger reaching the boiling point. "I don't know who you are anymore, Athon. You won't touch me unless I force you to and you won't let me touch you. Yet today I find you practically crawling into the pants of some bleached blonde half your age. What the fuck were you thinking?"

"I don't want to hurt you," Athon said.

"But you are! You make me feel undesirable and unimportant. No matter how much I love you, I can't live this way." Lauren pushed past Athon again, jerking her arm away when Athon reached out to stop her, and grabbed her purse and car keys. She ran out the front door and to the carport, fumbling with the keys to unlock the door. She pulled it open and started the engine, twisting in the seat to look behind her.

As the car began to back up, Athon placed her hand on the side window. Tears ran down her face. "Please, Lauren! Don't leave me! Please, baby, I need you! I can't make it without you! Please!" she begged as she tried to keep up with the car. When she couldn't run any longer she fell to her knees and buried her face in her hands, sobbing as the car continued to move away. Athon bent over at the waist until her forehead touched the ground. Her tears wouldn't stop. She trembled as she began to rock, feeling lost and abandoned. She struck her hand against her head, over and over. A hand grabbed her wrist and stopped her. She looked at the hand and up into shimmering cinnamon eyes. Lauren was on her knees next to Athon stroking her hair. Athon swiveled her body and laid her head in Lauren's lap and wrapped her arms around her waist while bursting into deep sobs.

When Athon finally stopped crying Lauren helped her up and led her back into the house.

"W–why did you come back?" Athon asked, her voice weak and hoarse.

"Because I promised you forever and always," Lauren whispered. "Staying is hard, but leaving would be harder."

Athon embraced Lauren tightly and held her. "I do love you, Lauren."

"I love you, too, baby."

Chapter Twenty-eight

AFTER THE BAR incident, Athon agreed to make another appointment with her psychologist. She was taking her medication regularly, but was embarrassed to discuss her diminished libido with a male doctor. She requested a female psychologist and was assigned to Dr. Francine Cortez who had worked with numerous men and women who were experiencing relationship problems caused by TBI and PTSD diagnoses. She was an older woman who patiently listened and never interrupted when Athon was talking.

"It's good to see you, Major Dailey," Dr. Cortez said as Athon took a chair across from her. She flipped open a chart on her desk and glanced over a page or two of in-patient notes. "How have you been?"

"Okay," Athon answered.

Cortez chuckled. "If you were okay, my dear, you probably wouldn't be here. Any nightmares?"

"A couple, but I can handle them."

"Do you recognize anyone in particular in your nightmares?"

Athon shifted her eyes to her hands and blinked several times as if trying to bat away what she had seen. "My crew," she answered so softly that Dr. Cortez had to lean forward to hear her.

Cortez took glanced at Athon's file. "No spouse?"

"I have a partner."

Cortez nodded and jotted down a note. "How is your relationship?"

Athon shrugged. "Okay."

"Do you touch her and let her touch you?"

Athon shook her head, refusing to look at Cortez.

"Why not?"

"I don't deserve her," Athon answered forcefully. "Okay. I wish she'd leave."

"Then you'd be alone. Is that what you want?"

"No," Athon mumbled. "But everyone leaves eventually."

"Tell me about her," Cortez said.

"What do you want to know?"

"How do you feel when you're together?"

"Fine."

"When was the last time you were intimate?"

Athon frowned. "That's none of your business."

"Isn't that why you're here, Major Dailey? Because you have an intimacy problem."

"I don't have a problem."

"Then when was the last time you were intimate with your partner? Or anyone else? Have you been with someone else?"

"No. It's just personal."

"Why? Because you can't perform?"

Athon glared at Cortez.

"Why do you think you don't deserve her?" Cortez asked.

"She's always been a better person than I am."

"Tell me about your parents?"

Athon shifted in her chair. "Not much to tell. My mother was a stripper."

"And your father?"

"Could have been anyone. Mom moonlighted as a prostitute and drug addict."

"What about your partner's parents?"

"Don't know much about her mother. Her father was a religious bigot. Refused to accept who she was."

"But you did."

"I loved her."

"That's past tense. Does that mean you don't love her now?"

"Of course I do."

"But you don't think you deserve her any more. Is it because you lost your crew? Because you came back and they didn't?"

"I should have died with them."

"But you didn't. You survived and now feel tremendous guilt. Tell me about them."

Cortez listened as Athon described each member of her crew, occasionally throwing in a humorous story about something that had happened. The only one she couldn't tell the doctor much about was Ricardo Ortega. He had only been with her a limited amount of time. However, she did manage to describe the meeting with his mother at her retirement ceremony. It had obviously disturbed Athon.

"I think you should write a letter to the family of each of your crewmen. Tell them what you told me, including the stories. I think it will help you let it go, as well as give them closure. Let them know your grief. It won't be an easy task, but will help you put them to rest in your mind."

Athon nodded. "I'll try."

Cortez took a deep breath. "Now about your partner. You should tell her how you feel. Don't keep it bottled up inside. It's not healthy. When you bury anger, it festers. I want you to start keeping a journal about what you're feeling. You don't have to share it with anyone unless you want to, but it can help to write out why you're angry or sad or happy. Can you do that?"

"I think so."

"Is there anything else we need to discuss?"

"I'm sorry to be so much trouble, Dr. Cortez."

"You aren't, Major. You've just strayed from the path and need a little guidance." Cortez stood and glanced down at her appointment calendar. "I'd like to see you again in a week. If you have any problems between now and then, don't hesitate to call me."

ATHON SPENT A few hours each evening writing down her thoughts about each member of her former crew. She would use them when she composed a letter to each of their families and attempt to explain why it had taken her so long to write and express her grief. She was emotionally drained by the time she crawled into bed next to Lauren. After her eyes adjusted to the dim light from a guard lamp in the old junk yard, she rolled onto her side and folded an arm under her head. She looked at the calm features of Lauren's face and watched her chest rise and fall evenly. Lauren's hand lay next to her head, occasionally twitching. Athon could tell by the movement beneath Lauren's eyelids that she was dreaming. She hoped it was a good dream. Lauren was always tired when she came home from work, but seemed to become more energized as she relived her day for Athon.

Even though intimacy remained a problem between them, Athon rose early each morning and prepared breakfast for Lauren. She packed a lunch, sometimes throwing in a special treat. Lauren called every day to see how Athon was doing. It was a routine and Athon needed routine. She even began to look forward to Lauren's brief kiss before she left for work each morning. Through most of October they settled into a more or less peaceful life together.

"DON'T FORGET OUR open house is tomorrow evening," Pat said as she stuck her head into Lauren's office after school near the end of October.

"I'm not likely to forget that, Pat," Lauren said with a smile. "I might just stay here after school tomorrow instead of wasting gas driving back and forth."

"My place isn't far from here," Pat said. "Why don't we go there for dinner and relax for an hour or two before we have to be back for the thundering herd?"

Lauren stuck out her bottom lip and nodded. "That sounds like a definite plan. I'll look forward to it," she said with a smile. "Thank you."

"Hell," Pat said with a light laugh, "if you're like me it's worth it to run around barefooted for a while."

"No argument there," Lauren said as she pulled her purse from the bottom drawer of her desk and turned off the lamp. She took her cell phone from her pocket as she followed Pat down the hallway toward the entrance to the school and toward the parking lot. They chatted as Lauren waited for Athon to answer. She smiled when she finally said, "On my way. Should be there in about forty minutes." After a brief pause she added, "Love you, too."

Pat shifted her briefcase from one hand to the other and unlocked her car. "She's a lucky woman," she commented.

"She won't think so when I remind her I'll be later than usual tomorrow," Lauren said as she tossed her purse onto the passenger seat and lowered her body behind the wheel.

"Tomorrow I'll be the lucky one."

"You won't think that after I eat everything in your refrigerator," Lauren said with a laugh as she closed her car door.

Athon greeted Lauren at the front door with a hug and a light kiss. While Lauren went into their bedroom to change into something comfortable, Athon returned to the kitchen to finish preparing dinner. Lauren was surprised when she re-entered the dining room, running her nails along her scalp and ruffling her hair. She heard the back door close and wandered into the kitchen in time to watch Athon spear a thick steak and drop it onto a platter. Two foil wrapped potatoes followed. Athon saw Lauren watching her and smiled while she unwrapped the foil.

"I hope they're not overdone," Athon said. The look on her face seemed almost child-like, as if she wanted to please an adult.

Lauren moved behind Athon and wrapped her arms around her waist, laying her head against her back. "They smell perfect," she said softly. She moved to Athon's side to help unwrapped the potatoes and smiled when she saw a small list leaning against the counter's back splash. Athon had made a list of everything she planned for dinner, including the way Lauren preferred her steak cooked, the kind of salad dressing she liked, along with a reminder to leave the green onion out of her salad. It touched her that Athon had taken such precautions and, for at least this one night, Lauren felt special.

"Thank you, sweetie," Lauren said softly, glancing at Athon as she concentrated on her work. She seemed to be nervous and Lauren ran her hand down Athon's back. "You okay?"

Athon nodded and cut the potatoes in half, setting them on the platters next to the steaks. She ran her hands down her hips and looked at Lauren.

"What's wrong, honey?" Lauren asked.

"Nothing," Athon replied, stepping closer and haltingly lowering her lips to meet Lauren's. Her hands rested at Lauren's hips and drew her closer as the tip of her tongue sought permission to enter by lightly stroking Lauren's full lips. Lauren brought her arms around Athon's neck as her lips parted to allow Athon's tongue to explore. The kiss was tender and ended only when breathing began a necessity. Athon hugged Lauren and whispered, "I love you, Lauren." She released her and looked down at the platters on the counter, clearing her throat before attempting to speak again. "We'd better eat these while they're still hot," she rasped.

Lauren stroked the side of Athon's face and smiled. "If they're half as hot as I am right now they're just fine."

Athon grinned sheepishly and carried the platters to the table to join the salads she had prepared. When they were both seated, Lauren cut a piece of her steak and closed her eyes as she chewed slowly, letting the flavor of the meat burst in her mouth. She was starving, but wanted to relax and enjoy the rare evening of tranquility.

Even though she hated to say or do anything that might break the contented mood, Lauren said, "I won't be home tomorrow night until later than usual." She saw the look on Athon's face. "We're having our Fall open house. It's only a couple of hours after school lets out so I thought I would just stay instead of coming home and having to turn right back around."

"What about dinner?"

"I'll grab something at a place near the school. I should be home about nine or nine-thirty at the latest."

Athon shrugged. "Guess it can't be avoided."

Lauren placed her hand over Athon's. "I have to be there, honey."

Athon leaned back and stood to clear the table. Lauren could feel her beginning to pull away and cursed herself for being the cause.

WHILE ATHON FILLED the kitchen sink to wash dishes after dinner, Lauren stepped behind her and lightly kissed the back of her neck. She ran her hands smoothly up Athon's sides. "I'm thinking about relaxing in the Jacuzzi for a while before bed. Maybe soak away any nagging tensions from the day. Do you mind?"

"Of course not," Athon said, rinsing soap from her hands.

Lauren squeezed Athon's upper arms and let a hand drift down Athon's back. Athon watched the sway of Lauren's hips as she moved away. She ached to touch her again, but was afraid. She flipped off the kitchen light and wandered around the house for a few minutes. She went into the bedroom and changed into her boxers and a clean t-shirt. Then she tapped on the bathroom door and went in to brush her teeth. She could feel Lauren's eyes on her back.

"This feels fabulous. Want to join me?" Lauren asked.

Athon turned and let her eyes rake over the dark body wavering beneath the bubbly water. She hated letting Lauren see the ugly scars on her body and hesitated. She turned away and lifted her t-shirt over her head. She bent over to remove her boxers and felt wet fingertips trace the curve of her ass. She didn't want to see the look in Lauren's eyes as she turned around, exposing the scars on her side and shoulder. Lauren scooted forward and bit her lower lip as Athon balanced herself on one leg to settle behind her. Lauren readjusted her body, pushing it back into the vee of Athon's long legs. She tilted her head back and said, "Comfy?"

"It does feel good," Athon admitted.

Lauren snugged her body against Athon's and ran her hands down her toned thighs. "So do you," she breathed.

Athon snorted a laugh. "That's a horrible line."

Lauren rolled onto her stomach. "It used to work," she pouted playfully. "When we were teenagers."

Athon leaned her head back. "I was so horny for you," she said with a smile.

"Do you remember the night you gave me this necklace?" Lauren asked as she fingered the heart-shaped object around her throat.

"It was the last time I saw you," Athon answered, her voice cracking.

"We were going to meet again the next night," Lauren continued. She looked up at Athon. "I was going to give myself to you that night...completely." She paused and ran a finger over the scar on Athon's side.

Athon stopped the movement of Lauren's hand and moved it away.

"It's part of you now and will never make you less desirable to me," Lauren murmured before she dipped her head below the water to kiss the white slash along Athon's waist. Water ran down her face as she resurfaced and searched Athon's stormy blue eyes. She moved up in the tub and pressed her lips against the scar on Athon's shoulder. She drew her knees up and raised her body to bring her breasts close to Athon's mouth.

"Please, baby," Lauren whispered hotly.

Athon ran her hands smoothly down Lauren's wet back and over the curve of her rear, squeezing it lightly, wishing she was that teenager again for Lauren and not the damaged adult she had become. No matter how much she wanted Lauren, wanted to feel her sweaty, passion-filled body move beneath her, hear her cry out Athon's name the moment before her body finally surrendered, Athon knew it would never be the same again. A piece would always be missing, perhaps lost forever.

"I can't. I'm sorry," Athon said, removing her hands from Lauren's body and moving her away to stand. The hurt she saw in Lauren's eyes forced her to turn away as she dried her body.

Chapter Twenty-nine

Duvalle, Texas
October 2010

PAT KICKED OFF her shoes as soon as she entered the small, comfortable-looking house she called home. She stepped onto the Persian carpet in the front room and wiggled her toes, burying them in the thick softness of its pile.

"I heard about this in one of the old *Die Hard* movies and tried it. Damned if it didn't work," she said, tossing her briefcase and purse onto a wingback chair that stood next to the fireplace. "Try it," she sighed. "You won't regret it. Just curl your toes into little fists."

Lauren laughed and slipped out of her pumps. She stepped onto the carpet and scrunched her toes. A surprised look crossed her face.

"Doesn't that feel good?" Pat asked and then shrugged. "Who knew?"

After a couple of minutes, she said, "Well, that's enough self-pleasuring for the feet. I put together a couple of chef salads before I left for work this morning and mine is calling my name. Make yourself comfortable." She pulled the jacket of her suit off and hung it on the back of a dining room chair as she walked toward the kitchen. "Iced tea okay?" she called over her shoulder.

"Sounds perfect," Lauren answered and she removed her jacket and mirrored Pat's actions. She looked around the tastefully decorated room.

Pat carried two large bowls of salad to the table and set them down. She returned to the kitchen and brought out a tray holding silverware, bottles of salad dressing, napkins, and two large glasses of iced tea. Once everything was in place she asked, "Would you like the fifty cent tour?"

"Sure," Lauren said. "I like to settle my body down a little before a meal."

Pat re-joined her. "Well, as you can see, this is the main room. I like it, but don't get to spend as much time in it as I'd like. If it snowed here more than once a decade, I'm sure I'd enjoy the fireplace more. Cleaning them is a bitch, but they are cozy." She moved down a hallway and Lauren followed her as Pat flipped on the lights in various rooms, pointing out the bathroom, guest room, office, and master suite. The interior of the single story home was more spacious than the outside revealed. When they returned to the front room, Lauren noticed several photographs on the mantel over the seldom needed fireplace. She strolled toward them, briefly studying each one. She stepped over to look more closely at one. "Is this you?" she asked.

"I was obviously much younger then," Pat said as she joined Lauren.

"Where was it taken?"

"On the reservation." Pat laughed. "I once was a wicked dancer."

The woman in the photograph was caught forever on film, her feet, covered by tall leather moccasins, a blur of movement. Braids decorated with beads and feathers fell over the shoulders of her turquoise dress, which was covered with rows of shells across the bodice and dozens of conical-shaped objects from her breasts to near the bottom of the garment.

"It's called a jingle dress," Pat said. "I remember my mother spending night after night putting it together. I loved the way it sounded when I moved."

"Do you still dance?"

Pat shook her head. "No. There's no future for Indian dancers anymore. Originally the dances had a religious meaning, giving praise to the gods and all that. It didn't matter if you were any good as long as the dance showed anyone watching what it meant to you. You followed the beat of the drum which symbolized your heart beating as one with the Great Spirit, or something like that. Then it gradually became a competition and most of the religious aspects began to disappear." She laughed harshly. "In the southwest, dancers now pawn their regalia in order to survive until powwow season begins again. It's a dying culture that doesn't want to admit it's sick."

"Where is your reservation?"

"Montana. I haven't been back since my parents died." Pat sighed. "Even though I complain about not being able to use the fireplace, I don't miss the cold weather."

"Are these your parents?" Lauren pointed to another picture.

"Yes. I don't have many photos of them." Pat smiled and lowered her voice to make it sound slightly creepy. "They believed when someone took your picture, they stole a piece of your soul."

"And this last picture?"

"Nona. She was much more traditional than I ever was. We used to argue all the time because she wanted to live the old ways. She and I were very close. I think she still lives in a teepee and burns buffalo chips to stay warm in the winter. She made the outfit in that photograph. It was beautiful work."

"And she's still in Montana?"

"She'll never leave the rez and she broke my heart." Lauren met Pat's eyes, already knowing what would come next. "We were lovers, but love wasn't enough."

"I understand," Lauren said. "I didn't mean to pry into your personal life."

Pat sighed loudly and said, "Let's eat so it will have time to begin digesting before we march into the fray once more."

ALTHOUGH LAUREN AND Pat were both thrilled by the number of parents that showed up, it seemed every one of them wanted to discuss, at great length, what the two women planned for the remainder of the school year. It was nine-fifteen before they escorted the last parent to the front entrance and said good night, inviting them to return to the school any time.

Lauren dropped into her chair behind her desk and laid her head on top of it. "Jesus! What a night!" she said.

Pat plopped in the chair across from Lauren and leaned her head back. "Thank God that only happens twice a year," she moaned. "I don't talk that much all damn day, let alone in two and a half hours. Fun, wasn't it?" Suddenly laughter bubbled up from her chest.

"And we get to come back again in a few short hours," Lauren said, joining in the laughter.

Their secretary stuck her head into the office. "I'm outta here," she said, causing another fit of laughter from the two women.

When they finally quieted down Pat smiled at Lauren. "I'm glad I had you to go through this with me. I really, truly, honestly appreciate having your support."

"Really, truly?" Lauren asked returning the smile.

Pat nodded. "Really, truly."

Lauren sat up suddenly. "Oh shit!" she said as she grabbed her cell phone and punched in a single digit. She tapped her fingers on the desk as she waited.

"What's wrong?" Pat asked.

"I promised I'd be home not later than nine-thirty and it's already a quarter to ten."

"It was a busier night than we expected," Pat said. "She'll understand."

When the answering machine picked up, Lauren left a quick message and opened the bottom drawer of her desk to withdraw her purse.

Pat pushed her body slowly out of the chair. "Hang on. We can walk out together."

A few minutes later they walked quickly toward their cars. Pat stopped and drew Lauren into a tight hug before they separated and got into their vehicles.

Lauren carefully stayed within the speed limit and glanced at the dashboard clock as she signaled to enter the drive of her home. She would be glad to fall into bed and let Athon massage away the fatigue that had settled in her bones. She opened the front door and smiled when she saw Athon.

"Hi baby," Lauren said. She walked to where Athon was standing and flung her arms around her. "It feels so good to finally be home."

"Where the hell were you?" Athon asked, grabbing Lauren's arms above the elbow and pushing her away.

"I called and left a message that I'd be late." Lauren turned her head and saw the red light on the answering machine blinking. She turned back to look at Athon. "Where were you?"

"Watching you."

"You came to my school?"

"Who is she?"

"Who is who?"

"Don't act innocent with me, Lauren. You're a lying bitch! I saw you with her!"

"I don't know what you're talking about."

Athon grabbed Lauren's wrist and jerked her closer, inhaling deeply. "I can smell her on you," she snarled.

Lauren tried to pull her arm away, but Athon tightened her grip. "Can't say I blame you though," Athon smirked. "Running your fingers through that long black hair must have really got your motor running."

"What are you talking about?"

"You're having an affair with that woman, the principal at your school," Athon said calmly, releasing Lauren's arm. Then the look on her face changed. "Just paying her back for hiring you?"

Lauren swung her arm to slap the smirk from Athon's face, but Athon caught her wrist again before the hand reached her. She twisted it behind Lauren's back and her voice turned hard. "You're mine, Lauren. You belong to me. Don't *ever* forget that."

"You don't own me, Athon! Let me go, godammit! You're hurting me."

Lauren rubbed her wrist when Athon released it. Athon jabbed her fingers against Lauren's chest, forcing her to back up. "You want her, admit it!"

"I like her, but there's nothing between us." When Athon jabbed her again, Lauren slapped her hand away and her temper flared. She leaned toward Athon. "I've been tempted, but I have *never* cheated on you. I don't know what you would have done with that blonde at the bar if I hadn't showed up."

In a menacing voice, Athon brought her face closer. "I would have fucked her brains out and enjoyed every damn moment."

Athon smiled at the stunned look on Lauren's face as the words assaulted her like a punch. Lauren backed away, tears filling her eyes as she gasped for air, until a wall stopped her and she slid to the floor. She wrapped her arms tightly around her knees and drew them to her chest, burying her face against her knees as she cried.

Athon stood over Lauren, breathing hard and shaking with rage. Her jealousy at the thought of Lauren with another woman was overwhelming. She grabbed the sides of her head to drive away the mental pictures of someone else's hands touching Lauren's beautiful, perfect body, other lips taking her full, pouty mouth, other fingers dipping into the molten heat of her passion. She saw Lauren's eyes, hazy with desire looking into someone else's eyes as her lips parted in release. She turned away and moved quickly down the hall toward the bedroom.

AFTER SHE CALMED down Lauren went into the bathroom and washed her face, now mottled from crying. She changed into her sleepwear and quietly slipped under the covers, careful to remain separated from Athon's sleeping body. She had just begun to surrender to sleep when her body stiffened as Athon's hand slid along her thigh and over her hip, pulling Lauren closer to her. Lauren closed her eyes and felt a familiar tingle as Athon's lips nibbled along her back and shoulders. She groaned when Athon's hand slipped up her abdomen to fondle her breast.

"I want you," Athon breathed in her ear, moving onto her elbow to pull Lauren onto her back.

Tears flooded Lauren's eyes and she knew she should push Athon away, reject her. But when Athon's hot mouth sucked in her breast and her hand stroked down her abdomen, Lauren pressed her hand against the back of Athon's head to deepen the contact. The muscles along her abdomen twitched and she gasped as tears ran from her eyes.

"I need you," Athon whispered as she began claiming Lauren's body.

Chapter Thirty

Duvalle, Texas
November 2010

AS USUALLY HAPPENED following one of Athon's outbursts, there was a relatively peaceful period for the next couple of weeks. Lauren never knew what awaited her when she entered their home at the end of each day. The continual roller coaster that had become her life was beginning to take a toll on her. She was certain others had noticed it despite her efforts to conceal it. She needed someone to talk to, someone who would allow her to vent, give her a chance to step back and observe her life.

Perhaps she was overreacting or was unrealistic in her expectations. She had spoken to every doctor available, but she'd never been able to meet with Dr. Cortez. As a civilian, as well as the lesbian lover of a member of the military, she would never be privy to anything Athon discussed with her doctors or, unless Athon told her, know what they had advised. Civilian doctors were of no help because Athon was not their patient and they only had Lauren's account of her lover's behavior. The one advice they all gave without hesitation was to be patient. Just be patient, but there was never a hint of how long she should remain patient. There was never any advice about how to make the pain of being cursed, ignored, belittled, and unwanted go away. Apparently there wasn't a pill for that. Despite her love for the Athon she remembered, and as much as she longed to be touched, she had begun to remove herself mentally from being touched by the new Athon who saw her body as nothing more than an object to relieve her anger and frustration. Aside from patience, the only other solution was to leave and start her life over as if the past had never existed.

LAUREN WAS PREPARING to leave at the end of a very long day when Pat tapped on the door to her office. "Got a minute?" she asked.

"Of course," Lauren answered with a nod.

Pat tossed a packet on Lauren's desk and sat down. "I think we need to attend that," she said. "We would be gone three days, but I think the time would be worth it. The district is willing to pick up the tab for the hotel, registration, and give a daily food allowance that wouldn't feed a chipmunk, but it's still more generous than I expected. We'd have to pick up the tab for transportation though. Interested?"

Lauren pulled papers out of the packet and looked through them. A dozen reasons why she couldn't, or wouldn't, leave Athon at home alone for three days sprang to her mind immediately. She flipped through her calendar.

"We can reschedule any meetings we might miss," Pat said as if she could read Lauren's mind.

"Can I have a day or two to talk to —" Lauren started.

"Tell her the district wants you to go. It's required as part of your position," Pat said with a shrug. "Do you really need her permission to do your job?"

"Of course not, but I won't lie about it," Lauren said, an edge in her voice.

Pat stood and looked down at her. "Every job has some degree of responsibility that comes with it. Anyone should understand that."

"Do you have any idea what the transportation cost might be?"

"The most inexpensive flight leaves here at four-thirty in the morning and arrives in Minneapolis about nine with one layover in Dallas. Round trip is three twenty-five. That rate remains the same for the next couple of days. Let me know in the morning and I'll have Lucinda make the reservations. Have a good evening."

Early the next morning, Lauren walked into Pat's office and dropped the packet on her desk. "Everything's filled out," she said. "Lucinda can make the reservations."

Pat picked up the packet and tapped the corner of the envelope on her desk. She looked up at Lauren and smiled. "I think you've made a wise decision, Lauren. Our students will benefit from what we learn and implement."

Lauren nodded. "I agree it's a program worth exploring." She glanced at her wristwatch. "Well, I need to get to bus duty." She smiled. "Thanks, Pat." Lauren's smile fell from her face as she made her way toward the bus loop. The only thing she hadn't told Athon the night before had been that she wouldn't be traveling alone. There was no reason to go through another argument because she would be traveling with Pat Stanton.

AN UNACCUSTOMED BLAST of frigid air greeted Pat and Lauren as they walked through the concrete parking structure of the Minneapolis airport searching for their rental vehicle.

"This conference better be worth it," Lauren said, her teeth chattering. "You couldn't find one in Florida?"

"Reminds me of home," Pat said, holding her hands folded in

front of her mouth to warm them with her own breath while they waited for the vehicle to warm up. She looked at Lauren. "Please tell me you know how to work the GPS on this thing."

"Didn't it come with instructions?"

"Check the glove box."

"That means I'll have to take my hands out of my pockets," Lauren said with a frown.

"Well, look at the bright side."

"And what would that be?"

"We're not at home listening to sniveling little kids with runny noses sneezing all over us," Pat said as she shivered and began laughing. "You needed this trip, Lauren."

"Me? This was your bright idea!"

"Yeah, well, the same conference is in Phoenix next month," Pat said.

"And you chose this!"

"Next month is Christmas break. It didn't seem like a good time and I was afraid you'd kill someone by snapping their head off if I waited much longer."

"What are you talking about?"

"Let's just say you've been a tad testy since open house. Problems at home or has my sparkling personality and witty banter worn thin faster than usual?"

Lauren looked at the lines of mid-size cars parked around them. "Has the engine warmed up yet?"

Pat crossed her fingers and switched the heater on. A stream of cold air was quickly followed by a rush of warmth. "Now look for the GPS instructions," she said as she glanced behind her and began backing up. "If it isn't in the glove compartment then watch for signs for the University of Minnesota. Our hotel is supposed to be only a block or two away."

As soon as Pat turned out of the parking garage, Lauren pointed to a large sign over the highway running adjacent to the access road. "University of Minnesota exit four miles."

"Can't get any easier than that," Pat said. As soon as she turned toward the college campus she said, "Now find us a place to get a cup of coffee and a lumberjack breakfast. My stomach is gnawing on my backbone."

After locating their hotel, Pat drove past it to an IHOP a couple of blocks farther down the road that ran along the perimeter of the university campus. The sun was shining brightly, but any heat it might have generated was quickly blown away by the brisk wind. They made their way inside an A-frame building and were assaulted by warmth, mouth-watering smells, and an abundance of patrons. The wait wasn't too long and they were soon seated in a booth, both grabbing for the thermos container of coffee. They sighed contently and placed their orders before shrugging off their coats and relaxing.

"I might need a serious nap after my stomach is pacified," Lauren said. "Getting up at two to catch a four-thirty flight is not my thing."

"Fortunately the flight back isn't at the ass crack of dawn," Pat said. "But a nap before lunch definitely has my vote. We don't have to pick up our registration materials until three. I think there's a mixer tonight. Other than that we're free until tomorrow morning."

"Isn't the Mall of America near here?"

"You got up at two in the morning so you can go shopping in Minnesota?"

"At least I could say I've been there," Lauren answered as the waitress set two platters of eggs, bacon, pancakes, and biscuits in front of them.

Conversation came to a halt as they both scarfed down the first three or four bites. Once their stomachs were temporarily mollified, they slowed to a more moderate pace of consumption. Pat picked up a piece of bacon and nibbled at it. "So, are you ever going to answer my question?"

"Which one?" Lauren laughed. "You've asked a dozen."

"What's making you so out of sorts lately? It can't be *moi* so it must be a problem at home. Am I right?"

"That's two questions," Lauren said in an attempt to divert the discussion to a topic she was more comfortable with.

"Are you still having problems with your partner? There, I can't get any blunter than that," Pat said picking up her coffee cup.

"It's not always bad, Pat. Athon's not a bad person. Sometimes she can't control what she does."

"Has she hurt you, physically?"

"Not really."

"You're waffling, Lauren. Yes or no, has she hurt you physically?"

Lauren set her fork down and wiped her mouth, "I *was* enjoying breakfast. No, Athon has never hurt me physically. She's never struck me."

"I've seen the bruises on your arms even though you've tried to hide them."

"She's grabbed my wrists or arms when we've argued and she's always released me when I told her to." Lauren looked down at the remains of her breakfast and pushed it away. "She's shoved me a couple of times and jabbed me in the chest, but she's never struck me, even though I probably deserved it a couple of times."

"No one deserves to be hit, Lauren. Listen to yourself. You're making excuses for her and it pisses me off." Pat reached across the table and covered Lauren's hand with her own. "The first day I met you, you were so happy, excited about what you were doing, friendly, inquisitive, but in three and a half months you've changed into this nervous, irritable woman looking for a victim to take your anger out on. I depend on you and wouldn't want to lose you. You're more than just another co-worker to me, Lauren. You've become my friend and I can't stand seeing you so unhappy. Tell me how I can help you."

Lauren looked down and sniffed. She picked up her napkin and wiped her eyes.

"Just having someone to talk to helps, Lauren. I'm a good listener."

"Something terrible happened to the woman I loved and she went away. I think she's trying to find her way back, but can't. I met her when I was sixteen years old," Lauren began. Over the next hour and despite many looks from their waitress, Lauren told Pat about her life with Athon before and after their twenty year separation. She told her what she knew about the events in Afghanistan and the injuries Athon suffered. She told her about the long wait for Athon to awaken and her final diagnoses. She told Pat about the name-calling, the verbal and emotional abuse, and the accusations. Lauren smiled sadly. "Her body came home, but she left a part of herself over there. It wasn't her fault and there wasn't a damn thing she could do about it. It's unfair for me, or anyone else, to blame her." She met Pat's steady eyes. "I miss her, but every now and then I still catch a glimpse of her. Some days are better than others."

"What do her doctors say?"

Lauren laughed. "You know that 'don't ask, don't tell' thing the military has?"

"Yeah."

"For me it's, 'don't bother asking because we ain't gonna tell you a damn thing'. The choices I've been given are to just pull up my big girl panties and deal with it or leave her alone and lost. Big whoop."

Pat exhaled a long breath. "You're a better woman than I am, sweetie. I'd've been out the door a long time ago."

Pat motioned for their check and laughed when she looked at it. "We've just eaten our entire food allowance for the day," she said. "Color me shocked as shit."

Chapter Thirty-one

Minneapolis, Minnesota
November 2010

BEFORE SHE UNPACKED and took a nap, Lauren sat on the edge of the bed and called home to let Athon know she had arrived in Minneapolis safe and sound. She was surprised when Bridget answered the house phone.

"How was your flight?" Bridget asked cheerfully.

"I don't know," Lauren answered. "I fell asleep as soon as we took off. I just got into my room and thought I'd grab a nap, but wanted to let Athon know I made it safe and sound. Is she there?"

"Sounds to me like you're planning to sleep the whole time you're gone," Bridget laughed.

"I could do that. I need to catch up on my sleep."

"Athon and Marty are workin' on that damned old camper. It finally sprung a leak. Want me to go get her?"

"No, just let her know I called. I hate to ask this because I know you're not a babysitter, but can you make sure she takes her meds while I'm gone. And I think she has an appointment with Dr. Cortez tomorrow."

"She's not a baby, honey."

"I know, I know," Lauren said, rubbing her forehead. "I just worry about her, that's all." She felt the sting of tears building in her eyes and took a deep breath. "I'm sorry, Bridget. How are you doing?"

"I'm finer than Georgia peach fuzz, sweetie. Me and Marty are havin' some renovations done to the house. Bein' over here means I don't have to listen to all that racket. Y'all will have to see it when it's done." She paused for a moment, then said, "Sounds like they're comin' in for a water break. Wait a sec."

Lauren heard voices and the phone receiver shuffling around as she swung her feet onto the bed and lay back.

"Lauren?" Athon asked. Her voice sounded happy.

"Hi, baby," Lauren said. A tear rolled down the side of her face. "I miss you already."

"You'll be back soon. Good trip?"

"So far. I stopped on the way to the hotel and had breakfast. Now I'm drowsy. It's freezing up here."

"Hot as hell down here. I'm running around in my shorts and a t-shirt."

"I'm jealous. Well, I'll let you go and get back to whatever you're doing. I only wanted you to know I arrived. The conference really gets under way in the morning. I'll call when I can, okay?"

"You don't have to call tomorrow, honey. Marty talked me into going fishing with him before the weather turns colder."

"Catch a bunch and we can have them for dinner when I get back."

"With hush puppies and cole slaw?" Athon laughed.

"Whatever you want, baby."

"I love you," Athon said, her voice low.

"I love you, too, sweetheart. Bye-bye." Lauren disconnected and covered her eyes with her hand as she wiped away her tears. Pat was right. She did need to get away.

THE JANGLING OF the phone roused Lauren and she groped around the nightstand to stop the annoying sound.

"Hello," she said, her voice raspy with sleep.

"Sorry to wake you, but I thought you might want to grab a bite to eat before the mixer," Pat's voice said.

"What time is it?" Lauren mumbled.

"Six-thirty. You must have been really tired. You okay?"

"I'll be awake in a few minutes. I promise."

"I'm down in the bar talking to a couple of other attendees for the conference. Put yourself together and join us. They have a pretty decent menu that won't break the bank. I can personally recommend the sliders."

"Sounds good. Place an order for me and I'll be down before they arrive."

"Good deal. See you in a few."

Pat stood and waved when she saw Lauren enter the bar and look around. Lauren wove her way through tables that had been moved to accommodate larger groups and smiled when she reached a table occupied by Pat and two other women.

Pat pulled out the chair next to her for Lauren. Once they were all seated and comfortable, Pat said as she pointed to the women, "This is Sylvia Jackson and Florence Simmons. Ladies, this is Lauren Shelton." Lauren shook the women's hands and then sat back as a waiter placed a platter with four sliders and a heap of curly fries in front of her.

"Wow," Sylvia said. "That was good timing."

"What would you like to drink, ma'am?" the waiter asked.

"Jack and Coke, please. Not too strong," Lauren replied as she picked up a curly fry. She looked at Pat and shrugged. "Since I'm paying I might as well get what I want." She turned her attention to the other two women. "Where are y'all from?"

Florence, who looked slightly younger than her companion said, "Milwaukee. We drove in after lunch today."

"Is it cold there, too?" Lauren asked with a grin. "I wasn't expecting it to be so cold yet."

Sylvia laughed. "It's Mother Nature's reminder that we'll be packing away the shorts and grabbing the long johns soon. It's supposed to blow out of here tomorrow and be a balmy fifty-five."

While Lauren ate, the four women discussed their schools and what they hoped to get out of the conference. Even though their demographics varied, their problems seemed to be universal — how to keep students motivated, how to get families more involved, especially with homework, how to improve test scores now that states were demanding more teacher accountability for student performance.

Sylvia, the principal of a Milwaukee middle school laughed. "I don't think I could go back into the classroom again now. We're told to expect so much from our teachers and they're so busy trying to do everything they're told, there isn't time for any real teaching. Sometimes, no matter what the teacher does, a kid just doesn't learn. Their retention level sucks from one year to the next. It's like they take a summer class in Stupid 101 or something." She leaned forward, resting her forearms on her chair, and clasped her fingers together in front of her. "If a student is failing a class, I have to call in the offending teacher and have him or her explain why the kid is failing. Is there anything they could have done to get the little bugger to pass? I have excellent teachers, people who want to honest-to-God *teach*," Sylvia lamented. "But their failure rates are unacceptable."

Florence chuckled. "We have a chapter of what's known as The Twenty Percent Club on our campus. Teachers who are members wear a little badge every day and dare administration to say something."

"What's The Twenty Percent Club?" Lauren asked. "I've never heard of that."

"It includes any faculty member who has any class, even one, in which twenty percent of the students failed," Sylvia answered. "I've checked everything they've done to make those students successful and most of them have gone way beyond the call of duty. In that particular group, for some reason, the students fail." She looked at Pat. "You know how it is. Do any of your teachers ever complain that the counselors have deliberately dumped every poor student they could find in one of their classes?"

"All the time," Pat answered with a nod.

"We always get blamed," Florence fumed. "I'm a counselor,

but a computer somewhere burps out the class schedules and it really doesn't care who goes where as long as everyone has a place to be each period."

"It's the same course, the same teacher, the same lesson taught in exactly the same way. Every class passes except one," Florence said. She shrugged. "And we don't know why."

"Maybe the students are all like that one Mrs. Fredericks had a couple of years ago. Remember that?" Sylvia asked with a smile.

Florence laughed so loud that other patrons of the bar turned to look in their direction. "I hope she found another position somewhere," she said between bouts of laughter.

"I heard she retired. She had the time in." Sylvia looked at Pat and Lauren. "We had this teacher, Mrs. Fredericks. She taught eighth grade science. Always been a decent teacher and enjoyed the kids. Anyway, one of the things a teacher can do, after working with the students a while, is make a referral for evaluation by the special education facilitator on our campus. You know, if she notices the kid might have a problem reading or whatnot. Mrs. Fredericks made a referral for one of her students who couldn't pass gas, let alone her class. The facilitator scheduled a meeting and notified the parent about the referral. Next thing I know, mom is jumping up and down on my desk, livid and demanding to know what the basis was for the referral."

Florence covered her mouth in an attempt to stifle another round of laughter.

"Anyway," Sylvia started again, "I escorted mom to Mrs. Fredericks' room and pulled her out of class for a moment to make the inquiry." She raised her right hand. "Then, I swear to God, Mrs. Fredericks said the reason for her referral was because the kid just *looked* stupid."

Pat and Lauren looked at each other and laughed loudly enough to draw further attention.

"I didn't know what to say to Mrs. Fredericks' response. I contacted my assistant principal to help me get this now thoroughly irate parent back to the office. I contacted Florence and had her make an immediate schedule change effective that same day."

"What did you do about the teacher?" Lauren asked.

"She began using quite a bit of the sick leave she'd accumulated over the years and left at the end of that semester. Personally, I chalked it up to battle fatigue. She just lost it. Kid failed the course with his new teacher, one of those newbie eager beavers, too. The next fall mom came back and informed us junior was ADD, ADHD, one of those problems almost every kid has these days, and had him enrolled in the special education program." She shook her head. "What a mess! I watch for teacher burn-out a lot more carefully now, let me tell ya."

Pat looked at Lauren. "See what we have to look forward to?"

"I can hardly wait," Lauren sighed as she chewed her last bite of food. "That was really good," she said as she leaned back. "Thanks for recommending it."

"I worried you wouldn't like it after I ordered for you," Pat admitted, rubbing her hand briefly down Lauren's back before resting it along the back of her chair.

"It was delicious and just enough to not ruin my girlish figure," Lauren said, returning Pat's smile.

With her stomach appeased, Lauren turned her attention back to the lively conversation. She felt relaxed and was enjoying the company without having to consider every word she said, fearing a negative reaction. Her drink hit the spot and she ordered a second. She didn't remember the last time she'd had an alcoholic drink, probably in Germany when she and Mandy polished off a bottle of wine while trying out a new recipe. Athon wasn't supposed to drink alcoholic beverages because of her medication and there was never any in the house, just in case. Athon wouldn't have cared if Lauren occasionally had a drink after a particularly arduous day, but Lauren felt safer, after the bar incident, not having the temptation around. She felt a pleasant buzz by the time she finished the second Jack and Coke and was glad she'd eaten. All thoughts of attending the mixer vanished as the four women continued their discussions about their schools. It had been a long time since Lauren had laughed so much.

An hour later, Sylvia stretched and stifled a yawn. "I think I'm going to have to call it a night," she said. "This is the most fun I've had in forever and it felt good to laugh about some of the ridiculous things we have to put up with. Now that I've bent your ears venting, maybe I can readjust my attitude. It gets out of whack at least twice a year." She patted Florence's arm and looked at her watch. "I was having such a good time that we've missed most of the mixer. You can stay if you want and I'll see you at breakfast."

Florence stood. "We left early this morning. I can read for a while before going to sleep." She smiled at Pat and Lauren. "It's been wonderful meeting you both. Maybe we'll see you in a session or at breakfast or lunch."

Pat stood and shook their hands, promising to get together again the following day. "Want to see if there's anyone still at the mixer?" she asked Lauren.

Lauren shook her head. "I can wait until tomorrow." She laughed. "I've talked so much tonight that I need to give my vocal chords a rest."

"You okay?"

"I haven't felt this good and been this relaxed in a long time." She looked down at her hands and said, "I should feel bad for having such a good time." She shifted her eyes to Pat and smiled. "But I don't. Thank you for making me get away for a while. You're an excellent friend."

"Ready to call it a night then?"

Lauren scooted her chair back and stood, grabbing the edge of the table to steady herself. Pat took her arm until she regained her balance.

"Remind me not to stand up so fast," Lauren said. "Sorry about that."

"Not a problem."

Lauren felt the warmth of Pat's hand through the sleeve of her blouse. It ran through her body, strangely comforting her. After they cleared the maze of tables, Pat removed her hand and placed it against the small of Lauren's back, guiding her toward the hotel elevators. Once they stepped inside and the doors slid quietly shut, Lauren licked her lips and suddenly couldn't think of anything to say. Both their rooms were on the same floor and Pat leaned forward to push the button for the fourth floor before leaning against the back wall.

"I'll walk you to your room," Pat said.

"You don't have to, Pat."

"My room's only three doors farther down," Pat said with a laugh. "Pausing for a moment isn't a hardship. Do you want to meet for breakfast around eight?"

"Sure." Lauren brought her hand up to Pat's arm. "We need to stop by registration so we can decide which sessions we're going to."

"I picked them up earlier while you were napping. Do you want to attend the same sessions or split them up so we cover more?"

"Whatever you think is best," Lauren said with a shrug. "Doesn't matter to me."

"We can decide over breakfast," Pat finally said when they stopped in front of Lauren's room. "Is your room all right?"

"Very nice," Lauren answered. "When I was at Carver, I think the district had a contract with No Tell Motel Incorporated." She shivered involuntarily. "I once shared a bed with two other teachers because when we saw the roll-away bed they wheeled in, none of us had the guts to sleep on it. I swear it moved when you looked at it."

Pat laughed as Lauren slid to key card into the lock. When she pulled it out, nothing happened. She tried a second time, but the light on the door remained red. Lauren made a growl in her throat and mumbled, "Locks hate me."

Pat took the card from Lauren and said, "Let me try. Mine fought back earlier." She jiggled the door and pulled it toward her as far as it would move. She slid the card in, holding it in place for a moment before withdrawing it quickly. She smiled when the locking mechanism blinked green. She turned the door knob and pushed the door open. "I think the card reader is out of alignment or something. You should tell the desk people in the morning and have it checked." Pat pushed the door farther open and held it as Lauren rested a hand on her waist and stepped around her. Once in the door Lauren turned to say good night and sucked in a breath, surprised how close she was to Pat. For a moment she paused and looked into Pat's eyes.

Pat's hand rose and lightly stroked Lauren's cheek. Her hand moved to the side of Lauren's neck and held it as their lips met. Lauren didn't push her away and deepened the kiss. She pressed a hand against Pat's back and slowly turned their bodies into the room. When the kiss ended neither woman was able to speak. Lauren wrapped her arms around Pat's neck and sobbed against her shoulder. She was cheating on Athon, seeking to bring her life back into balance.

Lauren lifted her tear-stained face, her eyes searching Pat's calm demeanor. She raised her arms and ran fingers through Pat's long raven hair, scooping it over her ears. She brought her arms over and around Pat's head, clinging to her as their lips met again. Lauren felt her body react. Words were unnecessary as Pat's touches, kisses, and tender strokes told Lauren everything she needed to know. It had been too long since her body had been treated in such a gentle, almost reverent way.

LAUREN STRETCHED AND groaned contentedly as she ran her hands down her naked body. She stopped and opened her eyes. She never slept in the nude. She raised the sheet and heavy bedspread and looked beneath them. She flopped back on her pillow and brought her hands up to rub her eyes with the heels of her hands. *Pat!* her mind screamed. Had it been a dream, a very vivid dream, or had she made love with Pat Stanton the night before? Two drinks? Come on! She wouldn't have done something so—so deceitful after only two drinks! She couldn't have. She closed her eyes and mentally ran down every part of her body. Her inventory only made it to her tender breasts before she knew. Oh my God! What can I say to her when I see her this morning? She rolled over and buried her face in the pillow. After taking a deep breath she sat up and jumped out of bed. She stared down at the bed. Her own scent mingled with a lighter, familiar scent all over the pillow.

After almost scrubbing the skin from her body to erase the scent of her infidelity, Lauren found Pat cheerfully eating breakfast with Sylvia and Florence in the hotel dining room.

"It seems like I'm always the last one to arrive," Lauren said with a smile.

"Did you get a good night's sleep?" Pat asked nonchalantly.

"I did." Lauren's eyes met Pat's. "Thank you."

"No problem," Pat returned. "The breakfast buffet is pretty good. They'll even make an omelet any way you want it while you wait."

Sylvia and Florence excused themselves while Lauren continued eating.

"You can go with them, Pat. I'll catch up in a little bit," Lauren said between sips of coffee.

"The venders will be here during the entire conference," Pat said with a shrug. "Are you better this morning?"

"I'm excellent this morning. I don't feel any particular burden on my shoulders and am actually looking forward to having a good day. How are you feeling after an undisturbed night of rest?"

"Very well." Pat finished her coffee and wiped her mouth. She looked at Lauren. "Have you ever read the children's book *A Dragon in the House*?"

"I don't think so."

"It was my favorite book when I was a child and still is. It's about this baby dragon that was brought into someone's house. The longer it stayed, the more it grew. The people in the house spent all their time stepping around the dragon, ignoring its presence until its legs protruded out the windows and doors. Then one day it stood up and walked off with the house before the inhabitants realized it was even there."

"I'm not ignoring or stepping around anything, Pat. I know what happened last night." She made sure she had Pat's eyes before continuing. "I—I knew what I was doing, but I'd rather not make an issue out of it. I cheated on my partner. It won't happen again, but I'm not sorry it did. If you want me to resign for personal reasons, I will."

"I don't want you to think I took advantage of you and I certainly do not want you to resign." Pat smiled. "Can we still work together?"

"Absolutely."

Chapter Thirty-Two

Duvalle, Texas
December 2010

LAUREN ROLLED ONTO her side. She shifted her body closer
to Athon's knowing her partner's body heat would warm her
quickly. Her hand slid over the cool sheet feeling for her, but the
bed was empty. She raised her head to look at the clock on the
nightstand and sighed. Two-forty-five.

"Athon?"

It wasn't unusual for Athon to rise in the middle of the night
and wander around their house, usually falling asleep on the couch
or in her recliner from exhaustion. Lauren turned on the light next
to the bed and swung her feet from under the covers. She pulled on
her robe and stopped to look out the bedroom window. Both cars
were still in the carport and she breathed a sigh of relief. There had
been times, when Athon couldn't sleep, that she would drive for
hours with no destination in mind. She seemed to be looking for
something, but didn't know exactly what. Lauren slid her feet into
her slippers, grabbed her cell phone, just in case, and left the
bedroom.

After flipping on the lights she thoroughly searched the
downstairs rooms. She smiled as a thought from the past struck her
when she saw the Christmas tree she and Athon had purchased and
decorated earlier that evening. It reminded her of the little
Christmas tree Athon placed on the table in the diner the last time
she saw her before they were separated so many years ago. It
reminded her of her arrival in Germany after they found one
another again. She fingered an ornament they had found in a little
shop in Kaiserslautern. It had been a perfect time as they made love
beneath the lights of their Christmas tree.

She started to back away when she saw an ornament lying on
the floor. She squatted down to pick it up and saw that it had been
smashed, as if someone had stepped on it. Lauren picked up the
helicopter ornament one of Athon's crew members had given her
before their final deployment. The sound of deep rolling thunder,
followed by a bright flash of lightning startled her and she dropped
it. As she knelt to pick it up again, she noticed small pieces of
broken glass on the carpeting near the fireplace. In front of the
hearth was a twisted picture frame, its glass broken. Lauren looked
at the picture and her breath caught in her throat. She dropped the

picture of Athon and her crew standing alongside their helicopter and walked quickly through the kitchen to the back door. A strong gust of wind tugged at her robe. Her hair whipped across her face and she twisted her neck to let the wind blow it away from her eyes as they searched the darkness.

"Athon!" she called, but the wind tossed her voice back into her face. She stepped away from the house and rotated in a circle for some sign of her lover. She lowered her head and pushed into the wind. There was only one other place she could think to look. It was where Athon always felt safest and the only piece of rusting junk she'd allowed to remain on the property.

When she finally made her way to the old camper shell, she placed one hand against the door frame and used the other to yank the aluminum door open. She caught her breath and looked inside. It was dry, with no sign Athon had been there. She secured the door and the rising wind pushed against her back as she retraced her steps to the house. She reached the safety of the carport before rain, ushered in by the wind and accompanied by lightning and thunder, began falling. It quickly grew from a light shower to a downpour.

WHEN HAD EVERYTHING gone so wrong? When had her life begun to unravel like an old piece of rotted cloth, one thread at a time until there was nothing left? The revolver rested comfortably in her hands as she leaned her head back and stared at the black sky above. Thousands of stars blinked through rapidly moving, gray clouds, beckoning her to join them. She closed her eyes, a sob escaping from her throat as a river of tears flowed down her cheeks and onto her neck. She didn't know why she was crying. She only knew that an indefinable pain gnawed at her relentlessly and she hurt deep inside. She could see the faces of everyone who had hurt her and those she had hurt even though they had never done a thing to her except cross her life's path for only a brief moment.

She shook her head and willed them to go away. She lowered her head and stared into the blackness surrounding her. She could see and hear them as they dodged behind the trees snapping in the wind. The ugly faces taunted her, tortured her, and refused to go away. Not even the downpour of rain that had crept across the field toward her could wash them away. The wind turned the raindrops into tiny cold knives that pricked at her skin. She slung her arms to knock them away, but there were too many. She wiped a muddy hand across her eyes to clear her sight; the scent of gun powder and oil filled her nose and she breathed it in deeply. She raised the revolver and aimed at those who deserved to die. Muzzle flashes exploded into the night, but the faces refused to go away, no matter how many times she fired. The faces laughed at her as she quickly reloaded, prepared to shoot until she no longer had the strength to pull the trigger. The more they laughed at her, the more her grief turned to rage.

LAUREN SPUN AROUND when she heard the gunshots, trying to determine where the sounds came from, but the wind tossed them away. She grabbed the cell phone from her robe pocket and pressed 9-1-1. As calmly as she could, Lauren gave her location and a brief explanation of what was happening. She knew she should stay on the line, but she had to find Athon. Without thinking she stepped from under the carport, cold drops of rain quickly soaking through her robe, chilling her skin. Her eyes scanned the wide field to the side of the house as she periodically wiped the rain from her face.

A flash of lightning illuminated the field for an instant and Lauren thought she saw something. Rushing forward, she stopped when she saw Athon on her knees in the mud, the rain forming small puddles around her. She was wearing only the t-shirt and boxers she'd worn to bed. She was slumped forward holding her head in her hands, rocking back and forth.

"Athon!" Lauren called out.

Athon jerked her head around. "Stop!" she called out as she brought her hand up. "Stay away from me," she screamed.

In another flash of lightning Lauren saw the pistol Athon now had pressed against her head. Reflexively Lauren stopped and held her hands out toward Athon. "Athon! No!"

"I can't live like this anymore," Athon cried. "I don't know who I am! Oh, Lauren, I'm so sorry."

Athon lowered the pistol and pressed it against her chest, over her heart. Lauren took a deep breath in an attempt to calm herself. The moment was broken by the wail of a siren moving up the driveway toward the house. A minute later, a police officer, weapon drawn, ran across the field to join Lauren. Sheriff Raynelle Cosper stopped and took in the scene before her.

Athon raised her pistol toward the two women. "Get off my fuckin' property!" she yelled.

"Take it easy, Athon. What's goin' on, girl?" Raynelle asked.

"Nothin' much. Just a little problem-solvin'." With her weapon still pointed at Lauren and Raynelle, Athon laughed, but there was no humor in it. She lowered her head and shook it. Then she jabbed the barrel in Lauren's direction. "I promised to take care of her forever," Athon said as if talking only to Raynelle. "If I'm gone, she can have the life she deserves."

Shrugging off Raynelle's hand, Lauren moved closer to Athon. "Without you, baby, I won't have a life," she said.

"Never took you for a quitter, Athon," Raynelle said as she inched forward. "Long as I've known you you've been a scrapper. Pudge thought so, too, kid. But right now you've run into somethin' that's a lot bigger than you and just need a little help."

"Please, baby" Lauren said gently.

Tears streamed down Athon's face, mingling with the rain water. "I'm sorry Lauren. They won't leave me alone."

"We can fight them together. There's nothing we can't do together," Lauren soothed.

"Make them go away," Athon said as her face crumbled and she brought her hands up to cover it. Raynelle placed her hand on the pistol and Athon relinquished her grip on it as Lauren enfolded her in her arms. She buried her face against Lauren and sobbed out her pain.

Raynelle pulled her rain poncho off and wrapped it around the two women as she guided them back into the house.

Once inside, Lauren said, "I have to get her out of these wet clothes. I'll be back in a little bit."

"Okay if I make a pot of coffee?" Raynelle asked as she brushed raindrops from her hair.

"Of course, Sheriff. There's a clean t-shirt in the laundry room. Throw your shirt in the dryer."

Lauren led Athon into their bedroom and started the shower. Then she stripped off Athon's clothes and her own and helped Athon into the shower, holding her in her arms as the warm water ran over their bodies. She rubbed her hands over Athon's back and up and down her arms until the coolness of her body faded away. She kissed her tenderly as she dried both of them and guided Athon into a clean t-shirt and boxers. She pulled back the covers and snuggled close, holding Athon until she was breathing evenly and fell asleep. She slipped out of the bed and dressed quietly before rejoining Raynelle.

"She all right?" Raynelle asked.

"For now," Lauren said as she filled the cup Raynelle handed her.

Raynelle adjusted her body on the couch in the living room and rested her elbows on her knees. "I'll have to file a report about this, Lauren," she said.

"I know," Lauren responded as she sipped her coffee and glanced at the living room clock.

"Does that pistol have a permit?"

"Yes."

"I'll unload it and let you do whatever you think is appropriate with it, but I wouldn't tell her where it is."

"Thank you, Raynelle. She has an appointment with her therapist the day after tomorrow. I'll call in and take tomorrow off to stay with her. I'm already off to take her to her appointment."

"I know this has been hard for you, Lauren." Raynelle cleared her throat. "No one would fault you if you—"

"I promised her forever. No matter what," Lauren snapped.

"I know you meant it, but sometimes they just don't come back. Somebody does. Just not the person who left."

"It's not her fault."

"Don't let yourself get hurt while she tries to find her way home."

A tear trickled down Lauren's cheek and she wiped it away. "I love her, Raynelle."

"You love who she was. She needs a lot more help than you can give her. Acting like her personal punching bag won't help her. You should call an ambulance and have her admitted to the hospital."

"She hates hospitals! I can't do that to her!"

"She hates who she's become! The last thread holding her together broke out there in that field. If I have to I'll swear she's suicidal and needs to be committed."

"You can't do that to her, Raynelle."

"I sure as hell can. I don't want to be called back here one night and find her dead body next to yours." Raynelle glared at Lauren. "Make the damn call!"

LAUREN FOLLOWED THE gurney as it was rolled quickly into the emergency room at the hospital at Fort Sam Houston in San Antonio. She had been allowed to ride in the ambulance with Athon and gripped her hand tightly. Athon stared at the ceiling of the vehicle, refusing to speak or look at Lauren. When she was awakened by the paramedics, she became combative. Lauren didn't know who Athon was seeing in her mind, but despite her hand-to-hand battle with the two large men, she was subdued. Wrist and ankle restraints were quickly and silently applied. Once the gurney entered the ambulance a technician took her vital signs and drew a blood sample. The pricking of her skin caused no reaction.

The gurney stopped next to the emergency room desk as paperwork was exchanged. Eyes that Lauren didn't recognize glared at her. "Don't do this," Athon said in a low voice. Unexpectedly, Athon raised her head and thrashed against the restraints holding her body on the gurney. "Don't do this, you bitch!" she screamed. Just as quickly, tears rolled down the sides of her face and her look became pleading. "Please, don't," she begged. "I promise to be good. Don't hurt me again. Please."

Lauren took her hand and brushed her other hand through Athon's blonde hair. Her fingers ached from the force of Athon's grasp as the gurney began to move toward an examination room.

"You can't go inside," the orderly pushing the gurney said. "The doctor will speak to you after her examination."

Lauren nodded, but Athon refused to release her hand. Lauren couldn't stop her tears as the orderly and a nurse pried Athon's fingers away. As the gurney rolled into the room, Lauren watched Athon's fingers clenching and opening as if trying to grasp her hand again. "Don't leave me here, baby. Lauren! Please don't leave me," Athon's voice continued to plead as the door to the room closed quietly. Lauren turned away and covered her face, releasing the tears she couldn't hold back any longer.

"MS. SHELTON?" A soft voice asked.

Lauren snapped her head up and stood quickly, looking at a young woman wearing light blue scrubs. "I'm Lauren Shelton," she answered after clearing her throat.

"Follow me, please," the woman said politely.

Lauren followed her through the doors leading from the waiting room into the emergency room. They walked past the room where Athon had been taken and turned down another long corridor. Maybe Athon had already been taken to a room, Lauren thought.

They stopped in front of a door and the nurse knocked lightly on it. When she heard a response, she turned the knob and smiled briefly at Lauren as she opened the door. "I have Ms. Shelton, Dr. Cortez," she said.

Lauren stepped into the room to face a short woman with gray hair. She remembered Athon describing her as a grandmotherly type who was a good listener.

"Thank you, Karen," Cortez said as she came around the desk and extended her hand. "It's nice to finally meet you, Ms. Shelton, even though the circumstances aren't the best. Please. Have a seat."

Lauren joined Cortez on a couch that sat against a side wall. "Where is Athon?" she asked.

"The Major has been sedated for now."

"She's not in the Army any longer. She retired in July."

"I know, but apparently she hasn't left the military completely behind. I understand you are her partner, is that correct?" Cortez asked in a soft voice.

Lauren hesitated, unsure how to answer the question. She raised her chin slightly and coughed. "That's correct."

Cortez smiled. "I am a civilian, Ms. Shelton. Quite frankly, I have little interest in anything other than the welfare of my patients. The Major has been quite open with me about your relationship."

"Can we drop the formality, Dr. Cortez? I just want to know what's going on."

The doctor leaned back. "Can you tell me what happened tonight?"

Lauren explained finding Athon and calling the police. Nothing unusual had happened before they had gone to bed. Athon had seemed fine through dinner and hadn't told her anything out of the ordinary that might have occurred while Lauren was at work. "The only thing we did last night was decorate our Christmas tree." Lauren frowned.

"What is it, Lauren?" Cortez asked.

Lauren shook her head. "While I was looking for Athon I found a broken ornament next to our tree. It was a little model of a rescue helicopter. Probably nothing. But then I found a shattered picture of her with her helicopter crew."

"Do thunder and lightning upset her?"

"Not that I've ever noticed." Lauren shrugged.

"I can't tell you what we've discussed during our sessions in any detail, but she is aware she has upset you with some of her behaviors. What exactly does she do that upsets you, Lauren?"

Lauren began to feel uncomfortable. "Most of the things I've read on the computer. She yells, calls me names, she's shoved me and pushed me around. She rarely touches me intimately any more or lets me touch her."

"She makes you feel unwanted, sexually."

"Yes. We've had sex periodically, but I feel like...I don't know."

"As if you weren't there."

"I suppose. Her body engages in sex and then she rolls over and goes to sleep."

"No foreplay?"

"No."

"Have you been with anyone else?"

Lauren couldn't meet the doctor's eyes and felt the burn of tears. Her voice sounded small and weak when she spoke. "Once. Last month with a woman I work with. Neither of us intended for it to happen. It just did."

"Athon never suspected?"

"Not that I'm aware of. I'm certain there would have been a

negative reaction if she knew. She's accused me of having an affair in the past."

Cortez patted Lauren's hand. "Athon has apparently had a break with reality. From what you've described it could have been caused by a nightmare or a flashback to something that happened during her last deployment, or it could have been caused by something even further in her past. Perhaps the two events overlapped in some way tonight and pushed her over the edge."

"What happens now? Can I see her?"

"I've had her transferred to a treatment facility. You won't be able to see her for...a while I'm afraid. Just know that she will be taken care of. Right now I'm concerned about you. The spouse or significant other of a Wounded Warrior suffers just as much, but in a different way. For years the military has denied that something like PTSD even existed. From the number of cases I've dealt with over the last few years, I hazard to guess they are incorrect. They are only now beginning to do anything to help these men and women and their families." Cortez stood and went to her desk. She wrote on a pad and handed it to Lauren. "That is the name and phone number of a military wife who has formed a group that meets periodically to discuss problems associated with PTSD and TBI. You're not alone, Lauren. I know you love Athon, but no amount of love can make her problems go away."

As Cortez walked to the door Lauren stood. "When will I know something?"

"Soon. Her mental health care providers are already putting a treatment plan in place."

Lauren joined the doctor at the door. "So I just go home and wait?"

"For a while."

Lauren took a deep breath and prepared to leave. Cortez stopped her and smiled. "Just so you know, she loves you too and hates herself for what she's doing. She knows she's doing things that hurt you, but cannot stop herself."

Lauren smiled down at the diminutive woman. "Thank you, Doctor." She walked down the corridor, distracted by looking for her cell phone and trying to find her way back to the emergency room exit. She heard someone call her name and turned to see the orderly who had taken Athon into an examination room walking toward her.

"Ms. Shelton?"

"Yes."

"Could I speak to you a minute, outside?"

She nodded and followed the middle-aged man into the waiting room and out the hospital exit. As soon as he was outside he shook a cigarette from a pack and offered her one. She shook her head and waited as he lit his and inhaled the smoke deeply, exhaling it in a long, gray stream. "This might not help, but there was nothing you could have done to prevent what happened to Major Dailey tonight. You did the right thing by having her brought in," he said.

"I hope you're right," Lauren said, shivering slightly from the cold damp air.

"I've been in the military and served as a medic with a combat unit when all hell broke loose over there. I want you to know that just last year, that was me in that room wearing restraints and my wife was standing where you are right now. Now take a bunch of deep breaths and do that every time you start to doubt you've done the right thing. She'll make it."

Lauren moved closer to him and hugged him tightly. "Thank you," she said. When they separated, she was surprised to see Raynelle Cosper ambling across the parking lot toward her.

"I figured you'd need a ride home sooner or later," the sheriff said.

Lauren nodded and followed Raynelle to her patrol car. The earlier downpour had tapered off to a light drizzle, but Lauren didn't seem to notice. She settled into the front seat and fastened her seat belt as Raynelle started the engine and backed away. Lauren was exhausted and was glad the sheriff didn't feel the need to ask questions. She closed her eyes, still seeing the tortured, panicked look on Athon's face.

Lauren gasped when a hand on her shoulder snapped her awake. She ran her hand over her face and looked around to see where she was.

"Do you have your keys?" Raynelle asked.

Lauren found her purse on the floor of the patrol car and rummaged through it. "I left in such a hurry," she mumbled.

Raynelle got out of the vehicle and walked to the back of the house, returning a few minutes later to open the car door for Lauren. "Back door was unlocked," she reported. "I checked inside and it's okay."

Once they were back inside the house, Raynelle said, "Get some sleep if you can. I'll let your school know you won't be in today."

Lauren didn't have the energy to argue as she removed her coat and hung it in the closet. She changed into a long sleep shirt and crawled into bed, pulling Athon's pillow against her body for comfort.

Chapter Thirty-three

Duvalle, Texas
December 2010

A SMELL BROUGHT Lauren out of a deep, dreamless sleep and she rushed from the bedroom toward the kitchen. She must have left something cooking on the stove. She grabbed the door frame to stop her momentum when she saw someone standing in front of the stove, stirring a pot. Pat looked at her and smiled. "Thought you might be hungry when you woke up," she said. "I make a dynamite chili even if I do say so myself."

"What are you doing here? What time is it? The school—"

"Will survive in my absence. It's out already anyway. I received a call from a Sheriff Cosper this morning. She told me you wouldn't be in due to a problem at home. There was only one problem I could think of so I left at noon to make sure you were all right."

"How did you get in?" Lauren asked with a frown.

"The sheriff stayed until I arrived and let me in. Next question," Pat said. "This is almost ready if you're hungry."

"I need to—"

"You need to rest and get your energy back," Pat said as she opened cabinets, searching for a bowl. "Sit down."

"Pat," Lauren said, unable to look at her.

"I'm only here because you shouldn't be alone," Pat said. "The sheriff said to tell you that someone named Bridget will be here with you this evening." She paused when she found the bowls. "I'm your friend, Lauren. That's all. Let me do what friends do."

"Can I at least get dressed?"

"You have five minutes," Pat said with a warm smile.

Lauren quickly changed into sweat pants and a t-shirt after washing her face and running a brush through her disheveled hair in an attempt to look presentable. She joined Pat at the dining room table and sat, drawing a leg up beneath her. She stared at the glass next to the steaming bowl of chili. "Milk?"

"Well, the chili might be a little spicy and milk's the best thing to put the fire out," Pat explained with a grin.

"It smells good," Lauren said as she dipped a spoon into her bowl and blew on it.

"I didn't have the recipe in front of me, but I've made it so many times that I think I got it right."

Lauren brought the spoon to her mouth and cautiously tasted the chili, letting it remain in her mouth for her taste buds to absorb the flavor. She nodded and pointed to the bowl with her spoon as she chewed and swallowed. "This is really good, Pat. I need your recipe. Athon loves..." she said with a hitch in her voice.

Pat didn't comment and continued eating, crumbling crackers to mix with the chili. "Maybe a little more chili powder," she said around a mouthful of food.

They continued to eat silently until their spoons scraped the last bite out of their bowls. Lauren looked embarrassed when she asked for a second helping. She sat back as Pat carried both bowls to the stove and filled them again.

"I don't even know where she is," Lauren said when Pat set the bowl in front of her.

Pat rested a hand on Lauren's shoulder. "They'll take care of her," she said.

"I'll be back at work tomorrow," Lauren said.

"Take whatever time you need," Pat said with a shrug.

"I can't sit around here feeling sorry for myself," Lauren said with a hint of anger in her voice.

"Whatever floats your boat," Pat quipped as she shoveled another spoonful of chili into her mouth.

"How can you treat this all so...so lightly?"

"I'm not, but I know a war can't be won in a single battle. You have to take it one battle at a time. Otherwise, you drive yourself crazy."

"Do you think Athon is crazy?"

"I didn't say that. She's definitely lost. For your sake, I hope they can help her find the path home."

"GOOD MORNING, MAJOR Dailey," a tall, distinguished-looking man dressed in civilian clothes said cheerfully. "Did you sleep well?"

"I guess," Athon said coldly.

"No nightmares?"

"No. When can I leave?"

"What do you remember about Tuesday night?"

"Last night?"

"Actually Tuesday was a couple of days ago. What do you remember?"

"Who are you?"

"I'm Dr. Chambers. You don't remember me?"

"If I did I wouldn't be asking who the hell you are," Athon snapped.

"Then we'll start from the beginning. I'm Dr. Leo Chambers, your primary physician while you're here."

Athon started to raise her hand to rub her face, but it was attached to the rail of her bed. Chambers saw the panic in her eyes and said, "I think we can remove these now." He watched her eyes dart around the room as he released the first soft restraint from her wrist. "We spoke for a few minutes Wednesday morning. Frank's fine, by the way. I spoke to him Wednesday evening. He said to tell you that he had your back and to quit worrying."

"He told us it was safe to make the pick up! He lied and they're dead! My whole fuckin' crew is dead."

Dr. Chambers showed no reaction to Athon's outburst and waited until she calmed down. "I'll let you get settled and have breakfast before I introduce you to the team that'll be working with you."

Athon blinked hard as she stared at Chambers. "Am I...am I crazy, Doc?"

He patted her shoulder. "Absolutely not, Major. You just need to learn a few coping skills." When she continued to stare at him, he said, "We need to find ways for you to deal with stress, anger, grief, guilt, and other things that cause you to overreact to certain situations."

She rubbed her hands together and looked at them. "You're not gonna get all up in my head, are you? It's not a pretty place."

"Eventually, we may have to take a peek."

"Can I see Lauren?"

"When you think you're ready to see her we'll schedule a visit."

"I don't want her to see me like this."

Chambers smiled. "She's already seen you at your worst, Athon. We've got a lot of work to do and it all depends on you."

FOUR LONG, EMPTY days and nights had crawled by. Now Lauren had a long, empty weekend to look forward to. The following week would be the last five days before students and staff were released for their Christmas break. It was the season she looked forward to the most, but she would be spending another two and a half weeks alone. There were people like Pat, Bridget, and Marty she could spend time with even though she knew she wasn't much fun to be around. She wanted to see Athon, she needed it. She needed a way to distract her mind and body. Alone all she did was think. What could she have done differently?

She jumped when the house phone rang shrilly. She picked up the receiver as she rested a hip against the couch. "Hello," she said.

A low voice, barely audible asked, "Lauren?"

"Athon? Oh my God, are you all right?"

"I'm okay. I miss you."

"I miss you, too, baby. When can I see you? I don't even know where you are for sure."

"I'm in a rehab place in San Antonio. Lauren?"

"I'm here, sweetie."

"I'm s...sorry," Athon managed as her voice cracked.

"There's nothing for you to be sorry about, honey."

"Forgive me."

Lauren didn't know what to say as tears rolled down her cheeks. She wiped them away and said the only thing she could think of. "Forever and always, Athon."

She heard Athon sniff and blow her nose. "If you want to, I can have a visitor tomorrow. I want you to understand."

"What time can I come?"

"Maybe after lunch, if that's all right. I don't want to keep you from anything."

"There's nothing more important to me than seeing you again. I'm sorry I took you there."

"No. You did the right thing. You had to protect yourself...from me, from who I've become."

"Do you need anything?"

"No."

"Tell me what you've been doing there," Lauren said.

"Tomorrow. I gotta go now."

"Wait! I don't know where you are."

She heard Athon speak to someone, but her words were muffled as if she was covering the handset. A moment later an unfamiliar voice came on the line. "Ms. Shelton, this is Abby Danner. I'm Athon's day nurse. She's in the polytrauma rehabilitation center at Audie Murphy Hospital on post." She gave Lauren directions to the new facility and told her where to go to visit a patient. Lauren heard another voice in the background. Abby's voice seemed to speak away from the receiver before she cleared her throat and said, "She wants me to tell you that she would understand if you didn't come."

Lauren's voice was strangled as she assured the nurse she would be there and said goodbye. She tried to remember what little Athon had said as she cried. Athon hadn't sounded like herself on the phone. Her voice seemed distance and unsure. Although it was nearly twenty-four hours before her visit, Lauren spent the afternoon deciding what to wear.

LAUREN WAITED AT the reception desk and looked around the facility that was still partially under construction. It was light and airy, but she was impatient to see Athon again.

"Dr. Chambers, Major Dailey's primary, would like to speak to you for a few minutes before you see her," the receptionist said. "He's on his way if you'd care to have a seat."

Lauren walked to a grouping of upholstered seats nearby and checked her clothing. She had chosen a pair of light tan slacks and Athon's favorite soft, forest green sweater. Athon loved to run her hands over the fabric, finding it soothing in some way. She didn't know what she would say to Athon when she finally saw her.

"Ms. Shelton?" a deep voice said as a man took a seat caddy corner to hers. He reached out to shake her hand firmly. "I'm Leo Chambers. My team and I have been working with Athon since her arrival."

"How is she?" Lauren asked.

"Probably different than you remember," he answered. He laughed, "Certainly not like the last time you saw her."

"I was surprised when she called last night," she said.

"It was her decision even though we weren't sure she was ready to see you yet."

"Will she be all right?"

"Eventually." Chambers leaned forward and rested his elbows on his knees. "We see patients who are dealing with post-traumatic stress disorder on a daily basis and many who have also received a traumatic brain injury. Fortunately, Athon's TBI has been diagnosed as mild. Also fortunately, the treatment for her TBI is pretty much the same as the treatment for PTSD. The two of them together account for many of her problems."

"But not all of them," Lauren said.

Chambers shook his head. "What do you know about her childhood?"

"Not much. She doesn't like to talk about it. She told me her parents were dead. Her mother died of a drug overdose, I think, and the man she thought was her father was murdered."

"You never met them then?"

"I saw her father once briefly, but never met her mother. Why is this important?"

"It may not be," he answered with a smile. "Sorry if I seem to be picking your brain, but to help Athon I have to know as much as possible about her. She's remained fairly quiet during our sessions, especially the group sessions."

"She's never been comfortable talking about herself and definitely not in front of other people."

"Has she ever discussed the time she was captured?"

"Never. All I know about is her rescue. She was in a coma after that."

"Have you contacted anyone in the group Dr. Cortez recommended yet?"

"No."

"You should. The women and men in the spouse's group have all experienced much of what you have. It does help to be able to discuss it with someone who's been where you are now."

Lauren looked at him. "I don't know what I'm supposed to do. Going to work every day, not knowing where she is or how she is, is tearing me apart." She sniffed as she tried to fight off the tears building in her eyes. "I don't want her to see me upset."

"But you *are* upset and *she's* the cause. She needs to know the effect of what she does and learn how to prevent it before it happens. You can't be afraid of letting her know how you feel. She's responsible for her actions, not you. She has to learn to deal with her pain and not shove it onto anyone else. When you see her act normally." Chambers stood. "I'll have you escorted to the visitor's room. And make sure you contact that group. No excuses."

Lauren followed a friendly candy-striper type to an elevator and then down a corridor that overlooked a covered area that held bench seats and picnic tables. Although she was anxious to see Athon again after abandoning her in the emergency room, she was just as afraid of Athon's reaction to being abandoned. The volunteer pushed open a door into a large room. Lauren looked around for Athon.

When she finally located her, she wanted to turn around and leave. She almost didn't recognize Athon, who was standing in front of a window, gazing at something outside. She looked thinner than Lauren remembered and her cheeks seemed to have sunken in. Act normally, Dr. Chambers had told her. She tried to force her face into a pleasant expression as she approached Athon. Her sneakers made a grating squeaking sound as she walked, drawing Athon's attention. When Lauren saw Athon's eyes she increased her pace and didn't stop until she held Athon in her arms, embracing her tightly. A few seconds later she felt arms encircling her as Athon buried her head in her shoulder. They stood embracing on another and rocking slowly from side to side for several minutes before parting. Athon rested her forehead against Lauren's and kept her eyes closed.

"I love you. I'm sorry," Athon murmured.

Lauren ran her fingers through soft blonde hair and kissed her cheeks and down to her neck. "I love you, too, baby," she said softly.

They located seats at a nearby empty table and Lauren

entwined her fingers with Athon's. Athon choked out a sharp laugh. "I don't know what to say. I had so much to talk about until I saw you." She looked up. "I wasn't sure you'd really come."

"Nothing could have kept me away," Lauren said. "How are you doing?"

Athon took a deep breath. "They keep me busy," she said, leaning back in her chair.

"You look thinner."

Athon shrugged. "I haven't had much of an appetite." One corner of her mouth curled up. "Food at home is better."

"I'll fix all your favorite things when you come home. Have they given you any idea when that might be yet?"

"I think soon for maybe a furlough over the holidays, but I might have to come back."

Lauren beamed. "Then you might be home for Christmas."

Athon looked down at their hands and tightened her grip. "I might not ever be the same. If you want to leave, I'll understand."

"Do you want me to leave?" Lauren asked.

Athon shook her head. "No, but I won't blame you if you do."

"What have you learned here so far, honey. Can we talk about it?"

"I'm learning how to cope with my anger before it gets out of hand. They say I'm doing pretty good so far." She looked at Lauren again. "I'm trying really hard." She laughed slightly. "It's exhausting being me, you know. How's school?"

Lauren rolled her eyes and smiled. "Exhausting! The kids get out for Christmas at the end of next week and it's like trying to herd cats."

Athon chuckled. "Have you talked to Bridget?"

"She calls every day to ask how you are. Tonight I'll have a lot to tell her. If she knows you're coming home for Christmas, I'll have to change the sheets in the guest room." What Lauren thought she saw in Athon's eyes hadn't been there in a long time. She glanced around the room before leaning closer to Athon and kissing her soundly. When she moved her lips away, she breathed, "I hope that wasn't against the rules."

Athon pulled Lauren into her lap. "Who gives a shit," she mumbled as they embraced. "God, you feel so damned good."

Chapter Thirty-four

San Antonio, Texas
December 2010

LAUREN ARRIVED AT the rehab center two days before Christmas. She was excited about having Athon home, but worry nagged at her. She had met with a group of women a week earlier. She recognized the things they described. Athon's descent into the terrors of her PTSD had occurred quickly, almost as soon as they returned to Duvalle. Many of the other women described how they coped with long-term, undiagnosed PTSD, some going back as far as the Vietnam period before manifesting into recognizable symptoms. The symptoms had always been there, of course, but hadn't reached their point of explosion for many years. They all believed that Lauren was fortunate to deal with her partner's behavioral changes so soon, but they all warned her that it could still be a long time before the interventions Athon learned at the hospital ended. It was an ongoing problem that would have to be continually fine-tuned. For her own protection they advised her to open a separate bank account in case she had to leave to protect herself. They recommended she purchase a second cell phone in case she needed to call for help and keep a weapon hidden, just in case. Lauren considered what they told her to be ridiculous. Athon would never hurt her physically. But what if she did? She hated thinking it could happen, but still visited her bank and purchased a pay-as-you-go phone, entering three numbers on speed dial. She felt guilty about not trusting Athon completely.

It was unusual in the San Antonio area, but a cold front moved across the region the day Lauren drove to take Athon home. She ducked her head as she hurried into the front doors of the rehab center. She was surprised to see Dr. Chambers lounging against the reception desk. He stood up erectly when he saw her.

"I hope we make it home before the streets ice over," she said as she shook sleet off her coat.

"I hope I can make it home after my shift," Chambers said with a laugh. "Looking forward to having Athon home?"

"Looking forward to a peaceful week lounging in front of the fireplace," she answered with a smile.

"Can we talk for just a minute?" he asked. "I promise not to delay you long. Her nurse will bring Athon down in a few minutes."

"Is there a problem, Doctor?"

"Athon is doing very well. She's adapting to the coping skills she's learned quickly. However, we haven't been able to get her to open up about her childhood or her captivity in Afghanistan. Oh, she's spoken about her treatment by her captors and her rescue, but we feel she's not divulging some information that could help her. One of her doctors believes something happened during those four days that brought back a painful memory from her childhood that she's not prepared to deal with yet."

"I don't understand."

"It's possible something occurred that released a childhood trauma. She won't discuss it because she doesn't believe it's related to what happened in Afghanistan."

"Will it create a problem at home?"

"I don't know and, frankly, I'm reluctant to let her remain at home more than a day or two. Because I don't know what might trigger an outburst, I think she should return to the center the day after Christmas at the latest."

Lauren frowned. "Have you confronted her about it?"

"We don't usually use the confrontational approach. Patients accept a memory and deal with it better if they divulge it voluntarily," Chambers explained.

"So Athon could be here until hell freezes over while you wait for her to tell you about this so-called childhood memory? Am I supposed to walk on egg shells until that happens, if it ever does?" Lauren's voice had risen, driven by frustration. Neither she nor Chambers heard Athon approach the waiting area.

"Not arguing over me, I hope," she said calmly.

Lauren stood and said, "As a matter of fact, we were."

"I'm doing better, I thought. I know I still have a lot to learn about what's going on in here," she said, tapping the side of her head. "But I'm working on it."

Lauren sighed. "I know you are, sweetie." Her eyes flashed as she glared at Chambers. "The doctor thinks there's something you're refusing to talk about or deal with. Something from your childhood." When Lauren saw the look on Athon's face, she knew it was true. "What is it, Athon? Please."

"There's nothing. I swear," Athon protested, not able to look Lauren in the eyes.

Lauren saw perspiration pop out on Athon's forehead despite the chilliness of the room. "You're lying," she stated bluntly.

The expression on Athon's face changed and she shouted, "You don't need to know. I can handle it!"

"Apparently not!" Lauren shouted back, taking a step closer to Athon, who was clenching her fists tightly against her thighs.

Chambers stood and nodded toward the reception desk. Lauren saw the receptionist pick up the phone and speak rapidly into the mouthpiece.

"Back off, Lauren," Athon warned. "You were here a couple of days ago, acting all lovey-dovey, like you fuckin' gave a shit about me. You're the liar! I trusted you!"

"Unless you tell me everything, I can't trust *you*!" She took a step closer. "Do you think I want to walk around afraid to say anything because it might set you off?" Another step. "Do you think I want to go to bed every damn night afraid of what you might do?" Another step. "Do you know what it feels like to be pushed away by your lover? Or be treated like a damn whore?" Lauren lowered her voice. "Tonight I was going to take you home. Tomorrow night we were going to celebrate Christmas together for the first time in two years. I had every intention of making love to you with nothing on but the lights of our tree. I want you so much it hurts to even think about it. I want you back whatever it costs."

Tears flooded down Athon's face as Lauren took the last step to take her in her arms. "Tell me, sweetheart, so we can both be whole again."

"I can't, I can't, I can't," Athon mumbled.

"Make it your gift to me this Christmas, baby," Lauren whispered as she held Athon against her. "You deserve to be free of whatever's tormenting you."

"I can't stand for you to see me as weak," Athon sobbed.

Two armed security officers entered the waiting area quickly. Chambers held a hand up, stopping them before they interrupted the scene. They stepped back, but remained nearby. Lauren leaned back slightly and used her hand to wipe the tears from Athon's face. She smiled and said, "Is there somewhere Athon and I can talk without everyone listening in." She placed her arm around Athon's waist and followed Chambers down a hallway. He opened a door and allowed the two women to enter alone.

Lauren sat in one of two upholstered chairs and waited for Athon to sit. But Athon wandered aimlessly around the room for a few moments. She didn't look at Lauren when she finally spoke.

"I was sound asleep," she said in a voice that was barely audible.

"When?" Lauren asked.

"I don't know exactly. I was nine or ten, I guess."

"Where were you, honey?"

"Some dump where me and Michelle were squatting." Athon laughed harshly. "We always lived in a dump, sharing space with cockroaches. Probably an abandoned trailer. Michelle could always find one of those."

"Were you there by yourself?"

"Usually. Most nights Michelle brought some asshole home with her that she'd fuck for a few bucks. That night wasn't any different except the asshole she dragged home was Hank."

"Your father?"

"According to her. But since she didn't keep score, who knows." Athon sniffed, ran her hand under her nose, and sighed.

Lauren started to ask another question, but Athon closed her eyes, as if seeing what was in her mind, and continued. "They must have been drinking and threw the bottle against a wall when it was empty. I heard it break. It woke me up. I smelled something pungent, but sweet. Might have been a joint. They laughed and then Michelle's squeaky bed hit the wall, over and over and over while they fucked. I don't know how long that went on and tried to block it out so I could go back to sleep." Athon turned, still not looking at Lauren and slumped into the other chair. "I think I dozed off for a while. Then I heard them arguing. Hank must have slapped her and she hollered. Something hit the wall of my room and I heard another slap and loud voices. I worked my way under the covers, afraid to breathe." She leaned forward and rubbed her hands over her face. "Michelle taught me to stick a chair under the knob on my door. You know, just in case." Athon barked out a laugh and shook her head. "Just in case. She never told me in case of what, just in case. When that door exploded off its cheesy hinges, it scared me half to death." She laughed again. "Guess that must have been the just in case." Athon's face twisted for a moment. Lauren covered her mouth as Athon went on. "Hands reached under the covers and grabbed my hair. I tried to knock them away, but hell, I only weighed about fifty pounds. Hank outweighed me by at least one-fifty. I grabbed his wrist and he jerked me from under the covers, then shook me off like I was a bug. I was scared and breathing like I'd run a mile. He was so damn drunk. I'd never smelled anything so bad and gagged. His chest was sweaty and hairy. The hair was all stuck together.

"Over his shoulder I saw what I thought was my salvation. Michelle was standing in the doorway staring at me. She had a cigarette in her hand and took a drag before stepping on my bed and dropping down next to me. I grabbed her hand wanting her to protect me. I was sure Hank was going to beat me. She shushed me and said, 'It'll be over soon.' I didn't know what the hell she was talking about. What would be over soon? Then...then..." Athon stopped and cleared her throat, looking around for something to drink.

Lauren looked in her purse and breathed a sigh of relief as she pulled out the half full bottle of water she'd brought with her when she left the house. Athon took it and chugged the remainder, letting the water dribble from the sides of her mouth.

Athon cleared her throat again and a new rush of tears ran down her cheeks. "Then I felt the pain stabbing into my body. I felt like I was being ripped apart. I wanted to scream, but Michelle put her hand over my mouth to muffle the sound. I pushed against Hank to get away, make the burning pain stop, but his weight was crushing me. I couldn't breathe except to take small, shallow breaths through my nose because of Michelle's hand over my mouth. Hank's grunting and the smell of him made me sick. I thought I was going to die in that filthy trailer. Finally, Michelle did the motherly thing and smacked Hank on the top of his head, telling him he'd done enough. He looked up and grinned at Michelle, then rolled off of me. I was crying from the pain and sucking in deep breaths when his weight was gone. He managed to get his fat ass up, looked down at his dick, all covered with blood, and laughed. 'I popped that little cherry real good,' he said. They staggered out of my room, shut the door as much as they could, and left me there. I didn't move all night and most of the next day. My whole body ached, but I couldn't move my legs and peed on the mattress. It burned and I stifled a scream, afraid he'd come back. I'm not sure when they left. Michelle didn't bother to kiss me goodbye," Athon said with a harsh sound that might have been an attempt to laugh. "I crawled to the bathroom. Didn't make it to school until the next week. I guess I figured if I never talked about it, it would be like it never happened." Her face crumpled as she sobbed out, "Guess I was wrong."

Lauren fell to her knees in front of Athon and soothed her as she sobbed out the pain she'd been holding inside for nearly thirty years. Athon's lips trembled when she tried to hold back the flood of emotions. "Then those assholes who had me threatened to rape me to death. They were hairy and stunk like Hank. They covered my mouth and nose and gave me their version of water boarding. I couldn't breathe. I was trying to think of a way to kill myself when Frank found me." She picked her head up and stared at Lauren. "I couldn't have stopped them from doing what Hank did and couldn't go through that again."

Lauren held her tightly. "You're safe now, baby. I have you."

"I...I can't go home," Athon sobbed.

"You're home as long as I'm holding you in my arms, sweetheart."

Athon raised red-rimmed eyes to search Lauren's face. "You mean it?"

"Forever and always, remember?"

"I was weak."

"You were a helpless child, Athon."

"I'm so tired, Lauren."

There was a tap at the door and Chambers stuck his head inside. Lauren looked over her shoulder as she held Athon close. "She's exhausted," she said.

When they got Athon back to her room, Lauren undressed her and helped her into bed, pulling the covers over her. She held her until she was sure Athon was asleep before kissing her on the forehead and slipping out of the room. Chambers was waiting for her at the nurse's station.

"She'll sleep well tonight," he said. "Probably for the first time in many, many months."

"I'll be back tomorrow," Lauren said. "I hated doing that to her. Do you think it helped?"

"Just being able to vocalize it helps. And now that we know the connection between her childhood and what happened in Afghanistan, we can work on finding a coping skill for her. It's late. I'll walk you to your car," Chambers offered. "I have to admit, Ms. Shelton, you really surprised me today. I've never seen that side of you before."

"I'm a school administrator, Dr. Chambers. It's not easy to scare me." Before she stepped out of the building she added, "This is the second time I've lost her and I hope it will be the last."

ATHON SPENT ALMOST a month at the rehabilitation center, learning coping mechanisms that might be useful if she found herself losing control or facing circumstances that rekindled her memories. Those techniques, along with an array of medications, traveled to Duvalle with her when Lauren came for her. She was surprised at the number of personal belongings she had accumulated. Lauren packed everything, except her personal journal. It had proven to be a very effective means of therapy. She could write anything in the journal. It never judged her and served as a relief valve for her thoughts. Perhaps one day she would allow Lauren to read them to understand thoughts that made her angry, sad, happy, or afraid. Within its pages, Athon had written many letters to Lauren, attempting to convey her frustration. She wanted to be close to her again, but thought Lauren wouldn't want her because she was weak. She knew it wasn't true, but hadn't been able to overcome it and couldn't tell Lauren what she needed. Very little conversation passed between them on the drive home. The weather was chilly and rainy. Not exactly a cheerful time of year.

"I made chili this morning. Thought it would be good on a day like today," Lauren said.

"Sounds good," Athon commented. She concentrated on watching mist gather on the windshield and form heavy drops that would eventually run down the glass, leaving a clean trail. It became a game to guess where the next droplet would form. She played the game in her head until Lauren paused to turn into their driveway.

Lauren walked to the back of her car and opened the trunk while Athon moved to the front of the carport and looked around the property. She barely remembered the last time she'd been here. Without a word, she turned her coat collar up and walked into the field behind the house. In the distance she could see where the old camper still rested. It had been her sanctuary against everything.

LAUREN PICKED UP Athon's duffle bag and a paper bag filled with miscellaneous personal items. She watched Athon cross the field and enter the old camper. It was where they had first kissed. It was where Athon always went when she needed...something. What did she need now?

Lauren opened the front door and carried Athon's things into their bedroom. Their bedroom. It hadn't been their bedroom for a long time. It was the room they both slept in, the room where Athon... She took a deep breath and unzipped the duffle. As she took out each item, her anger began to grow until she was grabbing items and slamming them into drawers. She finally stopped and covered her eyes with a shaky hand. Athon had taken her as if she were nothing more than a possession and then rolled away, leaving Lauren feeling used, violated. She had endured it to prevent another possible outburst. Now she was unpacking Athon's belongings like nothing had ever happened. She felt as much a victim as Athon was.

Lauren walked out the back door and stood under the protection of the porch. She wiped her face before stepping into the rain and making her way across the wide field toward the old camper shell. She paused before opening the door and going inside. Water dripped from her hair and ran down her face. Athon turned and looked at her before opening a storage cabinet and taking out a towel. She moved in front of Lauren and draped the towel over her head, gently patting her hair to absorb the water. Lauren took the towel from her and wiped her clothes.

"I'm angry," Lauren said.

"I know," Athon said softly. "I've put you through a lot."

"What are we going to do about it? I can't live in fear, Athon." Lauren shook her head. "That's wrong. I can, but I won't. Not anymore. It hurts too damn much. I want *my* Athon Dailey back."

"I wish I could give her to you."

"Me too." Lauren looked around the interior of the camper and a smile tugged at the corners of her lips. "This was her safe place. When she came here, there was nothing that could hurt her." Lauren stepped closer to the cab-over bunk. She ran a hand over the mattress cover. "I kissed her for the first time in here. I fell asleep safe in her arms. This was where I was going to make love to her for the first time. My father ruined that trying to save my soul." She chuckled. "If he only knew." She lowered her head to the mattress and took a deep breath. "It still smells like her."

Lauren stood up straighter when she felt Athon's hands come to rest on her shoulders. "Don't," she said. The hands slipped off and Lauren could feel the space between them grow cooler. She stared at the mattress for a moment longer, then turned and found the blue of Athon's eyes. "I've missed her so very much." Her hand caressed Athon's cheek.

Athon stepped closer, taking Lauren's hand and bringing it to her mouth. "Please don't be afraid of me," she said.

Lauren wrapped her arms around Athon's neck, holding her tightly. "Just hold me, baby," she whispered. "I know you're in there."

Athon crawled onto the mattress and held a hand out to Lauren. When Lauren joined her, Athon rested an arm around her waist. Lauren felt her body relax and closed her eyes. She was sixteen again.

Lauren didn't know how long she'd been asleep when a loud boom of thunder woke her. Periodically, a flash of lightning illuminated the inside of the camper and Athon's arm was no longer draped over her body. Lauren rolled over and saw Athon pressed against the wall of the camper, her eyes wide.

"It's all right, honey," Lauren said calmly. "The storm will pass."

"I'm sorry. I'm trying."

Lauren reached out. "I know. Come here."

Athon slowly moved closer and Lauren ran a hand through her sweat-covered hair. Her clothes were damp and she was shivering. Without speaking, Lauren brought Athon's shirt up and over her head. She unfastened Athon's bra and opened a cabinet over the bed to pull down a blanket. She tucked it around Athon's body and drew her closer. She kissed her forehead and stroked her back through the blanket. Athon buried her face against Lauren's neck. A few minutes later, she kissed the side of Lauren's neck and pushed onto her elbow. Athon's hand moved up Lauren's abdomen and stopped short of her breasts.

"Don't stop," Lauren breathed as her hands found their way

into Athon's hair and she tilted her neck to give Athon more skin to tease.

Athon lifted her body over Lauren's. She shifted her mouth to cover Lauren's, her tongue searching her mouth. Athon pulled away and straddled Lauren's body to pull her shirt and bra off together. Lauren raised her hips and struggled to remove her slacks.

"You're so beautiful," Athon said, her hands running down Lauren's sides, her thumbs stroking over the dark, hardening nipples. "God, I want you so much."

Lauren smiled and sat up enough to run her hands up Athon's back and flip her over.

"You're safe with me," she said softly as she kissed Athon for the first time in months.

Chapter Thirty-five

Duvalle, Texas
October 2012

LAUREN FLIPPED ON the blinker and waited for an opening in the traffic. She tapped her fingers impatiently on the steering wheel. Two patrol cars blocked the ravaged drive as she slowly approached them. She lowered the window of her car and smiled at the officer as he approached her vehicle.

"This site is closed, ma'am," the young man said courteously.

"I'm supposed to meet Sheriff Cosper here. My name is Lauren Shelton."

The officer stood and brought a hand up to the small radio attached to the shoulder of his uniform. Lauren heard a response, but couldn't understand a word of the garbled-sounding reply.

"Back your car up!" he shouted to the second officer before he leaned down again. "Sheriff Cosper said to veer left at the fork and you can't miss them."

"Thank you, Deputy," Lauren said as she began to pull forward.

She was excited and nervous about what was happening, but knew Athon needed it. It had been two long, busy years since Athon's breakdown. When she finally came home Lauren had worried she would have a relapse. There had been arguments, but Lauren stopped analyzing everything she did, fearing Athon's reaction. She became herself gradually as the months passed. Now she was confident she and Athon had surmounted ninety-nine percent of their problems. She was proud of how much her partner had overcome.

What a difference twenty-two months had made. Lauren smiled, remembering how she'd thought Athon was crazy when she purchased Tiny's business. Things hadn't gotten much better for about a month, until the day Athon found her future.

Lauren was tired after what seemed like an endless day. She hadn't even had time to change from her work clothes when the back door opened and Athon entered, dragging a bleeding teenaged girl behind her. The girl's sandy brown hair fell over her eyes as she tried to get away from Athon's grip. "Lauren!" Athon called out.

Lauren walked into the kitchen in time to see Athon, who was also bleeding from a cut under her left eye, shove a filthy girl into a chair at their small table. Every time Athon shoved her down, the girl jumped back up and tried to make a break for the back door. "Don't make me tie your ass down, kid," Athon hissed.

"Better people than you have tried," the girl snapped back.

"Do we have a first aid kit?" Athon asked.

"Under the sink," Lauren answered, taking a glass from the cabinet and filling it with tea. She leaned against the counter. "What's with her?" she asked before she took a sip.

"Caught her stealing from the shop," Athon said, flipping open the red plastic box.

"I told you I wasn't stealin'. What are you, deaf or somethin'?" the girl snapped.

"I'm guessing you're responsible for the blood," Lauren observed, shifting her gaze to Athon.

With a half-grin, Athon answered. "I chased her, but a tree behind the shop did most of the damage." Athon grabbed the girl's chin and turned it toward her to use a wet cloth to wipe away a trail of dried blood.

The girl jerked her head away. "I can give you a matching black eye on the other side," she threatened as she grabbed the cloth. She ran it over her face, looking at Lauren with each wipe. She nodded toward Lauren and grinned, waggling her eyebrows and revealing deep green eyes. "Who's the smokin' bitch? She yours?"

Athon tapped the girl on the forehead to get her attention. She smiled at Lauren and winked. "I'm hers and she's not a bitch. She's very special." She pushed the girl's head back and placed a butterfly bandage over a cut.

The girl ducked around Athon's hand to look at Lauren again. "You get tired of grandma here, I'll be around," she said.

Lauren chuckled. "Looks like you have competition, baby."

"Damn straight." The girl licked her lips. "You wouldn't believe the things I could do to that bitchin' fine body."

"Hey! Watch your damn mouth!" Athon ordered loudly.

Lauren set her glass down and moved behind Athon, running her hands around her waist. When Athon turned to face her, Lauren took her lower lip between her teeth and brought her into a sizzling kiss. When they separated, Lauren glanced down at the staring girl and licked Athon's taste from her lips. "I've got what I want, honey, and nothing you've got can come close. What's your name?"

The girl seemed mesmerized. "S-Shelby. Da-a-a-amn."

Lauren held out a hand. "Semi-nice to meet you." While she shook hands with Shelby, she looked over her shoulder at Athon.

"She staying for dinner?"

Athon looked down at the teenager and shrugged. "I dunno, are you?"

Shelby became the first in a long line of abused and abandoned teenaged girls Athon brought home. Aside from the original camper, she added six additional camper shells, which stayed occupied most of the time. Pudge's Place, as it became known, was a safe place where young girls could remain if they attended school and obeyed Athon's rules.

Lauren followed the old road to the left and around a curve. She saw Sheriff Cosper talking to a group of men and honked her horn before pulling to the side of the road and parking behind Raynelle's patrol car. Various pieces of heavy equipment idled in the area as Lauren picked her way carefully toward the sheriff.

"Am I late?" she asked.

"We were waiting for y'all to get here," Raynelle answered. "Hey, Shelby," she said to acknowledge the tall girl climbing out of the passenger door. Shelby smiled and threw a hand up.

"Game tonight?" Raynelle asked.

"Senior night," Shelby said as she meandered around until she stood next to Raynelle.

"Sorry. I couldn't get away from school any sooner," Lauren apologized. "Shelby wanted a haircut before tonight's game."

Raynelle reached up and ruffled the short-cropped hair. "Adoptin' Athon's style, huh. Looks good on ya."

Shelby blushed and pushed dirt around with the toe of her sneaker. "Thanks, Sheriff."

Raynelle hooked her thumbs in her equipment belt, looking at Lauren. "So how you like bein' back at Carver, Principal Shelton?" she asked with a grin.

"I love not driving an hour to get to work," Lauren said with a laugh. "I miss the people I worked with at the middle school, but there's a lot I think I can contribute at Carver. It's so different from when Athon and I were there. Speaking of, where is Athon anyway?"

Raynelle squinted and pointed toward a bulldozer idling down the road. "Couldn't let her drive the damn thing, but she finally agreed to just ride along. Stubborn ass," Raynelle muttered.

"How come you never found yourself a good woman, Raynelle?" Lauren asked as she leaned closer to the sheriff.

"Ain't many around. Besides, I don't want to be responsible for anyone but myself. Too set in my ways," Raynelle said with a shrug.

"It's never too late, you know."

"Pushy broad, ain't ya? Well, let's get this show on the road," Raynelle said, letting out an ear-piercing whistle to get everyone's attention. She raised her arm and moved it in a circle over her head.

Lauren saw Athon, wearing a bright yellow hard hat, jump onto the track of the bulldozer and stand behind the driver as he revved the engine and shifted gears, lowering the steel blade almost to the ground. He shifted gears again and looked over his shoulder at Athon as the machine lumbered forward toward a derelict old mobile home whose roof had caved in years earlier. Lauren watched Athon's face as the blade bit into the old wreck and pushed through it steadily. In less than thirty minutes the mobile home had been reduced to a pile of rubble. The bulldozer backed away to make room for a front loader to begin scooping the remains away, including Athon's ghosts. Nothing there would hurt her again unless she let it in.

AS THE BULLDOZER backed away and prepared to demolish the next abandoned mobile home, Athon patted the driver on the back, shook his hand, and jumped to the ground. She began to walk away when she shielded her eyes with her hand and saw Lauren and Shelby standing next to Sheriff Cosper. A smile cut across her face and she jogged toward them.

"Wasn't that great!" Athon said loudly over the noise of the machinery. She reached out and hugged Lauren. "I've never felt so free," she whispered. "Thank you for being here."

Athon released Lauren and looked at Shelby. "Great haircut," she said with a grin.

"Cool, too," Shelby said, bumping Athon's shoulder and running her hand through her hair.

"You'll like it when a hot chick feels the need to run her fingers through it," Athon kidded.

Raynelle interrupted the moment. "The sign out on the highway's coming down in a day or so," she said.

"What's going in here now?" Athon asked, looking back at Lauren.

"A moving and storage company of some kind," Raynelle answered. "Well, I guess I should get back on patrol."

"Sheriff Cosper, can you give me a lift back to school? I have an exam this afternoon," Shelby asked.

"I'll drive you back, sweetie," Lauren said.

"Nah. I need to talk to Sheriff Cosper anyway," Shelby said. She winked at Athon. "Besides, you got other things to do. See you at tonight's game!"

"Walk me to my car?" Lauren asked, sliding a hand around

Athon's waist as the sheriff and Shelby walked away.

"I suppose you have to get back to school pretty quick," Athon said.

"I didn't tell my secretary how long I'd be gone. Why?" Lauren asked with a coy smile.

Athon pulled Lauren behind a tree near her car. "Oh, I don't know. I was just thinking, with the kid gone and all, this would be a really good day to lounge in bed all afternoon," she said as she lowered her head to kiss Lauren's neck.

"All afternoon, huh?" Lauren asked, tilting her head to expose more of her neck for Athon.

"I think I could handle that," Athon said as she slid her hands slowly up Lauren's sides. Her thumbs stroked the sides of Lauren's breasts causing a hitch in her breathing.

"You can handle anything you want, baby," Lauren breathed as she found Athon's lips and kissed her greedily.

They broke apart reluctantly at the sound of approaching voices, still grinning at one another. Lauren ran a finger down the middle of Athon's chest. "Welcome home, soldier. Can I give you a lift?"

Other Yellow Rose Titles You Might Enjoy:

The Chosen
by Verda Foster

In the feudal kingdom of Ryshta, there are masters and there are slaves. The servants labor for their arrogant lords, who treat them little better than animals. That's the way it's always been. But the slaves are waiting for the coming of The Chosen One, the prophesied leader who will take them out of their bondage.

A chance encounter separates Roslin, daughter of the king, from her privileged world. She takes refuge in a peasant community where she finds herself drawn to the charismatic Brice, leader of the slaves' rebellion. Is Brice indeed the Chosen?

The old order is eventually overturned and the slaves win their liberty. But in the new, free world, the unveiling of a carefully kept secret has as much impact on the ex-slaves as the rebellion had on their ex-masters. And Brice and Roslin have to face their own challenges as they explore their love for each other. A gripping story of love, battle and outstanding moral courage.

ISBN 978-1-61929-027-3

Available in print and eBook formats

Mountain Rescue: The Ascent
by Sky Croft

When your heart has been broken, can you ever trust again?

This is the question that Dr. Sydney Greenwood finds herself asking, when she relocates to a village in the Scottish Highlands, seeking a fresh start.

There, she joins the local Mountain Rescue team, and finds a new challenge in the form of Kelly Saber—an expert climber with a hidden past—who tests Sydney's resolve to stay single.

Amidst harsh terrain, turbulent weather, and life or death rescues, the two women must learn to trust each other, not only on the mountain, but in matters of the heart.

This is the first in the Mountain Rescue saga, how Saber and Sydney meet, the beginning of their relationship, and their first tests as a couple, both on and off the mountain. This is...The Ascent.

ISBN 978-1-61929-098

Available in print and eBook formats

It'sElementary
by Jennifer Jackson

Tolerance and acceptance are growing in society, but don't tell that to a parent of a school-aged child. Teachers are supposed to be straight, wholesome, and good examples for the children they teach. This is why one vague rumor about a slightly effeminate teacher at Baxter Elementary resulted in a mob of angry parents demanding his removal. Victoria was a first hand witness to the carnage, which is why she vowed to never let her personal life mingle with her professional life. It was a good plan. That is until a most-certainly-not-her-type, absolutely adorable, first-year teacher got under her skin. And, when a confused and desperate parent targets her protégé, Victoria must decide which is more important: her career or love?

ISBN 978-1-61929-084-6

Available in print and eBook formats

Strength In Numbers
by Jeanine Hoffman

Bailey ran out on her best friend, Jay, years ago but wants to make amends if she can. Sharon has buried herself in work for so long she isn't sure she knows how to do much else. Riley, a one-time LPGA golfer, has traveled and played the field while competing on some of the finest golf courses of the world. And, then there is Jay whose heart was broken by Bailey so many years ago - she hasn't fully trusted anyone since. All four women have things to face about themselves and the others. Fate brings them together to face a crisis none of them ever expected. Their lives will turn upside down, and the outcome can only be determined if they will believe that there is *Strength in Numbers*.

ISBN 978-1-61929-051-8

Available in print and eBook formats

More Brenda Adcock titles:

The Sea Hawk

Dr. Julia Blanchard, a marine archaeologist, and her team of divers have spent almost eighteen months excavating the remains of a ship found a few miles off the coast of Georgia. Although they learn quite a bit about the nineteenth century sailing vessel, they have found nothing that would reveal the identity of the ship they have nicknamed "The Georgia Peach."

Consumed by the excavation of the mysterious ship, Julia's relationship with her partner, Amy, has deteriorated. When she forgets Amy's birthday and finds her celebrating in the arms of another woman, Julia returns alone to the Peach site. Caught in a violent storm, she finds herself separated from her boat and adrift on the vast Atlantic Ocean.

Her rescue at sea leads her on an unexpected journey into the true identity of the Peach and the captain and crew who called it their home. Her travels take her to the island of Martinique, the eastern Caribbean islands, the Louisiana German Coast and New Orleans at the close of the War of 1812.

How had the Peach come to rest in the waters off the Georgia coast? What had become of her alluring and enigmatic captain, Simone Moreau? Can love conquer everything, even time? On a voyage that lifts her spirits and eventually breaks her heart, Julia discovers the identity of the ship she had been excavating and the fate of its crew. Along the way she also discovers the true meaning of love which can be as boundless and unpredictable as the ocean itself.

ISBN 978-1-935053-10-1

Pipeline

What do you do when the mistakes you made in the past come back to slap you in the face with a vengeance? Joanna Carlisle, a fifty-seven year old photojournalist, has only begun to adjust to retirement on her small ranch outside Kerrville, Texas, when she finds herself unwillingly sucked into an investigation of illegal aliens being smuggled into the United States to fill the ranks of cheap labor needed to increase corporate profits.

Joanna is a woman who has always lived life her way and on her own terms, enjoying a career that had given her everything she thought she ever wanted or needed. An unexpected visit by her former lover, Cate Hammond, and the attempted murder of their son, forces Jo to finally face what she had given up. Although she hasn't seen Cate or their son for fifteen years, she finds that the feelings she had for Cate had only been dormant, but had never died. No matter how much she fights her attraction to Cate, Jo cannot help but wonder whether she had made the right decision when she chose career and independence over love.

Jo comes to understand the true meaning of friendship and love only when her investigation endangers not only her life, but also the lives of the people around her.

ISBN 978-1-932300-64-2

Reiko's Garden

Hatred...like love...knows no boundaries.

How much impact can one person have on a life?

When sixty-five-year old Callie Owen returns to her rural childhood home in Eastern Tennessee to attend the funeral of a woman she hasn't seen in twenty years, she's forced to face the fears, heartache, and turbulent events that scarred both her body and her mind. Drawing strength from Jean, her partner of thirty years, and from their two grown children, Callie stays in the valley longer than she had anticipated and relives the years that changed her life forever.

In 1949, Japanese war bride Reiko Sanders came to Frost Valley, Tennessee with her soldier husband and infant son. Callie Owen was an inquisitive ten-year-old whose curiosity about the stranger drove her to disobey her father for just one peek at the woman who had become the subject of so much speculation. Despite Callie's fears, she soon finds that the exotic-looking woman is kind and caring, and the two forge a tentative, but secret friendship.

When Callie and her five brothers and sisters were left orphaned, Reiko provided emotional support to Callie. The bond between them continued to grow stronger until Callie left Frost Valley as a teenager, emotionally and physically scarred, vowing never to return and never to forgive.

It's not until Callie goes "home" that she allows herself to remember how Reiko influenced her life. Once and for all, can she face the terrible events of her past? Or will they come back to destroy all that she loves?

ISBN 978-1-932300-77-2

Redress of Grievances

Harriett Markham is a defense attorney in Austin, Texas, who lost everything eleven years earlier. She had been an associate with a Dallas firm and involved in an affair with a senior partner, Alexis Dunne. Harriett represented a rape/murder client named Jared Wilkes and got the charges dismissed on a technicality. When Wilkes committed a rape and murder after his release, Harriett was devastated. She resigned and moved to Austin, leaving everything behind, including her lover.

Despite lingering feelings for Alexis, Harriet becomes involved with a sex-offense investigator, Jessie Rains, a woman struggling with secrets of her own. Harriet thinks she might finally be happy, but then Alexis re-enters her life. She refers a case of multiple homicide allegedly committed by Sharon Taggart, a woman with no motive for the crimes. Harriett is creeped out by the brutal murders, but reluctantly agrees to handle the defense.

As Harriett's team prepares for trial, disturbing information comes to light. Sharon denies any involvement in the crimes, but the evidence against her seems overwhelming. Harriett is plunged into a case rife with twisty psychological motives, questionable sanity, and a client with a complex and disturbing life. Is she guilty or not? And will Harriet's legal defense bring about justice — or another Wilkes case?

Recipient of a 2008 award from the Golden Crown Literary Society, the premiere organization for the support and nourishment of quality lesbian literature. Redress of Grievances won in the category of Lesbian Mystery.

ISBN 978-1-932300-86-4

Tunnel Vision

Royce Brodie, a 50-year-old homicide detective in the quiet town of Cedar Springs, a bedroom community 30 miles from Austin, Texas, has spent the last seven years coming to grips with the incident that took the life of her partner and narrowly missed taking her own. The peace and quiet she had been enjoying is shattered by two seemingly unrelated murders in the same week: the first, a John Doe, and the second, a janitor at the local university.

As Brodie and her partner, Curtis Nicholls, begin their investigation, the assignment of a new trainee disrupts Brodie's life. Not only is Maggie Weston Brodie's former lover, but her father had been Brodie's commander at the Austin Police Department and nearly destroyed her career.

As the three detectives try to piece together the scattered evidence to solve the two murders, they become convinced the two murders are related. The discovery of a similar murder committed five years earlier at a small university in upstate New York creates a sense of urgency as they realize they are chasing a serial killer.

The already difficult case becomes even more so when a third victim is found. But the case becomes personal for Brodie when Maggie becomes the killer's next target. Unless Brodie finds a way to save Maggie, she could face losing everything a second time.

ISBN 978-1-935053-19-4-

Soiled Dove

In 1872, sixteen-year-old Loretta Digby fled her home in Indiana to escape an abusive step-father. Rescued from the streets of St. Joseph, Missouri by brothel owner Jack Coulter, she turns to the only work available. By twenty she became a much sought after prostitute catering to St. Jo's most influential men and dreaming of the day she can leave her past behind and start her life anew. Jack is enraged when he discovers his favorite employee's plan to leave. Bloody and beaten, Loretta is rescued by a young prostitute, Amelia Benson, and customer Reverend Cyrus Langford. Working with teacher, Hettie Tobias, who is traveling west for a teaching position in Trinidad, Colorado, Loretta and Amelia leave their former lives behind.

In the foothills of the Sangre de Cristo Mountains outside Trinidad, Clare McIlhenney has been struggling for years to make her father's dream of owning a cattle ranch in the west come true. Working with a few ranch hands and her foreman, Ino Valdez, Clare has slowly built the ranch over the last twenty years while overcoming everything that should have stopped her.

In the spring of 1876 Loretta and her friends arrive in the dusty Colorado town. Her first meeting with Clare McIlhenney is less than inspiring. When Clare is injured, over her strenuous objections, Ino hires Loretta as a temporary cook and housekeeper for the ranch. Over the next few months, Clare struggles with her unwanted attraction to the much younger woman, unable to forget the events of her past that led to the deaths of everyone she had been close to. Determined to never lose anyone else, Clare closed off her emotions and became a distant and disliked stranger to everyone around her.

Will Loretta be able to keep her past a secret and find a new life? Will Clare open herself up to loss yet again and put her own prejudices behind her? In a story of the struggles in a harsh and unforgiving time will the two women find peace at last?

Recipient of a 2011 award from the Golden Crown Literary Society, the premiere organization for the support and nourishment of quality lesbian literature. Soiled Dove won in the category of Historical Romance.

ISBN 978-1-935053-35-4

The Other Mrs. Champion

Sarah Champion, 55, of Massachusetts, was leading the perfect life with Kelley, her partner and wife of twenty-five years. That is, until Kelley was struck down by an unexpected stroke away from home. But Sarah discovers she hadn't known her partner and lover as well as she thought.

Accompanied by Kelley's long-time friend and attorney, Sarah and her children rush to Vancouver, British Columbia to say their goodbyes, only to discover another woman, Pauline, keeping a vigil over Kelley in the hospital. Confronted by the fact that her wife also has a Canadian wife, Sarah struggles to find answers to resolve her emotional and personal turmoil.

Alone and lonely, Sarah turns to the only other person who knew Kelley as well as she did—Pauline Champion. Will the two women be able to forge a friendship despite their simmering animosity? Will their growing attraction eventually become Kelley's final gift to the women she loved?

ISBN 978-1-935053-46-0

The Chameleon

Six years ago Detective Christine Shaw left her happy life and a good job in Texas to follow her libido to New York City. She's still a cop, but her stewardess girlfriend has flown the coop and Chris hasn't been able to fill the void. Everything in her life begins to change when she and her partner are assigned to a high profile case.

The murder of Broadway star Elaine Barrie propels Chris into a whole new world. A fan of the murdered actress since she was a teenager, Chris isn't prepared for the secrets she uncovers during their investigation, including her attraction to the daughter of her number one suspect.

Was the victim any of the personalities witnesses describe, or was the real person a chameleon, satisfying the expectations of each person she met?

ISBN 978-1-61929-102-7

OTHER YELLOW ROSE PUBLICATIONS

K. E. Lane	And, Playing the Role of Herself	978-1-932300-72-7
Helen Macpherson	Love's Redemption	978-1-935053-04-0
J. Y Morgan	Learning To Trust	978-1-932300-59-8
J. Y. Morgan	Download	978-1-932300-88-8
A. K. Naten	Turning Tides	978-1-932300-47-5
Lynne Norris	One Promise	978-1-932300-92-5
Paula Offutt	Butch Girls Can Fix Anything	978-1-932300-74-1
Surtees and Dunne	True Colours	978-1-932300-529
Surtees and Dunne	Many Roads to Travel	978-1-932300-55-0
Vicki Stevenson	Family Affairs	978-1-932300-97-0
Vicki Stevenson	Family Values	978-1-932300-89-5
Vicki Stevenson	Family Ties	978-1-935053-03-3
Vicki Stevenson	Certain Personal Matters	978-1-935053-06-4
Cate Swannell	A Long Time Coming	978-1-61929-062-4
Cate Swannell	Heart's Passage	978-1-932300-09-3
Cate Swannell	No Ocean Deep	978-1-932300-36-9

Be sure to check out our other imprints,
Quest Books, Troubadour Books, Mystic Books, Silver Dragon
Books, Young Adult Books, and Blue Beacon Books.

About the Author

Originally from the Appalachian region of Eastern Tennessee, Brenda now lives in Central Texas, near Austin. She began writing in junior high school where she wrote an admittedly hokey western serial to entertain her friends. Completing her graduate studies in Eastern European history in 1971, she worked as a graphic artist, a public relations specialist for the military and a display advertising specialist until she finally had to admit that her mother might have been right and earned her teaching certification. For the last almost thirty years she has taught world history and political science. Brenda and her partner of sixteen years, Cheryl, are the parents of four occasionally grown children, as well as five grandchildren. Rounding out their home are three temperamental cats, a Poodle mix, and a Puggle puppy who snores like a freight train. She is looking forward to retirement sometime in the future. She may be contacted at adcockb10@yahoo.com and welcomes all comments.

www.ingramcontent.com/pod-product-compliance
Lightning Source LLC
Chambersburg PA
CBHW031225260626
47169CB00007B/2187